Felicia Ferguson's  bit as good as her award-winning Choices She Made." This is the kind of story you can't put down—the tug of the truth will keep you wondering until the last page.

A testimony to being truthful and doing the right thing, When Secrets Come Calling is a love story wrapped up in a tough crime case. As sweet as an Alabama summer and as gut-wrenching as a coastal hurricane, this one is a keeper.

LENORA WORTH (USA TODAY BESTSELLING AUTHOR OF DISAPPEARANCE IN PINECRAFT)

When Secrets Come Calling

FELICIA FERGUSON

When Secrets Come Calling

Published by Salt and Light Publishing
Destin, FL

Copyright ©2024 by Felicia Ferguson. All rights reserved.

No part of this book may be reproduced in any form or by any mechanical means, including information storage and retrieval systems without permission in writing from the publisher/author, except by a reviewer who may quote passages in a review.

Paperback ISBN: 979-8-9900866-0-9
Hardcover ISBN: 979-8-9900866-1-6

FICTION / Romance / Suspense

Cover by Hannah Linder.

This is a work of fiction. Characters, corporations, institutions, organizations and geographical locations in this novel are either a product of the author's imagination or, if real, used fictitiously without any intent to describe actual conduct. Any resemblance to actual persons living or dead, events or locales is entirely coincidental.

All rights reserved by Felicia Ferguson and Salt and Light Publishing.

For Mom and Dad

Chapter One

Monday, September 17
Montgomery, Alabama

Thumping country music pounded the leather and wood grain interior of Maddox "Dax" Carpenter's King Ranch F250 with tales of love, summer, and broken hearts. Though he mouthed the words, neither the drum's beat nor the guitar's whine penetrated the whirl in his brain.

Pop. Arrested. For a robbery and murder forty years ago.

Dax stared almost unseeing through the windshield as a line of traffic sped down I-85 like a summer Saturday at Talladega Speedway. He swiped a hand down his cheek. The dampness made him blink, shattering the comforting bubble of numbness.

The man who had tucked him in bed, said nighttime prayers for protection and sleep, threw footballs for hours, and taught him honor and discipline. That man could be a killer, a thief, and a liar?

Could have been for all of Dax's life.

At least according to the police's evidence and this mysterious finger pointer. Dax grabbed the collar of his Titans player t-shirt and tugged it up, wiping his tears. The police were wrong. They had to be. And he would prove it.

He had no investigative skills. He could only dissect an offensive playbook, but he knew someone who could. Caitlin Fitzhugh. Dax had looked her up before setting his GPS for Montgomery and merged into the mad crush of Atlanta traffic. She still worked at the Alabama State Division of Investigations. Still wore her auburn hair in that same short pixie from five years ago if it wasn't an old ID picture.

He hoped it wasn't old. He liked seeing her as he'd known her. Liked thinking she was the same woman he'd fallen in love with—although, it was more likely she wasn't.

She worked as a cold case expert, searched for justice for other families. Would Pop's arrest be enough for her to overlook their past and help him? It had to be.

He grimaced. But maybe not. He had loved her—still did, if he was completely honest with himself. And that was a cardinal sin to her.

But he was at least going to try. *For Pop.*

Clutching a yellow medical progress report, Assistant Special Agent in Charge Caitlin Fitzhugh pushed open the door to her glassed-in office at the Alabama State Division of Investigations. Four weeks had passed since she'd torn her rotator cuff during an arrest. The injury had stuck her in a sling, immobilizing her arm for an agonizing five weeks.

While her physical therapist had released her from the sling that morning, freedom from desk duty remained another four long weeks away. Her lips bunched together as the recommendation taunted her from the tiny print. She shoved her door closed, then gasped as pain shot through her shoulder. Eyes watering, she took in a deep breath and gave her shoulder a gentle rub.

Okay, he's right. Four more weeks it is.

Pushing the pain aside, she focused on the new stack of files on her already cluttered desk. Additional paperwork came with the Assistant Special Agent in Charge title, but she suspected her new supervisor regularly cleared out his inbox as little "enjoy desk duty" gifts. She frowned and flipped open the top file, skimming the contents.

Routine background checks. Again.

Rolling her eyes, she closed the file and settled behind her desk. Maybe her email would provide something more interesting.

A flurry of movement tugged her gaze from her inbox and through the glass wall dividing her office from the bullpen. Caitlin's jaw dropped. At six feet, six inches, Dax Carpenter would be hard to miss, however, the years of weight training drew every eye within a hundred yards.

But it wasn't his height or even his muscled physique that made Caitlin's heart quicken and her breath stutter. No, that was thanks to the memories flickering across her mind. Their shared moments—of laughter, delight, and yes, of love. Biting her lip, she closed her eyes in a long blink, willing those images back into the deepest recesses of her heart.

By the time he reached her door, she'd nearly succeeded. "Dax."

His mouth flinched into some semblance of a smile. She studied his face, the pained brackets around his eyes, his tense cheeks, the dark green of his usually hazel eyes. Worry skirted through her. This was not a social call.

"What happened?" Despite her resolve to keep her distance, she rose and stepped around her desk. Her fingers itched to touch him, to soothe his desperation. It had been five years. How could he still have such an effect on her? She pushed the question aside. This wasn't personal. And she couldn't let it be.

Dax gestured helplessly, then swallowed hard. "My dad's been arrested."

Caitlin's jaw dropped. *Okay. That would explain ...* She pointed to the chair in front of her desk, hoping it would hold up under his bulk. As he took his seat, she returned to her own, her heartbeat slowing to its normal pace. *Space between us is a good thing.* "Tell me what you know."

Dax ran a hand over his face. "Not much. Mom didn't have many details. All I know for sure is someone called in a tip to the Gulf Shores Police Department over the weekend and accused him of committing a robbery and murder forty years ago. The police picked him up from the house this morning and took him back to Gulf Shores for questioning."

Thrill skimmed up Caitlin's spine. A hot lead on a cold case. There was no buzz like it. Her gaze met Dax's, and guilt twisted her gut. This wasn't a case. This was a life. Dax's life. His father's life. She knew the answer before she asked the question, but still she asked, "If he's in Gulf Shores, why come to me?"

"You're a cold case expert, right?"

She glanced away. *By circumstance, not choice.*

"I want you to look into this case. He's my dad. I know him, and I can't believe he would do this. I think he's being framed, but I don't know why."

Caitlin shook her head.

No. No. And no. She wouldn't—couldn't—reopen the door to him. But it didn't seem like he would take a personal no for an answer. Maybe a professional one would send him back out of her life? "Dax. I can't just horn in on another agency's investigation. My help has to be requested. And given the Gulf Shores P.D. now has new information to work with, I highly doubt they'd ask."

"I'm asking, Caitie. Please."

Caitlin's breath caught. Between the fear in his eyes and the achingly familiar whisper of her nickname, her resolve melted. But this still had bad idea written all over it. She pulled her gaze away from him and searched the bullpen for one final, desperate excuse. Her Special Agent in Charge, Bill McWorter, stood at the far end talking with two state troopers.

"I'll have to clear it with my supervisor, and given our ... past ... uh ... relationship, he's not likely to okay it."

"Just ask, will you? I trust you. No matter what happened between us, I know you'll find out the truth."

With a nod, Caitlin squared her shoulders and took in a deep breath. *Don't leave me hanging with this one, too, God.*

Chapter Two

Monday, September 17
Montgomery, Alabama

Caitlin flagged Bill down with a two-fingered wave and a tilt of her head toward his office. His brow furrowed, and he glanced over her shoulder into her glassed-in cubicle. With a nod, he turned and pushed through his door. "What's up, Fitzhugh?" He stepped behind his desk.

"Sir, I have a citizen's request for a cold case consult that just turned hot a few hours ago. The man in my office is the suspect's son, Dax Carpenter."

Bill snagged a pair of reading glasses from his desk and flipped through a stack of case files. He nodded, then flicked a curious glance toward her above the rims of his glasses. "I thought he looked familiar. What's the problem?"

Tucking her hands in her pockets, Caitlin shifted from one leg to the other. "I can't work this case."

Bill closed the file, one eyebrow lifting. His dark eyes pierced her with speculation. "You 'can't'? Fitzhugh, you're on desk duty—you've got the time and, according to the outgoing SAC, you've got the talent. So far, I'm not seeing a problem."

Caitlin stifled a frustrated sigh. McWorter might know her record, but he didn't know *her*. Of all the times for her mentor and former boss to retire. Ted would've trusted her read on the situation—would've let her make the call and gone on about the day.

Pursing her lips, she searched for a reasonable excuse for him to deny Dax's request. But as much as she hated airing her personal life, it was the only card she had to play. Hopefully, it worked. "Sir. I know him."

Bill didn't look impressed. "Don't we all? He's Alabama's favorite son. National championship wide receiver, twelve-year career in the NFL, just inducted into his college's Hall of Fame."

Her cheeks heated, and she shook her head. "No—we … uh … dated."

Bill's brow wrinkled in confusion. "When? Last week?"

"No. Five years ago."

A slow, knowing smile crawled up one side of his face as his gaze grew mischievous. "And for how long?"

Caitlin swallowed her ire and prepared herself for the merciless ribbing looming on the horizon. "Six months."

"Were you engaged?"

"What?" *Engaged?* Her wounded heart leapt at the thought. "No." Her mouth worked to find more of an explanation even as she shoved the girlish dream aside.

But the gleam in Bill's eyes told her no excuse would get her out of Dax's request. In fact, he seemed to take fiendish delight in imagining the possible scenarios it could create. "Then I don't see there's a problem." His one-sided smile grew to a full-on knowing smirk. "Unless you don't think you can handle it."

Caitlin's eyes narrowed. The past with Dax was long dead and buried. She swallowed a resigned sigh. *Yeah, even I don't believe that.* But she was a professional. "No, sir. I can handle it. Just thought you should be aware. In case it comes up later—at the trial."

"Ah. Thanks for the information. But I'm sure the Gulf Shores P.D. wouldn't mind having a second set of eyes on this—especially *your* set of eyes. Reach out to them and see what they say." The teasing twinkle in his own gaze told her he was happier about the rare chance to give her grief than to add to the department's already prestigious reputation.

Seeing there was not a chance for even an ungraceful exit, she crossed her arms. "All right then, but I'd like to bring Ethan and Shannon in on it as consultants." Her brother, Ethan, and his wife owned a digital consulting firm regularly used by the department, so she was certain of Bill's agreement. They would be assets to the investigation and could also provide a much-needed buffer between her and Dax. At least she hoped so.

Bill waved at her as his desk phone rang. "Do what you gotta do, Fitzhugh. Keep me updated. Oh, and congratulations on getting out of the sling."

Caitlin shut Bill's door behind her, eyes lasering in on Dax where he continued to sit in front of her desk.

Keep your focus, Caitlin. Push through and find the truth. It's what you do.

Dax Carpenter's involvement had no bearing on the case. A family needed closure. Perhaps even two, depending on the truth of Mark Carpenter's involvement. Squaring her shoulders, she took in a fortifying breath and headed back to her office.

She pushed through the door and motioned Dax back to his seat when he started to stand. "Okay, my SAC doesn't see any issues with our past and in my working this case. It looks like you've got your consultant."

Dax's eyes gleamed as he ran a hand over his bald head. A memory flickered through her. Dax standing in front of his kitchen sink shaving cream and razor in hand as he went to work removing the stubble. Her leaning against the counter wearing his old team jersey and teasing him about his ego and early male pattern baldness.

Caitlin jerked her thoughts back. *Stop it. Now.*

"Caitie? You okay?" Concern bracketed his eyes as he watched her.

Clearing her throat, she gripped her sidearm like she would her blanket as a child. "Yeah. But we're going to need some ground rules, Dax."

His head bobbed in a quick, agreeable nod. "Name them."

"First off, you can't call me Caitie. Especially not here. No one but family calls me that."

A flash of something crossed his gaze. Had he wanted to be considered family? *Of course he did, dodo. You were the one who ended it.*

"You want me to call you by your title? What is it? Something like *Assistant Special Agent in Charge Fitzhugh*?" Dax's gaze warmed as his lips twitched into a teasing smile. "That's kind of a mouthful."

Caitlin rolled her eyes as her breath hitched in a wry snort. "No, Caitlin is fine."

"Okay, what's the next rule?" Dax crossed his arms and leaned his elbows against her desk. His gaze intent, but mirth lurked in the shadows.

Her breath caught. Rules? How about no looking at her the way he was looking at her?

He laced his fingers together, and a shiver slipped over her skin. No touching?

Her mind blanked. "Um—I'll get back to you on that."

She gripped her sidearm again, but this time she pulled the gun and holster from her belt. Laying them on her desk, she sat and leveled a serious look on Dax. "For now, you need to get out of here so I can start getting what I need together."

Dax's humor sobered. He nodded and stood. "I'm heading to Mom and Pop's house in Elba. I'll be there as long as she needs me." His eyes dropped to her cell phone where it lay on the desk. "If you need to reach me, my number hasn't changed." He glanced back up, piercing her with a look filled with memory. "If you still have it."

Caitlin smashed her lips together and gave a rueful nod. "I do."

Dax's cheeks wrinkled with a quick, pleased smile. "Good." He paused and glanced around the office. The bullpen bustled with agents taking calls, discussing cases, and for the most part ignoring them. "Thank you, Caitlin."

Her name was slathered with gratitude but laced with history, brushing her with as much intimacy as her nickname. She gripped the arms of her desk chair and felt the wheels shift beneath her. *So much for stability.* She forced a nod and, without another word, Dax left.

Grabbing her mouse, Caitlin clicked through folders, pulling up the case file request forms, and started typing. The sooner she could get them, the sooner she could kick Dax Carpenter out of her life again.

Out of her heart was another matter altogether.

Chapter Three

Monday, September 17
Montgomery, Alabama

Caitlin tugged the stack of background checks closer to her. They were scut work, but at least they'd keep her mind occupied while she waited for word from the Gulf Shores Police Department. Unfortunately, she doubted they'd be enough to distract her from Dax's re-entering her life.

She'd worked her way through a third of the stack when her cell phone rang. Still clicking through files on the agency's database, she glanced at the screen, expecting to see *spam call* in a pop-up banner. But instead, *Mom* glowed from the display. Closing her eyes, Caitlin answered the call.

"Everything okay, Mom?"

"Oh, of course. Why wouldn't it be?"

Caitlin's eyebrows lifted at the words and tone. Mom was too chipper. "Because you know I'm at work, and you never call me here unless something's going on. Spill."

Mom's sigh wafted into her ear, tired, exasperated, and maybe a bit sad. Caitlin turned her full attention to the conversation as Mom continued talking. "I had to run an errand today and left your father at the house while I was gone."

Over the last year, Daddy's dementia had spiraled downward, leaving Caitlin wondering how long Mom would be able to care for him at home. "Doesn't he normally go with you?"

"The last time I took him to the store he wandered off and when the sales person asked if he needed help, Daddy couldn't remember why he was there. I heard someone describe him over the loudspeaker while I was bagging apples. I found them up at the customer service counter, and he almost hit the manager who was only trying to keep him from wandering off again. It was a nightmare. Today, I only planned to be gone thirty minutes—less actually since the store is just around the corner, and I only needed a few items ... I'm baking pies for the church potluck this weekend."

Caitlin rolled her eyes as Mom veered off on a tangent. Shaking her head, she said, "And what happened with Daddy, Mom?"

Thankfully jerked back from her foray into the side story, Mom continued, "Oh, well, given it was supposed to be a short trip, I thought he'd be safer at home."

"And what happened with Daddy while you were gone?"

Mom huffed, but obliged. "Well, he apparently decided he was hungry and tried to make a can of soup. I had told him before I left that I'd pick up something for him on my way back —you know how much he enjoys the barbecue from Duley's, and I thought it'd be a nice treat."

Caitlin's inner cop bristled at the wandering conversation. "Mom, focus. Did he burn down the house?"

"What? No, but he did forget to put the soup in the pan, and when I got home the whole kitchen was filled with smoke."

Caitlin sighed and shook her head. "Mom, we need to talk about what to do now. Caring for Daddy is becoming too much for you. I know you retired from giving private lessons, but when's the last time you played your piano?"

Mom didn't answer.

"That's what I thought."

"Well, your daddy likes his TV shows, and the last time I tried to play, he started yelling at me."

Though Caitlin hadn't been there, Mom had relayed the full story in the hours after it had happened. Daddy had not only yelled, but he'd also thrown the remote at the wall, smashing it into bits—that was, if they were talking about the same "last" time. Caitlin pinched the bridge of her nose and took a deep breath.

The daddy she had known all her life had adored Mom. And vice versa. Dementia had slowly turned him into someone neither of them recognized—and definitely not someone he would want to be.

"Look, Mom, every time we talk, you sound worn out and exhausted. Just like you do now. And with his diagnosis, it's only going to get worse. You need help. Or we need to talk about putting—"

Mom's voice crashed through the phone filled with blustering excuses. "No, he may be your father, but he's my husband."

"We could at least help out from—"

"No. You and Ethan are busy with your careers, and I hate pulling you away from them. And of course, Luke is off on his own adventures. I'll manage." She paused and uncertainty tinged her tone. "I just wanted you to know in case someone happened to mention something."

Caitlin's eyes narrowed. "Why would someone mention something?"

"The next-door neighbors called the fire department when they heard our smoke detectors going off."

Of course, they would. Caitlin dropped her head in her hands.

Something had to be done. But she was not winning this conversation. Maybe Ethan could talk some sense into Mom. He was the oldest and the favorite—although Mom would deny it with her last breath. "Thank you for the heads-up, Mom."

They talked for a few more minutes about generalities. As the conversation wound to a natural close, Dax's return and request sat on the tip of Caitlin's tongue. Mom and Daddy had known him. More than that, they had liked him. Dax and Daddy had talked Alabama football for hours on end. In fact, those long circular conversations tipped Caitlin off that something wasn't quite right with Daddy.

She should tell Mom about Dax's request. But what would Mom think about his sudden reappearance in her life?

Caitlin bit her lip. Mom would probably call it divine intervention. And then get her hopes up that it would grow into more. Even though it couldn't. Caitlin shook her head and ended the call. Mom had enough on her plate—no sense in adding to her disappointment.

She tapped her text app and selected the running group text with her brothers. Typing in Mom's news, she added a request for a sibling phone call to discuss options as soon as possible. Three dots appeared almost immediately. But with Luke's career in Army special ops, she highly doubted his name would be attached to them.

Born ten years after Caitlin, she and Ethan, who were only two years apart, had long teased Luke he was Mom and Daddy's "oops" baby, tagging him with the nickname "Fluke" early on in his life. And he certainly broke the family mold, choosing the military and regular deployment to hotspots around the world over local law enforcement and sticking around Montgomery. Caitlin would worry about him if he wasn't so perfectly suited for his career. Instead, she enjoyed knowing her baby brother kept the country safe and loved every minute of it.

Given his duties, the family could go weeks without hearing

from him. However, when those weeks turned into months, Mom would send out a text requesting proof of life, to which he'd often respond with pictures of Mount Ranier or other sites around Tacoma where he was based.

Come to think of it, last word we had was July Fourth. May be time to send another proof of life demand Luke's way. Maybe this news would be enough to snag a few minutes of his attention —if he was in the country.

Ethan's name and comment popped up on the screen, recommending Luke set the date and time, and agreeing a sibling meeting was definitely needed. That settled, Caitlin flicked over to her individual message conversation with Ethan.

CAITLIN: May need a consult on a cold case I just picked up. Y'all available?

ETHAN: Me, not until next week—at a conference in Texas. But Shannon is. Doctor wanted tests done before we try again. Results back any day now so consulting gig would be a good distraction.

Caitlin skimmed her thumb over Ethan's words. *Yeah, I bet it would.* Last month, Shannon miscarried for the second time in a year. While every conversation with her sister-in-law indicated Shannon had bounced back emotionally, tests had to be a blow. She and Ethan had just got their marriage back on track after he'd overextended their business investments, and they'd almost lost everything. The pregnancies were supposed to be a celebration not another battle to fight.

Caitlin tapped out a short, affirmative response then moved to her message conversation with Shannon.

CAITLIN: Got a bone for you to gnaw on SIL, you interested?

SHANNON: Every time. Come by the office in the morning?

CAITLIN: Done. I'll bring breakfast.

SHANNON: Must be a big ask. You never feed me. LOL! See you then!

Caitlin smiled despite herself.

You have no idea how big, Shan. But before she could ask, she needed to know the right questions. Caitlin scanned the Gulf Shores P.D.'s paperwork and found the main office line. Grabbing her desk phone, she jabbed in the number. Even though the request was only a few hours old, it wouldn't hurt to follow up.

After a brief explanation for the reason for her call, the PBX operator transferred her to the detective in charge of the case.

"Detective Osgood."

Introducing herself, she gave an expanded summary for why she'd called.

Osgood's seeming reluctance buzzed between them. "Can't say we need help from big leagues what with the tip we're working now. Especially since it's a family member requesting it."

Relief coursed through her. Finally, a plausible excuse not to work the case. Cops were territorial about jurisdiction and could be bears to work with. Osgood just might fall into that category.

But she winced a moment later. Her professional pride tweaked. Professionalism overruled her heart. "I understand, Detective. And I'm not trying to elbow in and take over. I'm simply letting you know I'm available if you do need help." *Please say no.*

The phone line was silent for a minute. Had he hung up on her? But then he cleared his throat. "Well, I guess it can't hurt to have another pair of eyes on it. What'd you say your name was again?"

She ran a hand over her forehead. "Caitlin Fitzhugh."

"You're the one who closed the Stacey Rhodes murder about a year ago, aren't you? She was the runaway they pulled out of Mobile Bay."

Caitlin's eyes narrowed. "Yeah, that was me."

"Stacey was a friend of my cousin's girl." He paused, and she sighed at their heartbreaking connection.

Why does this small world have to be so evil?

Osgood cleared his throat. "All right, then. The hard copy of the case file will take a week, but I'll send you a digital copy by the end of the day. Still gotta get the witness's statement typed in, and you'll need it for the full picture."

Surrendering to the inevitable, Caitlin squared her shoulders. She could do this. In reality, she had to do this. If not for Dax, then for Missy. She cleared her throat. "I'll take what I can get, Detective. You'll be my first call if I come up with anything." She dropped the phone receiver into its cradle and stared at it as the promise curled in her stomach. What if she did uncover something damaging? Could she really break Dax's heart again? But then, wouldn't she be doing that anyway when the case was over, and she walked out of his life once more?

She closed her eyes as the meeting with Dax washed over her. The earnest plea in his voice. The memories of them lurking in his eyes. The easy way her nickname fell from his lips.

She huffed and willed her heart to return behind its invisible wall. *Can't win for losing.*

But she'd agreed, and she'd see it through to whatever end. She was a professional. And this is what she did—to honor Missy.

Chapter Four

Monday, September 17
Elba, Alabama

Dax pulled into Mom and Pop's driveway and cut the truck's engine. His arms draped over the steering wheel as he studied the home where he'd grown up. Despite months of baking under the scorch and humidity of the Alabamian summer, the yard gleamed a healthy green—compliments of Pop's mindful watering and fertilizer. Mom's roses stood tall, their reds and pinks a perfect accent to the painted-white brick exterior and black shutters. A white swing glider sat to one side of the porch softened by a pale blue cushion bleached by years of morning sunlight.

A bronze house sign was tucked to the right of the front door. *Home of the Carpenters*. It was the perfect southern family home. But were the appearances true? Dax drummed the dashboard.

Thirty-eight years ago, Mark Carpenter answered an electrician's call from Susan Jones about her fritzing breaker box. The job was a routine fix—a simple replacement of a couple of breakers. But the electricity between them was immediate and unforgettable. A year later they married, and Mark moved in. Ten months after that, Maddox Dean Carpenter was born.

But what had happened forty years ago? Did Mom have any idea, any sense, that Pop wasn't who he said he was? And if she did, where did that leave Dax? Unable to trust not one but *two* parents?

He needed answers, and he could only find them in that house. On the field, he was proactive, insightful, reading plays and always ready to grab the ball. But now, with the proverbial ball in the air, he could only sit frozen in his seat.

The front door opened, and Mom stepped onto the porch still in her housecoat and bedroom slippers despite the afternoon hour. She lifted her hand in a sad wave, then gestured for him to come inside. Dax nodded and unbuckled his seat belt.

You have to go. There's no punting this.

But still, he sat.

In the next few minutes, the life and the father he'd known could be gone. And then what?

The *Monday Night Football* theme song blared from his cell phone. Dax grabbed the phone from where it lay upside down on the passenger seat. Maybe Caitlin already had information?

But when he turned it over, he groaned.

Gene Anderson, his producer.

Dax rubbed his face. Tapping the green button, he readied himself for the much-deserved reprimand.

"Carpenter, what in the world?" Gene barely took a breath before launching into his rebuke. "You can't just run out on the studio like that. Higgins is scrambling for some pre-recorded replay to cover your spot. Do you want the desk job at ESPN or not? 'Cause stuff like this isn't gonna cut it in the big leagues—heck, it doesn't cut it here."

While Dax waited for a break in Gene's tirade, he scrambled

for some sort of explanation. He always thought best in the scramble, right?

Gene had lost both of his parents in a car accident last year. So if there was one thing he would appreciate, it was a family emergency. "Look, Gene. I'm sorry. But I got a call from my mom. Something's happened to my dad. I had to leave."

Dax listened as Gene's breath whooshed over the phone. "Ah. Okay then. I can cover today for you with management. How long will you be out?"

Dax swallowed his relieved sigh, grateful he wouldn't have to explain further. "I don't know. I just got here. But it may be a few days—if not longer."

"I'm gonna need your latest on the upcoming Alabama-Texas A & M game by the end of the week. And this ditch today has to be the only hiccup, my man, or that ESPN job is history."

"I understand, Gene. Give me today to get things sorted out here, and I'll finish up the story tomorrow or the next day. I won't let you down."

"It's not about letting me down, Dax. You've got the biggest dog in this hunt."

Dax ran a thumb over his national championship ring and nodded. Yeah, he did. But after Pop's arrest, would he have any dog at all? He ended the call with more promises of a stellar report, then climbed out of the truck.

It's time to find out.

"Mom?" Dax called as he pushed open the door. He scanned the living room to the right. The leather couch he'd given them for their anniversary last year sat against one wall across from the seventy-inch TV, Pop's birthday gift from the previous year. Just across the hall, Mom's upright piano, an antique store find sometime during his childhood, still graced what should have been the formal dining room. Creased music books with whatever piece Mom had practiced for the Sunday service were propped against the piano's music rack.

Mom's voice, tired and ground down by thirty years of classroom teaching, drifted from further inside the house. "In the kitchen. Sweet tea in the fridge."

Dax dropped his keys on the entry sideboard and headed back, ducking under the door jamb. Mom sat on the bench of the breakfast nook, cradling a full glass of tea in her hands. He ignored the offer of iced tea and reached for her. He tugged her from her seat and into his arms.

She sagged against his chest as a single sob slipped between her lips. She rested there, like bone china in his hands. After a moment, she gave him a tight squeeze, took in a deep, steadying breath, and eased back.

Pain and confusion warred in her copper-colored gaze. No, Mom had no idea about Pop's potential past. But he wasn't sure if that made anything better. "We'll figure this out." He pulled her back into another hug, then let her return to her sweaty tea glass.

He grabbed a kitchen chair and straddled it certain the impertinent act would make her smile—if not call him to task. But it did neither. Pressing his lips together, he waited for her to find whatever words she had to explain the morning's events.

As a retired elementary school teacher, she'd always had a wide vocabulary she wasn't afraid to use, and no topic was off limits for discussion. She'd always considered every subject a learning opportunity—but more than that, she seemed to relish "stomping out ignorance."

But as the silence continued, it seemed she'd finally reached a subject beyond her.

"Mom." He prompted her softly, reaching his hand across the table.

Slowly, she nodded and gripped it, but she couldn't hide her tremble. Her usual authoritative tone quivered. "I can't wrap my brain around this, Dax. Your daddy. A robber and a murderer? How is this possible?"

"Nothing's been proven yet, Mom."

"But this witness—" Her voice broke as tears gathered in her eyes.

He gave her hand a long squeeze before releasing it. "Is from forty years ago. He may not be right."

Pain wrinkled the corners of her lips as she shook her head. "But if it is true, what else is he hiding? Another—"

"Shhh, Mom. What is it you always say, 'Don't borrow trouble'? All we know right now is someone reported they think Pop did something. And the police are doing what they have to do, which is ask questions."

But would they ask questions if they didn't have good reason? His gaze drifted out the window into the backyard where he and Pop had spent hours running plays and tossing the football. *Could that man really be responsible for killing someone?*

Mom's shoulders eased a fraction even as his own tightened. Maybe telling her about Caitlin would give them both a bit of peace.

He tapped her hand, drawing her eyes to his. "I made a stop on my way here. To see Caitlin. To ask for her help."

Awareness flickered through Mom's gaze. She leaned against the bench, studying him. "Are you sure that's a good idea?"

Dax glanced away. "No. I'm not. But this is our family. And she's an expert in old cases." He pulled his gaze back to her, willing certainty into his eyes. "Besides, I trust her."

Mom rubbed the back of her neck. "Just don't get your heart broken again, son."

Dax flashed what he hoped was a reassuring smile. *Yeah, I'll do my best.*

Chapter Five

Monday, September 17
College Station, Texas

Ricky Adams slumped against the bar, smothering a curse as pain shot through his gut.

"You okay, boss?" Antoine, his long-time bartender and the closest thing he had to a son, watched him with dark, worried eyes under a back-turned Astros ball cap.

Ricky pushed off the bar and took a deep breath, praying for a break in the pain that even morphine couldn't completely kill. Closing his eyes, he pulled another breath in and out of his mouth. Slowly the stabbing eased to its usual dull throb. He gave a quick nod, then grabbed the tray of glasses, intent on the sink behind him.

"Man, give me those. You've got enough to deal with." Antoine jerked his head toward the barstools. "Go sit."

Ricky winced, but eased onto the barstool. He let his gaze wander around the interior of the Silver Shooters, landing on the pool tables and arcade games at one end and skipping to the tables and booths at the other. In the middle was a space that doubled as a dance floor and occasional game day mosh pit.

For the last forty years, this place had been his saving grace and hideout all rolled into one. Twenty years of bartending-turned-managing became ownership after his old boss died and willed it to him.

As one of the original bars in College Station and close to Texas A & M's campus, the dive atmosphere and strong drinks made it a local favorite. When the doors opened at three, customers in search of quick bites and discounted drinks kicked off the crowd. The college kids descended around ten to close them out at two.

Game days, though, were a whole different breed of crazy. And Saturday had been huge—in more ways than one. First, he'd caught that clip from Alabama's Hall of Fame induction ceremony where a face from the past stared out from the screen. Then A & M decimated University of Louisiana-Monroe in a blowout game. The bar had been packed with people who spilled off the expansive front porch and into the parking lot. Ricky had made sure to savor every minute of it—he had too few left on his clock.

And now he needed more. Thankfully, the doc thought he could buy Ricky some time by cutting him open later this week. Even though the surgery wouldn't cure him, he'd take what he could get. He still had things to do. Hand off the bar. Clear his conscience.

Both seemed insurmountable given his fatigue and pain level. But what was the old saying? "You eat the elephant one bite at a time?" He'd taken the first bite on Saturday afternoon with his call to the Gulf Shores Police Department. The next bite would be the deposition where he'd spill his and Doug's secret for the record.

Whitney, one of the college students who waitressed part-time, set her tray of dirty glasses down with a soft thump, jostling him from his pondering. She flashed him a supportive smile before reaching for a rag to wipe down the tables.

The whole staff knew about his death sentence known as colon cancer. However, he still hadn't told them his estimated time of departure. Whitney ran her arm across her forehead, scattering her long tawny bangs, then propped her elbows on the bar. "Glad it's looking like an easy day. Gotta tell you, game night Saturday liked to kill me, Ricky."

Antoine reached across the counter and flicked her shoulder. Hard. Eyes widening with disbelief, he shook his head. "Seriously? When's the last time you thought before you opened your mouth, Whit?"

Whitney blanched then turned red. "Oh my gosh. Ricky. I'm so sorry. I ... Mom always said my mouth ran quicker than my brain."

Ricky shrugged and patted her arm. "Forget it. It is what it is. And I don't want y'all walking on eggshells around me. You never have before."

Antoine leveled a doubtful gaze on him, and Ricky gave a quick, decisive nod. "I mean it. Both of ya'."

Antoine sighed then grabbed Whitney's tray as she left to wipe down the tables. Ricky watched him clean the glasses, holding them up to the light to check for smudges or cracks before racking them back behind the bar. Antoine would do well by the Silver Shooters. If the dang lawyer would ever call and tell him the will was ready.

Once he signed and filed the papers, all that would be left was the when and how to tell Antoine—yet another secret Ricky would have to reveal. While the lawyer was concerned about Ricky's plans for Antoine and the bar, willing it away wasn't that out of the ordinary. After all, that was how Ricky ended up with the Silver Shooters.

A familiar name blared from the surround sound speakers on the TVs by the pool tables. Ricky turned on the barstool, gaze latching onto the repeat SEC Network highlight reel, and listened to Dax Carpenter's insights on the Alabama players. Guilt clenched Ricky's stomach. From everything he'd seen, Dax was a good kid, a hardworking one who deserved the success he'd found. But his being a good kid didn't make up for Doug's actions.

Someone had died because of them. Because of what they'd done. Ricky never understood how he'd managed to carve out a life while looking over his shoulder. But maybe it was a matter of will. He'd just put one foot in front of the other and lived, regardless of the possibility one day someone could walk into the bar and nail him. Maybe some part of him even wanted that. And why he never changed his name.

Ricky rubbed his gut, a vain effort to soothe the constant ache. But something had finally caught him. Not the police. Not some private investigator. No, it was a hell of his body's own making. Cancer literally ate him alive. He'd come to think of it as his payback. Payback he certainly deserved. Although Ricky wasn't a praying man—wasn't too sure God would want him after all his screw-ups early on—when the diagnosis came, he'd asked the Big Man to do him a favor and let him leave this world with a clear slate.

And then a few months later, Ricky turned on the University of Alabama's Hall of Fame ceremony. He couldn't believe it at first. But there was no doubting it. God had heard his prayer. But more than that, he'd answered it.

The news banner had listed Dax Carpenter's parents as Mark and Susan Carpenter. But Ricky knew in his gut that man, Mark Carpenter, was Doug Bewley. Something about the eyes, deep set and missing nothing, and the glimpse of a scar above his right eyebrow, silvery under the bright stage lights. It was the same place Doug had gotten cut during his shoving match with Mic. Stunned, Ricky had picked up the phone and bared his sins to the Gulf Shores P.D. detective on duty.

Ricky ran his fingers through the tufts of hair that were just starting to grow back from the chemo and radiation. How had

Doug/Mark lived with himself all these years? Did he ever think about what he'd done? How they were responsible for a man's death? For Mic's death?

Mic, who never did anything to them but hire them for a job and treat them right while they worked. Mic, who only wanted to keep his ex's nose out of his business. Mic, who wanted to do the best he could by his kids.

Ricky wasn't clairvoyant or anything. They were all Mic talked about. His boy who was gonna grow up and take over The Broken Flip-Flop. His little girl who was his princess.

If he'd had a dad like Mic, maybe his life would've been different. Maybe he wouldn't have gone off on larks with Doug, come up with those crazy stupid ideas about hitting up easy joints and blowing the money on booze and beach life.

But no, his dad had been a bum. Skipping out on child support before finally skipping town completely—leaving Ricky with a mother who spent more time drunk than sober.

Antoine laid a comforting hand on his shoulder and squeezed. "Man, you shouldn't be here."

Ricky shrugged. "Wanna be here as long as I can. Gonna be in the hospital soon enough and in the ground not much longer after that."

Jill, his head waitress, slipped her five-foot-nothing frame behind the bar and grabbed the soda gun, spewing out the first of several Mountain Dews that she'd drink on her shift. She took a long swallow, eyes narrowing in warning. "Don't say that."

Ricky spread his hands wide. "It's the truth." A slow breath slipped between his lips as his gaze flicked between Jill and Antoine. "And if it's one thing I'm starting to appreciate, it's telling the truth."

Antoine tugged at his ball cap, then blinked hard. His dark eyes softened with fondness. "No matter what, Ricky, you've been good to us. And that says something. At least to me."

Jill tucked her arm around Antoine's shoulders—a feat in

itself given his greater bulk and height—and nodded. "And me too."

Ricky blinked away his tears. "This place and all y'all are the best part a' my life." He let his gaze wander around the bar again as Dax Carpenter's spot wound up. Ricky gave a slow, decisive nod, then turned back to Antoine and Jill. "Need to tell you both something. In case people come around asking questions."

Chapter Six

Tuesday, September 18
Pike Road, Alabama

With a travel tray of coffee in one hand and bags of chicken biscuits and hash browns in the other, Caitlin pushed through the entry door to Ethan and Shannon's offices. She nodded to Wendy, the receptionist, who jerked her head toward the door marked Private and grinned.

"Shannon's in there—and hungry."

Caitlin shook her head. "When isn't she?"

Shannon's roadrunner metabolism was famous amongst the staff, and new employees learned to keep their hands off her stash of snacks.

The phone rang, cutting off any further comment as Wendy greeted, "Starline Security, how may I direct your call? I'm sorry, he's out for the week ..."

The rest of her explanation disappeared behind the door while Caitlin slipped into Shannon and Ethan's inner sanctum, which she jokingly nicknamed their "bat cave." She shivered as the temperature dropped a good thirty degrees. Blue and green lights glowed from the rows of server towers lining the glassed hallway that led to Shannon's office. Using her elbow, she knocked once, then backed through the door.

"Shan, this place becomes more like an igloo every time I visit. What gives?"

Shannon twisted a strand of her long, dark hair, shadows skirting across her brown eyes. "Ethan's upgraded servers mean lowering the office temperature."

Caitlin grimaced. Those new servers were what led to their almost losing the business fourteen months ago.

But Shannon's cheeks curved in a reluctant smile. "As much as their purchase put us in a financial bind, we do need them. He just signed a contract with a hospital group in Pensacola after one of their offices got hacked and someone stole patients' records."

"Yikes for them, but great news for y'all."

"Yeah, this client puts us completely back on track, and Ethan's thinking we'll even turn a nice profit this year. God certainly does use bad things for good—you just have to survive the bad in the interim."

Caitlin cleared her throat with a pointed look toward Shannon's cluttered desk and then the bag of food. Shannon's deep faith might be something Caitlin admired, but admiration didn't mean she shared it—or was comfortable with it. At least not any more. Too much bad had happened for her.

Shannon flashed a sympathetic smile and lifted her head toward the bare conference table in the far corner of her office. "So tell me about this bone you brought me along with breakfast. I'm guessing it's meaty."

Ignoring Shannon's rampant curiosity, Caitlin tugged out the sandwiches and hash browns, taking time to distribute the napkins. She shot a glance to Shannon whose answering look read, "You're stalling." Shannon's brows lifted as she took a bite of her sandwich and chewed.

Unable to deny the silent accusation, Caitlin bit her lip. She pulled off a corner of her sandwich wrapper, watched the steam rise from the breaded chicken, and tried to find the words. Finally, she blurted, "It's about Dax Carpenter's father."

Shannon's eyes widened around her bite. "The NFL player you dated a while back?" she choked out as she cough-swallowed.

Caitlin nodded.

Shannon gulped a mouthful of coffee and leaned toward Caitlin. "Oh, I liked him. You two were good together. I never understood why you broke it off."

Hoping to divert Shannon's romantic dreams, Caitlin waved a hand. "Well, I guess we can't all be as lucky as you and Ethan are."

Shannon took a bite of her sandwich and leveled a serious, but kind look at Caitlin. "You know luck has absolutely nothing to do with it. It's all choice, commitment, and God."

Caitlin winced, hiding behind her coffee cup. "Yeah, I guess so."

Shannon polished off her sandwich and soon her hash browns disappeared. She cast a longing look toward Caitlin's share. "You know if you would just take Ethan up on his offer and come to work for him, your dating life might improve."

Okay, this is totally not going where I need the conversation to go. Time to shut it down.

Caitlin pushed her uneaten hash browns toward Shannon. "A. I'm not looking for a relationship. And B. I'm not a tech nerd. That's your skill set."

Shannon bit her lip and studied Caitlin's offering as if deciding its worthiness as a bribe. She picked up the hash brown patty, but her gaze grew thoughtful and her tone serious. "I'm sure Ethan could find something for you. I know he worries about you—especially after your injury. Of all the fields you could've gone into, law enforcement is the absolute last one that any of us would've expected."

35

"Oh, I don't see that. Daddy was a police chief."

Shannon devoured the hash browns and wiped her fingers on the thin paper napkin. "Yes, but you have the most beautiful voice. You should have stuck with opera like you planned. I mean I get the whole thing with what happened to Missy, but ..."

Caitlin sighed. And there it was. The source and cause of every choice she'd made since college. Appetite gone, she wrapped up her unfinished sandwich and pulled out the case file, setting it open on the table in front of Shannon. It was an obvious and abrupt change of topic, but hopefully Shannon would take the hint.

"Robbery and murder at a popular restaurant forty years ago in Gulf Shores. The new witness ID'ed Dax's dad, Mark Carpenter, as the robber—and killer of the restaurant's manager. Said they were partners in several robberies all along the Gulf Coast."

Shannon blinked. "I'm sorry, what? Murder?"

Caitlin nodded as she flipped to the case notes. "Yeah. You heard right."

Shannon skimmed the printouts, intrigue gleaming in her eyes. "Wow. And what do you think?"

"I'm not sure. I've only got what they've converted to digital—still waiting on the full case file. But looking at what's in it—how extensively Dax's dad would have had to cover his tracks for those forty years, the credibility of the accusing witness after all that time—it doesn't seem possible. And yet ..."

"And yet something's tickling that gut of yours, right?"

"Yeah, unfortunately."

Shannon set the papers aside. "All right then, tell me the story."

"The morning of Wednesday, July fifth, nineteen-seventy-eight, Michael "Mic" Prescott, the restaurant manager of The Broken Flip-Flop, was found dead behind the bar."

"Gunshot?"

"No, oddly enough. Coroner said it was blunt force trauma."

Shannon's lips twisted in consideration. "So heat of the moment, then yeah?"

"That's the way it reads to me and to the original investigators."

"What else?"

"The cash register and safe were open and cleaned out. No telling how much had been taken. But could easily have been several thousand dollars, given it was July."

Shannon's brows lifted. "Wow. Did they have any leads?"

Caitlin shook her head. "Nothing definite at the time, but now, yeah. This witness, Ricky Adams, said he and Mark, or Doug Bewley as he was known then, were buddies. They did small robberies together for living expenses and basically as a lark. When Mark/Doug accidentally killed Prescott, they got scared. Ricky wanted to go to the cops because he didn't want to get blamed for the death, but Mark/Doug argued Ricky was just as guilty because he was there. They decided the best thing to do was go their separate ways and disappear."

Shannon skimmed the pages. "That would definitely turn a case cold."

Caitlin leaned her elbows on the table. "So Ricky runs to Texas, gets a job as a bartender at a sports bar, and when the owner dies, he inherits the place. A few months ago, he got a terminal diagnosis. Saturday, he's working at the bar and has the SEC channel on. A clip of Dax's college hall of fame induction ceremony runs, and in it someone pulled Mark up on stage. Ricky recognizes him, calls in the tip, and here we are."

"How can I help?"

"Outside of some deep background checks on these names, I'm not sure yet. I just really wanted a second pair of eyes. And—"

Shannon's lips quirked in a sympathetic smile. "And someone to tell you you're not crazy for taking on this case?"

Caitlin huffed. "Yeah, this has bad idea written all over it. If I find out the witness is right, Dax will hate me. If I find out they're wrong, I've reopened a door I thought was closed forever."

Shannon's nostrils flared. "Why do you care if he hates you?"

Caitlin swallowed a curse. Shan was on the scent.

Caitlin played with the loose edge of the sandwich's wrapping paper, hoping she could fudge her way out of the hole she'd dug. "I don't know. I guess … he is a great guy … and I really did like him …"

Shannon's mouth dropped open as her gaze sharpened. "Wait, so are you still in love with Dax?"

"No. Not at all. Of course not."

Ugh, what is it about Shannon that always makes me overshare?

"We didn't work together. *Couldn't* work together." Caitlin shifted her eyes from Shannon's disbelieving gape to the dregs of her coffee. "But he's a good human being. And I don't want to be the person responsible for ruining his view of his dad."

Shannon lifted a single brow. Doubt creased the corners of her mouth. "Uh huh." She crossed her arms over her chest and leaned back in her chair. "You know Mark Carpenter is responsible for ruining Dax's view of him, not you. I think you just don't want to admit you made a mistake and ended something you shouldn't have."

Heat stole up Caitlin's neck as she tugged the file across the table and shuffled the papers into some semblance of order. But Shannon's comment whirled in her head. Had she made a mistake?

No. It had to be done. I couldn't risk—

The *Law & Order* theme song rumbled from her purse. Shannon snorted and shook her head. "I still can't believe that's your ringtone."

Caitlin chuckled as she reached for the phone. "You're one to talk. Yours is the *Leverage* theme."

Shannon's smile widened into a smirk.

Caitlin read the number on the screen. "I need to take this. Looks like it may be the detective at Gulf Shores P.D."

Shannon nodded and cleared away their breakfast. Caitlin placed a hand over her re-wrapped biscuit as she answered the call.

Detective Osgood jumped right into the details. "Mark Carpenter lawyered up, and we spent yesterday questioning him, but all he'd say was he didn't do it. We've got the eyewitness statement but with nothing else corroborating it, we can't hold him. I did tell him he has to stay in town until the investigation is finished. His lawyer wasn't happy, but they agreed."

Caitlin didn't know Mark all that well, and even then, her experience was five years old. "You think he's a flight risk?"

Osgood hmphed. "I wouldn't have put it past him to do a duck and run back then. But now? Nah, he's too adamant he's innocent." Flipping papers fluttered in her ear. "Funny enough, though, there's no record of Mark Carpenter before 1978 except for a Social Security number and birth certificate."

Shannon returned to the conference table and slid into her chair, watching Caitlin. Her brow furrowed as she tried to piece together one side of the conversation.

Caitlin's gaze sharpened. "I have a consultant who researches this type of evidence. She's helped me solve several cases over the past few years. If you'll give me the information, I can ask her to run it and see what she can find."

"Done. I'll email the digital case file to you when we get off. It'll still take a week to get the hard copy to you. But if you want to come to Gulf Shores and see it sooner, we'll roll out the red carpet."

"Thanks. I'll have to clear it with my SAC since I'm still on desk duty after an on-the-job injury, but I'll let you know."

"Happy to have all the help we can get, Fitzhugh."

Caitlin's automatic reply of "my pleasure" sat frozen on her tongue. Swallowing the words, she opted for something more truthful. "I'll keep you posted." She ended the call as Shannon lifted her brows, questions lurking in her brown eyes. "Looks like you've got something to start with. With the exception of his birth certificate and Social Security number, Mark Carpenter didn't exist before 1978."

Shannon tugged the file toward her. "Oh, I love a secret." She flipped it open and jotted the information down on a sticky note.

Something told Caitlin more secrets would be revealed before this was all over. Possibly even some of her own.

Chapter Seven

Tuesday, September 18
Montgomery, Alabama

Caitlin leaned against her car door and groaned when she ended the call with Bill McWorter, allowing her curse free rein. Not only had he approved her trip to Gulf Shores, he'd sounded almost like he'd help her pack. Had she been that much of a pain during her desk duty? Or was he just happy to finally have something to needle her about?

Caitlin closed her eyes and shook her head. *Probably both.*

Bill really wasn't a bad guy, and he was a good boss—although still new enough to the department for that opinion to change. But she cherished her reputation as a consummate professional and did whatever she could to maintain that image—Missy deserved that dedication.

Pull yourself together, Fitzhugh. She climbed into her car, and a reminder alert dinged from her phone. She tapped open her calendar and read the entry for her physical therapy appointment tomorrow morning.

Yeah, that's not happening.

Flicking to her contact list, she dialed the PT office's number, then returned to her calendar. No telling how long the case would take. She calculated the possibilities until the receptionist answered.

"Yes, hello. This is Caitlin Fitzhugh, and I need to cancel my physical therapy appointments for this week and next."

A perturbed hum cut across the airwaves. "Let me just pull up your file. All right then, I see the PT ordered another four weeks of therapy before reassessing your ability to return to full duty. You do understand canceling these appointments will likely delay that, right?"

Caitlin bit her lip. She did. And that would be the perfect excuse not go to Gulf Shores. She *was* only a consultant on Mark's case—even though the ASDI would still sign her paycheck. And a medical excuse would be an acceptable and reasonable excuse to get out of the commitment, despite Bill McWorter's approval. She could argue that taking on the case would delay her full return to his team and possibly impact their case solve rate.

Guilt pricked at her. The excuse was lame. And Bill would see right through it—leading to even more merciless ribbing.

Oh, put your big girl panties on, Caitlin. It's done. You're in it.

She pinched the bridge of her nose and once again pushed aside the emotions that threatened to spill through their invisible wall. "I understand that. As does my boss. But if the PT will email me any additional exercises I can do, I'll make sure I'm still complying with his treatment plan." She forced a wry chuckle. "Maybe I'll even be better when I get back."

The receptionist exhaled her doubt, but agreed. "Please check your email by the end of the day. If you have any questions about the exercises, reply to that email."

Caitlin thanked her and ended the call. Tucking her phone in her briefcase, she turned on the engine. Time to get packing.

Caitlin flicked through her closet, pulling blouses and pants from their hangers mentally creating multiple outfits using the same pieces. She folded each and smoothed them into place in the suitcase, then turned back to the closet, contemplating adding more options. Just in case. Then she shook her head. While she wasn't a clothes horse, she tended to overpack. Worst case, she could have clothes laundered while she was away.

She headed to the bathroom for her toiletries as her phone rang. She slipped her phone out of her back pocket and read the area code. *615. Tennessee.* Her gut clenched. A shiver whispered across the back of her neck. Grabbing the bathroom door jamb, her eyes darted to the date on the phone's screen. It was too early for the yearly call. Then did that mean …?

She stabbed the green button and answered, flinching at the quiver that laced her greeting. "Special Agent Fitzhugh."

"Caitlin Fitzhugh?"

The voice sounded young, eager, quickening Caitlin's pulse. Maybe this time there was news. "Yes. And you are?"

"Special Agent Greg Kidd with the Tennessee Bureau of Investigations. Agent Fallon retired, and I've been assigned Melissa Hargrove's cold case."

"And?" Again, Caitlin's voice quaked. But this time Kidd heard it.

"Oh … no … oh, I'm sorry. So sorry. There's nothing new on the case. I didn't mean to get your hopes up."

Tears pricked her eyes. She smashed her lips tight against the four-letter word that wanted to leap out as Kidd stumbled to cover his gaffe. "I just wanted to touch base. Let you know I'm now your contact on the case."

Caitlin managed to pull words together. "You must be new to family notifications too."

Kidd groaned. "Ah, yeah. I'm sorry. Today's my second day here. I guess I should have waited a few months for the yearly call. But there's not much to do while I'm waiting to qualify for my firearm carry, and I wanted to get a jump on my assignments ..."

The explanation rambled in her ear, but Caitlin didn't listen —couldn't listen—as the memories and hopes crashed through her in an awful mélange of crushing disappointment. When Kidd fell silent, she cleared her throat, lashing the ever-present ache back behind its invisible wall. "Okay then. Have you called Brenda, Missy's mother?"

"Ah, no. Thought I'd start with you—what with your job and all. Thought maybe—"

"Good. I'll call her. If she sees your caller ID, she'll have much the same reaction I had, and more likely worse."

"Yeah, I can see that—and I am sorry. I just ..."

Caitlin forced herself to find some sort of grace. "I get it. You're new and eager." Those were positive traits when harnessed well. And it sounded like it was up to her to rein Kidd in. She took in a quick breath. "I hope you use both well. Fresh eyes on the case with new energy can be a good thing."

Kidd's relieved sigh flickered between them. "Um. Thanks. Hey, uh, when you have time, I'd like to talk about the case, especially given your expertise and friendship with the vic—uh, Missy."

Good catch, Kidd. He was young, overeager, but apparently teachable and empathetic too. He could do well in the job.

Caitlin patted her cheeks dry. Her gaze caught on her half-packed suitcase on her bed. "Yes. We can talk, but I'm on my way out of town to work my own cold case that has fresh leads. Why don't I contact you when I get back?"

"Sure. Sure. That would be great." Curiosity laced Kidd's reply, but he only added, "And yeah, if you'd let Ms. Hargrove know the case contact has changed and give her my cell number, that'd be great."

Caitlin agreed and ended the call. She glanced at the suitcase then at her bathroom, but instead of returning to her packing, she headed toward the living room and her briefcase. She tugged a worn case file out of the back, not that she needed to read it. No, she'd memorized it within hours of receiving the copy from the Tennessee Bureau of Investigations when she'd gotten her state trooper shield.

> 05/18/03. Melissa "Missy" Hargrove, DOB 03/01/82, blonde/blue, mole on inside right elbow, last seen wearing white Belmont Music t-shirt, blue jeans, and pink Converse shoes reported missing by roommate and best friend, Caitlin Fitzhugh, after not returning to their Belmont University dorm room the night of 05/17/03. Fitzhugh reports she last saw Hargrove at or about three p.m. in the practice rooms in the Performance Arts building. Hargrove was practicing her cello for her performance final and stated she would be home by eight o'clock.
>
> Teacher's Assistant, Jason Ball, confirmed Hargrove left the practice room at seven-thirty, stating she would see him the next day for class. Bell reported Hargrove appeared to be in good spirits when leaving.
>
> Security camera footage recorded Hargrove leaving the building at seven-thirty-seven. A canvass of the area was conducted the morning of 05/18/03. A cello case and cello, confirmed by Fitzhugh to belong to Hargrove, were discovered under the magnolia trees ten feet from the back exit on 05/18/03 at seven-fifteen am. Neither the cello nor the case appeared damaged outside of customary wear. No other signs of a struggle were found at the scene. Mother, Brenda Hargrove, was notified of disappearance by campus security on 05/18/03 at seven-fifty-five am. Contact

attempted with father, Donald Hargrove, at same time. Notification confirmed at one-twenty-three pm 05/18/03. Dental records requested. Dentist of record: Dr. Raymond Barnes, Montgomery, AL

Case turned over to Tennessee Bureau of Investigations on 05/22/03.

Case closed as unsolved on 01/31/04.

Caitlin stared at the copy of Missy's photo. Missy had moved to Pike Road, Alabama joining Caitlin's seventh grade class after her parents' divorce. For Missy's mom, it was returning home after living her married life in Nashville. Missy, an only child, had grown up coming to see her grandparents in the area.

Caitlin had been assigned to be Missy's homeroom buddy, but it wasn't long before they were inseparable. As much as Caitlin loved her brothers, she and Missy were kindred spirits—cleaved together by a joint love of music and the same birthday.

When the police had come to their dorm room, she'd taken the most recent photo she had and torn it in half, removing herself. The original had been of the two of them at their spring concert. Taken by Daddy with Mom, Ethan, Luke, and Brenda grinning with pride, Caitlin had slung her arm around Missy's shoulders as she held her cello and bow in a pantomime of a final flourish.

And Missy's performance had been amazing. The orchestra director for the Nashville Symphony even complimented her finger work, hinting at the possibility of a chair opening up after she graduated. Caitlin absorbed the photo and the pang that always accompanied it. Joy radiated from Missy's eyes, and her smile spoke of dreams on the edge of coming true.

Two months later, she was gone.

Caitlin closed the file with a sigh. "Where are you, Missy?"

She'd asked the question with every review of the case file. With every thought of her bright, talented, Jesus-loving soul sister. And on its heels, came the other question that haunted her. "Where were you, God?"

She shoved the file back into her briefcase. As Kidd had said, there was no news on Missy's case. But Mark Carpenter had a lot on him. Slapping the leather flap shut, Caitlin padded back to the bedroom.

Focus on what you have. Not what you want.

Chapter Eight

Tuesday, September 18
Elba, Alabama

Dax slid his empty plate and fork across the table to Mom. Possibly for the first time in his life with her, they had eaten in silence. Well, he had eaten, but she had pushed her eggs and toast around the plate until finally chucking the cold remnants down the garbage disposal.

She rinsed the plate, tucked it and the fork in the dishwasher, and shoved it closed. After drying her hands on a dish rag, she shuffled over to the coffee maker to top off her mostly full mug. She raised the pot to Dax in silent question, and he shook his head.

The wall phone shrilled, breaking the silence and drawing his gaze. Dax glanced at Mom. Worry, and even fear, flashed through her eyes.

The phone rang again.

Dax pointed to the phone. "Want me to get it?"

She smoothed her hands over her housecoat. This morning's choice was blue with tiny flowers. The color usually brightened her eyes, but today's battle with dark circles and pale cheeks were too much to offset. Gaze dull, she stared at the phone.

It rang again.

Dax eased out of his chair, careful to not startle her, and picked up the phone. The long cord drooped then twisted. Another item he'd asked to update, but Mom liked always knowing where the phone was—since she regularly lost her cell phone around the house.

A lolling, easy lilt poured through the speaker. "May I speak with Susan Carpenter?"

Dax glanced over his shoulder. Mom's eyes widened, and she shrank back against the counter. His lips lifted in a quick, comforting smile. "I'm sorry, but she's unavailable. This is her son. I can take any messages for her."

"Ah, you must be Dax, then."

Dax's brows creased at the casual, but knowledgeable response. "And you are?"

"Peter Broussard. Your father's attorney."

Dax's hand clenched around the receiver as his pulse skittered. Tucking the phone to his chest, he turned to Mom. "It's Pop's attorney. Do you want to talk to him?"

She shook her head and sagged against the kitchen counter.

Dax's voice firmed. "What's going on, Mr. Broussard?"

"Peter, please. And your father is being released." Peter's native New Orleans accent rolled across the phone-line as if he was inviting them over for dinner. "Can y'all come collect him?"

Dax flicked a quick glance toward the clock. "Yes, I can leave in an hour and be down there around lunchtime."

"Pack a bag for him because he's not been completely cleared, so he has to stay in Gulf Shores. Since it's not high season, you should be able to find a hotel easy enough. I can make recommendations if you need them."

Dax's mind whirled. *Not completely cleared? Stay in Gulf Shores?*

"Peter, what is going on? What did Pop tell the police?"

Peter's agreeable tone took on a dubious tinge. "He swears it's a mistaken identity."

Dax leaned against the wall. Breath left his lungs in a hitching sigh. "But the cops don't believe him."

"No, but they also don't have enough to charge him, so they're calling him a 'person of interest.'"

Dax closed his eyes. "Which is just as bad these days."

Peter made a clicking sound and resignation filled his voice. "It isn't the best, but it's not the worst. I'll give you my cell number. Call me when y'all get to town, and we'll meet up at the jail."

Dax hung up the phone and relayed the conversation to Mom. "Do you want to go with me? You can stay here—"

Mom crossed her arms, somehow making her threadbare housecoat seem regal. Her lips firmed as she shook her head. "No, I'm his wife. I need to go. I'll pack bags for both of us and take my own car. You can follow me."

Dax opened his mouth to argue, but swallowed the words as he absorbed the steel in her eyes. "What can I do to help?

Caitlin pulled her official car into the parking lot at the Gulf Shore Police Department and swallowed a curse. Dax's truck was already there. At least it could be Dax's truck. The University of Alabama emblem on the Georgia tag wasn't a dead giveaway—not with the area being known as the Redneck Riviera.

But the black exterior coupled with the King Ranch logo and 4x4 decal, made it at least a dead ringer for the truck he'd owned when they'd dated. She could do a quick license plate search, but that would be an abuse of power—and juvenile. And besides, his presence shouldn't be a surprise, given Osgood's information about having to release Mark.

Osgood. Dang. She'd yet to give him the full run-down of her involvement with the Carpenter family. However, that time was fast approaching. Shaking her head, she grabbed her briefcase and headed inside.

Caitlin introduced herself to the desk clerk. Although two men in tuxedoes didn't appear with a roll of red carpet, the clerk did offer coffee, muffins, or anything else Caitlin wanted while she waited for Osgood. She refused everything, having tanked up on her way down, and settled in to wait.

Pulling out her phone, she sent a quick text to Shannon, asking for updates on the searches she'd started that morning. Shannon's immediate and indignant reply popped on the screen. A gif of a woman sitting at her desk drumming her fingers.

Caitlin chuckled. "I'll take that as a no."

The door to the main station area opened, drawing her gaze. A second later, she'd wished it hadn't. Dax stood behind his mom, Susan, holding the door while she shuffled through it. Susan looked as if she'd aged twenty years instead of five. Her gaze landed on Caitlin, and her lips lifted into a quick, but almost-relieved smile.

There was no avoiding the greeting and really, Caitlin didn't want to. Susan would have been the perfect mother-in-law. "Hi, Susan." Caitlin stood as Susan reached for her hand.

"It's good to see you, Caitlin. I wish it were under different circumstances."

Caitlin nodded, her gaze shifting to Dax, and her heart fell as his eyes met hers. Pain deepened the lines in his forehead and pinched his lips, a reaction she'd seen many times before in the faces of family members who'd walked into her office. It was a terrible look on them, but a gut-wrenching one on Dax. Caitlin balled her hand into a fist to keep from reaching for him, from pulling him into a hug and telling him everything would work out.

She couldn't guarantee that outcome anyway. "I heard Mark's being released?"

Dax nodded. "We just met with his lawyer, and since he can't leave the area, I'm going to find a hotel for us."

A hotel. Great. Thankfully, there was no shortage of those in Gulf Shores. But they could not end up at the same one. Even a newbie defense attorney would use that detail to rip through her claim of unbiased participation in the case. "Do you know where?"

Dax shook his head. "Any suggestions?"

"As long as it isn't the Hampton Inn, you're fine."

Susan looked confused, but understanding lit Dax's eyes. "Got it. I'll steer clear of it."

"Caitlin, Dax said you agreed to consult on the case. I'm very grateful."

Oh, don't be grateful yet, Susan. I could be your worst nightmare.

But Caitlin pulled what she hoped was a comforting smile out from under the guilt. "Even though Dax requested my help, please remember I'm an unbiased consultant. This has to be as clean as possible in case ..." She let the thought trail off. After all, everyone knew the potential outcome.

Susan pulled a tentative smile over her lips. "Oh, of course. But I will say, it's so good to see you again. It's been a long time."

The memories, the emotions, hung between them. Dax had taken her to Elba a few times toward the end of their relationship to visit his parents. During their first visit, Caitlin discovered she and Susan shared a mutual love of old movies and older books. They would talk Grace Kelly and Jane Austen, while Dax and Mark would man the barbecue.

And if there was time, Susan would pull Caitlin to the piano and coax her into singing the choir's part of the pieces she'd planned for their next church service. Away from her own mother's well-meaning questions and guilt, Caitlin had relished the opportunity to sing for the simple joy of it.

Susan's cheeks curved with sadness, and a wisp of regret flickered across Caitlin's heart. *Looks like Mom isn't the only mother who's unhappy with how everything ended.*

The side door opened again, revealing a burly man in a sport coat and khakis with a detective's shield clipped to his belt. He leaned into the waiting area as his dark eyes scanned the room, absorbing the scene before zeroing in on Caitlin. "Would you be ASAC Fitzhugh?"

Caitlin tucked her heart back behind its invisible wall. "That would be me. You must be Detective Osgood."

He extended his hand, wrapping Caitlin's almost twice around. A heavy gold signet similar to Dax's national championship ring circled Osgood's ring finger. But instead of a crimson A, a gold Greek Omega gleamed from a purple background. "I'm Tyrone, but please call me Ty."

"Caitlin. And it's a pleasure." She forced a smile, but the words were true. She slid a quick glance to Dax and Susan, more than ready to escape Susan's disappointment.

As if sensing the tension, Ty flashed an easy smile. "Ready to get started?"

You have no idea.

"Let's do this."

Chapter Nine

Tuesday, September 18
Gulf Shores, Alabama

Ty gestured Caitlin back to an array of desks in the department's bullpen with a sweep of his thick arm.

"I've got you a space to use for as long as you want, and there's a conference room down the hall if you want to spread out. Coffee's in the breakroom just beyond it. The CCTV footage has been converted to digital and is on the department servers." He pulled an index card out of a file on his desk and handed it over. "And I've got your login and temporary password right here."

Caitlin's brows lifted. "You weren't kidding about the red carpet."

Ty's lips pulled back in a wide grin as he tugged out his chair. "We do our poor best."

Caitlin snorted and sat in the chair at the desk across from him. She made quick work of the login and password change, then gave the screen a cursory glance. *Pretty basic setup. Good.*

Turning her attention to Ty, she said, "I read through the

digital files. Tell me what wasn't in them. Anything missing from the original case file? Forty years is a long time."

Ty flipped through a file on his desk. "The higher-ups converted a lot of the cold files to digital around the time I got my detective shield. So that was twenty years ago. Only reason I remember it is because the IT guys were chasing their tails my whole first week on the desk."

Caitlin nodded as he handed her the file. "Which means we may not even know what we're missing until we go looking for it. Been there."

"But the most obvious things I couldn't find were a couple of sheets of the detective's notes from the witness interviews."

Caitlin frowned as she read through the old statements. "And who was the witness?"

"A waitress who worked at the restaurant. Doesn't read like she saw anything—but she found the body."

"Okay, so probably nothing earth-shattering then. Tell me about this Ricky Adams. Is he local where we can talk to him?"

"Nope, and unfortunately, he's in pretty bad shape. Colon cancer, got to stay in Texas for his treatments. We did the interview via video call, and when it comes time, the ADA will have to go there for the deposition."

"Think he'll be around long enough to testify?"

Ty shrugged. "He said his doctors say at most six months, but they're doing surgery sometime this week to buy him some more time. Ricky says the odds are good. The DA's office won't splurge for a trip to Texas to take the depo in person until we have solid evidence."

Caitlin swallowed her frustration. Budgets were a pain, but she understood. "All right. Let's get them some then. What about the CCTV footage?"

Ty rolled around to her side and pointed to a file folder on her screen. "It's in there. Cameras covered the entrance and the bar, but the robbers wore long hippie-type wigs with headbands."

Her mouth dropped open. "You're kidding me."

"Nope." Ty's grin wrinkled his cheeks and brightened his dark eyes. "There was a July Fourth party that night, so everyone was dressed up. Completely obscured any ID—especially since it looks like the robbers knew where the cameras were located. Prescott must have struggled with one while the other emptied the safe, but it doesn't show exactly what happened."

Caitlin found the coroner's report while Ty pulled up the video. She scanned the report, noting the pertinent details. "Evidence collected at the scene found the victim's hair and blood on the corner of the bar, which is consistent with the wound according to the medical examiner."

Ty nudged her arm, drawing her attention back to the screen. "Okay, here it is. The two perps enter, look around, and then head for the cash register and the safe below it."

Caitlin watched one man paw through the register, then duck down behind the counter. A moment later, the other one turned. "That must be when Prescott catches them."

Ty nodded. "Something happens off-screen. The suspects run out the front door—obviously panicked."

The footage ended, and Caitlin studied the screen. "Where's the transcript of Ricky Adams's statement? I want to run through it against the camera footage."

Ty clicked to another folder on the screen and pulled up a document. "Want me to print you a copy?"

Caitlin nodded. "That'd be good."

The printer next to their desks whirred.

She grabbed the print out from the tray, skimmed the video back to before the robbery, then clicked play. "Okay, so Ricky said they'd waited until the restaurant closed up and watched the bartender leave. So here's the bartender wiping down the bar. He empties the cash register and puts the money in a bank bag, then into the safe."

Caitlin paused the video and scanned Ricky's statement. "But according to his witness statement, Ricky said he actually got money from the register." She studied the bartender on the grainy video. "So that's inconsistent, but not surprising."

Ty shrugged. "Yeah, the last thing you want is a witness to be absolutely right."

"Especially after forty years." Caitlin pressed play again. "We can give him a pass on that." She glanced to the time on the video. "Okay, thirty minutes after the bartender leaves, they enter. Odd they didn't wait longer than that."

Ty clicked his tongue. "Not the brightest crayons in the box?"

Caitlin huffed. "But bright enough to go forty years without being caught."

"Yeah, there's that."

"Ricky goes for the register like he said." She paused the video and looked back to the notes as Mark/Doug turned. "Ricky said he'd cracked the safe and was going for the money when he heard Prescott call out. So that must have been what grabbed Mark/Doug's attention. Okay, that fits."

Caitlin watched the screen, waiting for Ricky to reappear from where he had bent down behind the bar. A moment later Ricky jumped up, obviously panicked.

"This must be where Mark/Doug pushed Prescott. Ricky said there was no attempt to explain—Mark/Doug just reacted." She paused the video again and flipped through the case notes. "Was there a gun at the scene?"

Ty shook his head. "Surprisingly enough, no. Not on the perps that we can see. Ricky said they never used them. And there wasn't one at the bar or restaurant."

"Something else must have made Mark/Doug panic enough to push Prescott and knock him into the bar. Interesting."

Ty leaned back in his chair with huff. "Yeah, but there's still nothing on the video that backs up Ricky saying Mark Carpenter was his partner."

Caitlin's eyes unfocused as she replayed the video in her head. Slowly, the timing and her knowledge of crime patterns gelled. She tossed a glance to Ty. "Did the original investigators check any of the earlier footage?"

He clicked through the folder on the screen and shook his head. "The converted case notes don't mention anything earlier than the day of the crime itself." He turned a curious glance her way. "And Ricky didn't say anything about being there earlier. Think Mark/Doug might have cased the place on his own before robbing it?"

"It's not unusual." Caitlin shrugged and turned back a few pages to skim the itemized evidence report. "But there's no mention here about the original investigators looking at earlier footage either." She heaved a frustrated sigh. It had been forty years and investigative protocols regarding digital security had evolved. But it still made her job harder. "Let's at least go back to the first of what we do have."

Ty clicked back to the beginning of the footage and sped through the morning until he saw one of the staff opening the restaurant for lunch then slowed it back to real-time. Caitlin scoured the footage for similar body types and clothing since hairstyles and faces were out of the running. "Let's bump it up a bit."

Ty increased the speed times eight. Images blipped across the screen as patrons, waitstaff, and bartenders went about their day. By the time they reached five o'clock, there was still no sighting of Ricky or Mark/Doug. But at seven o'clock, Caitlin spotted one of the wigs.

"Pause it." She pointed to the screen and glanced to Ty. "There he is. Same wig, same headband."

Ty leaned in. "Yep. We got him checking things out. Great catch." He put the video back to real-time, and they watched the scene play out. Mark/Doug elbowed his way to the bar from the entrance. "There's the manager, Mic Prescott, behind the bar with the bartender. What was his name?"

Ty checked the file. "Jimmy Gates."

Caitlin nodded. The scene continued to play. Mark/Doug lifted a finger and pointed to the beer tap. The bartender nodded and filled the drink, sliding it along the bar until Mark/Doug caught it in his hand. He nursed the beer for a few minutes, watching the crowd, then left a few bills on the bar and headed to the entrance, taking care to hide his face from the cameras.

Caitlin tapped the screen. "Check out Prescott and Gates. See how Prescott kind of shrugs and smiles as Mark/Doug walks away? And Jimmy shakes his head—even knows exactly which beer to serve? There's a familiarity there."

Ty scratched his stubbled chin. His fraternity ring gleamed under the fluorescent light. "They definitely knew him. Which gives weight to Ricky's claim—even though it doesn't fully corroborate it."

"Yeah. But something's bugging me." Caitlin fiddled with the top page of the case file as the video replayed in her mind. "Will you forward it to when they came in that night?"

"Sure. What'd you see?"

"I'm not sure."

With the video cued back up, they watched the scene again. As the one perp dashed off camera and then back into view, Caitlin pointed at the screen. "Right there."

Ty's brows furrowed. "What about it?"

"Watch the perp's hand. It goes to his forehead like he's wiping at something. Look when he pulls his hand away."

Ty leaned in closer. "Blood? You think it's his?"

Caitlin nodded as she tugged the case file in front of her and pulled out Mark's photo. "I'm thinking, yeah. Check this out." She tapped the photo, then glanced at Ty. "Mark has a scar above his right eye. The perp wipes what looks like blood from the right side of his face."

"Maybe Mic tagged him hard enough to leave a scar."

"Exactly."

Caitlin clicked play and watched the rest of the scene. She tapped a finger against the file as she stared, unseeing, at the screen, while her mind twisted and turned the evidence trying to make it fit. "Did anyone re-interview Jimmy Gates after Ricky made his statement?"

Ty folded his arms across his chest and leaned back in his chair, the springs squeaking under his bulk.

"I followed up, but that's a no-go. He was injured breaking up a bar fight about twenty years ago in Orange Beach. Took a bottle to the head and got a traumatic brain injury. Died not long after that." Ty unfolded his arms and swung his chair back to his side of the desks. "Don't think he would've been much help anyway, though. They said that blow messed him up pretty good. Guess what they say is true, 'No good deed goes unpunished.'"

Caitlin's stomach churned. *God, I hope it isn't. Otherwise, I may be in for some serious penance after this case.*

Shaking off Ty's foreboding words, she closed the case file and stood. "All right, then. I'm going to head over to the conference room. I want to spread out and look at all the evidence piece by piece. Where's that coffee pot you mentioned?"

Chapter Ten

Tuesday, September 18
Gulf Shores, Alabama

Dax adjusted the leather duffle bag on his shoulder and tugged Mom's rolling suitcase through the hotel room door. From behind them, Pop sucked in a quick breath. Mom ducked under his arm and walked in, mouth dropping open. "Dax, honey, this is lovely, but we can't afford it."

Dax came in behind her and placed his hands on her shoulders, giving them a reassuring squeeze as he surveyed the suite. There was a small kitchenette, living area, and king bed, complete with private balcony and a stunning Gulf view. "I wasn't sure how long we'd need to be here, and I wanted you to be comfortable." He released her shoulders and looked at Pop. Hurt, anger, frustration, and worry circled and danced in Dax's stomach.

"But—" Mom's objection drew his gaze back to her overwhelmed expression.

Dax's lips lifted. "No buts, Mom. I've got it covered." He cut his eyes toward Pop.

Pop reached a hand out to him. His shoulders were loose but pain thinned his lips. "Son, we need to talk."

Dax flicked his gaze to Mom.

If he lied about this, what else has been hiding? Her earlier question hung between them as Dax read the silent plea in her eyes. *Don't leave yet.* Mom bit her lip, and she rubbed the back of her neck. Dax winced. Yeah, the car ride from the jail had to have been difficult. But did he really want to hear Pop's side? Did she?

He could beg off. He needed a workout, and of course, there was the pressing issue of his Alabama-Texas A & M spot. Given Mom and Pop's solid support of his career, either would be acceptable excuses. And yet, could he leave Mom with Pop without knowing his side of the story?

With a sigh, Dax released Mom's suitcase handle. "Yeah, we do." He dropped his duffle bag, pointed to the kitchenette table, and they each took a seat—Mom on his side as they faced Pop.

Pop flinched as he registered her choice. But then he nodded. "I know you both have a lot of questions, and most of my answers are going to be, 'I don't know.'"

With a steady and firm voice, Pop leveled an unwavering look between them. "You know I grew up in the Florida panhandle, and my parents died in a car accident when I was eighteen. After that, I lived in Orange Beach doing odd jobs for a while. This person, this witness, has to be confusing me with someone else."

Dax watched Mom out of the corner of his eye, gauging her reaction to Pop's claim. She was doing a great job of staring a hole in the table top, and her fingers looked ready to break under her own grip. He laid a light hand on her shoulder and gave her a comforting squeeze. "Do you know who this witness is?"

Pop leaned back in the chair and scratched at the narrow silver scar above his right eye. "No, they wouldn't tell me his name. And I have no idea who it could be." His gaze firmed and certainty radiated from the dark depths. "But that's beside the point. You both know me."

Mom glanced away, her lips tensing. Dax sympathized. That actually was the question.

Pop laid his hands on the table palms up in a silent plea. His steady gaze met Dax's eyes. "Do you really believe I could rob or even kill anyone?" He reached for Mom's hand, but she slipped it off the table and onto her lap.

Pop's lips flinched, but his voice remained steady. "Susan, how many times have I worked for free because someone couldn't afford my services even though they desperately needed them? Remember Cowell Jenkins? How his water heater burned out, and I gave him the one I'd bought to upgrade ours with? Why would I do that if I wasn't the man you both know I am?"

The story was news to Dax, but he watched the memory flicker in Mom's gaze. It did fit with the man he knew Pop to be.

And yet, the police wouldn't have brought him in for questioning unless there was some truth in their evidence too.

Pop reached for Mom again, a plea in his dark eyes. "This is a hiccup, Suz. After forty years together, are you really ready to throw what you know about me out the window on some misidentification?"

Everything in her seemed to deflate under his persuasion. Slowly, she nodded. "You're right. I do know you, Mark." She took his hand and flashed a wan smile, but hope lit her eyes.

Dax's shoulders eased. The witness was wrong. And now he was doubly glad he'd asked Caitlin for her help. Taking Pop's other hand, Dax gave it a squeeze. "We'll get this figured out."

Dax paced his suite, notes in hand, rehearsing his commentary on his picks of player match-ups to watch in the Alabama-Texas A & M game. He'd done most of the legwork prior to getting the news about Pop's arrest so all that remained was putting together his spot and getting it recorded. Unfortunately, the "putting it together" part was not going well.

He glanced at his notes, then looked at the wall as he envisioned the one fan out there who really wanted to hear his insight. "Number fifty-seven, wide receiver, Keyshawn Owens is a powerhouse pitted against ...wait, something's not right." Dax checked his notecards then ran a hand over his head with a groan.

"*Forty*-seven, doofus. Fifty-seven is the center." He tossed his cards on the couch and stalked to the window. A barge dotted the distant horizon, and a pair of sailboats steered out toward the lowering sun. Sugar-white sand lapped by clear, aqua-green water beckoned him with its promise of peace.

"Yeah, maybe a run on the beach would help." He shot the notecards a dark look. "Getting nowhere on this anyway right now."

Tucking his feet into flip-flops, Dax grabbed his phone, earbuds, and a bottle of water from the fridge. He reached the beach access a few minutes later, slid off the flip-flops, scrolled through his music app, choosing his usual running playlist. But when the thumping beat hit his ears, he tapped pause.

Closing his eyes, he focused on the slap and shush of the water as it met the shore. No, that was the music he needed. He tucked his phone and earbuds into a zippered pocket then set out in an easy barefoot jog on the wet sand. Up ahead, beach chairs and umbrellas clustered around two large coolers as a pair of surf fishing rods bobbed and pulled nearby. Four adults sat in an animated conversation, while six boys of varying ages played touch football.

Dax smiled at their innocent pleasure. Eager encouragements and gentle ribbing floated toward him as the football was thrown, caught, and the teenaged receiver dashed over the imaginary goal line. He dropped the ball, turned, and threw his arms in the air like goalposts.

But a moment later, his jaw fell open, his arms lowered, and he ran back to his friends. Grabbing two of them by the arms, he whispered and shot quick glances over his shoulder at Dax.

Busted. Dax slowed and prepared for the crush of admiration. His fame was Caitlin's least favorite part of dating him—and the reason for her breaking things off. He shook off the memory and focused on the present. Cheeks curving with a friendly grin, he waved to the boys.

"Oh, man. You're Dax Carpenter. This is crazy." The boy who made the "touchdown" turned and yelled back at the adults. "Dad! It's Dax Carpenter."

The man pushed back his ratty-on-purpose Roll Tide ballcap and scratched his head, eyes narrowing then widening with recognition. As the boys peppered Dax with questions, stats, and praise, the man dug something out of a beach bag and shuffled through the loose sand toward them.

"Dax Carpenter." An amazed smile danced over his lips. "Man, I watched you play at Alabama—always knew you'd make it to the pros. That Iron Bowl game where you scored two touchdowns after running thirty yards the first time, and snagging the ball one-handed the second time. Man, I'll remember that 'til the day I die."

He took off his ball cap and held it and a Sharpie out, flashing a sheepish smile.

"I know you're on vacation or whatever, but would ya' mind?"

Dax shook his head with an easy grin. "Of course not." He signed the brim, including his college jersey number, then glanced to the boys. "How about the ball?"

The teenager who scored the "goal" looked from Dax back to where the ball lay in the sand, eyes widening with disbelief. "You mean it? I'm mean yeah. Let me get it."

They chatted a bit while the teen dashed off, and Dax learned the two families were visiting from Tuscaloosa on the kids' fall break. The boy returned with the ball and watched with awe as Dax again signed and added his jersey number and the encouragement, "Keep playing."

After a bit more conversation, Dax returned to the water's edge, giving them a brief wave. The father looped an arm around his son's shoulders as they walked back to the group. Snippets of their words caught the breeze, rehashing the interaction and debating the best place to display the hat and the ball at their home.

Dax returned to his jog, the sand melting under his feet. He and Pop had been much the same back in the day. When Dax first showed an interest in football, Pop had been right there, encouraging him, practicing with him for hours on end, even attending the pee-wee games. But as he grew up, Pop stopped going to the games.

Dax had asked him to come to his first game as a starting wide receiver in high school, certain Pop would be eager to cheer him on. Pop, however, shook his head and said something like, "Crowds aren't my thing, son."

Dax had been disappointed, but the more he thought about it, the more he realized Pop was a loner. He worked by himself as an electrician. He tinkered alone with an old Mustang GT in his workshop. He would go to church with Mom for Sunday service, but few of the other gatherings.

Dax had learned to accept it. Besides Dax had always felt loved. Pop always wanted to talk or throw balls, always had an encouraging word. But what if Pop's self-isolation wasn't a preference? What if he'd been hiding?

Dax stumbled as the questions crowded him, peppering him with uncertainty. Desperate to outrun the doubts, he ramped up into the familiar sprint drills drummed into him over the last twenty years. But still more condemning memories rose.

Pop had skipped Dax's college national championship as well as all of the NFL games, despite the offer of box seats. And it had taken almost an act of God and Mom's bribery to get him to the college Hall of Fame induction ceremony.

That's where Pop had been pulled up on stage by a well-meaning member of the team's staff. Where he'd been caught on camera in a film clip that had played on the SEC Network across the South. That allowed the witness to label Pop as someone other than who he'd always claimed to be.

Had Pop given in to Mom's demand he attend because he figured after forty years, he was safe? Dax's stomach clenched as the sweat suddenly chilled against his skin. If Pop had been hiding rather than preferring isolation, did Dax really know him at all?

He pulled out his phone and opened his texts. Scrolling through the list, he paused at Zebedee Reeves's name. The date next to his name was from two months ago. He tapped the message and scanned the conversation. Zeb's oldest son, Marco, had been starting pee-wee football.

Zeb's career, marriage, and three kids under the age of seven made prioritizing friendships difficult. But Zeb was still his closest friend—had been since they'd met at the Titans' rookie training camp. And Dax could trust him without question. Maybe he could help Dax sort out the truth. He tapped out a quick text asking Zeb to call when he got a chance.

Dax scrolled through his contacts list until he found Caitlin's name. Her reaction to his reminder his number hadn't changed played across his memory. Since he hadn't changed his, maybe hers hadn't either?

Worth a shot.

Needing some amount of grounding against the confusion thrumming through him, he clicked on the message icon and typed out a quick text.

DAX: Thank you for looking into this. I really appreciate it.

He waited a moment, but then decided he hadn't really expected an immediate reply, if any. Brushing off the disappointment, he tucked the phone back in his pocket. He returned to his run, and did his best to push all thoughts of Pop, Caitlin, and what to do about either of them out of his mind.

Chapter Eleven

Tuesday, September 18
Gulf Shores, Alabama

Caitlin pulled her rolling suitcase behind her, mentally exhausted from the review of the video and setting up the evidence board and eager to disappear into her hotel room. A young couple chattered up ahead as they corralled their toddlers, each carrying a small plastic pail and shovel. The mom's neck and arms were an alarming shade of pink.

That would be me after a day on the beach—even with sunscreen.

They passed by her, discussing how to best schedule dinner, bedtime, and sunset on the beach. Caitlin smiled. Their accents tagged them as native southerners. But not from Alabama. Maybe Georgia?

Clutching the bag of fast-food dinner around her melting strawberry milkshake, she scanned the hallway for her room. Finding it, she pushed inside the heavy door and gave the layout a quick, cautious survey, an old habit instilled by police training and years of crime scene visits. But thankfully nothing malicious met her experienced gaze, freshly reset for the new guest.

Dropping her bag and briefcase by the closet, she plopped on the loveseat and pulled her fast-food salad and fries from the paper bag and took a long sip of her shake. Figuring the lettuce would cancel out the extra calories of the ice cream, she'd splurged on the shake. Besides after all the bombs over the last two days, she needed the comfort of carbs and fat grams.

A ding sounded from inside her briefcase. Popping a fry in her mouth, she pulled out her phone and read the banner and the message.

DAX: Thank you for looking into this. I really appreciate it.

"Dax, we can't be doing this." She shook her head. "But I didn't set this as a rule, so yeah, I guess texting is fair game."

She bit her lip as a deep ache welled within her. She could blame it on fatigue, on the stinging in her shoulder, on any number of things that had loosened her grip on her emotional wherewithal. But she couldn't ignore the pang of guilt. She should be with him. Holding his hand, holding *him*, as he faced this nightmare. Caitlin closed her eyes against his words.

She had her own nightmare—a daily reminder of why she couldn't be with him.

But she also knew she couldn't leave him hanging. Not when she knew his heart and the unknown he faced. Opening her eyes, she stared at his words, her fingers poised over the keyboard for some sort of reply. But what could she say?

As much as her heart wanted to comfort him, her mind overruled it—and with good reason. Her phone records could be subpoenaed by Mark's defense attorney. If there was anything damaging in the messages with Dax, that could be enough to place doubt in the minds of a jury about her objectivity—even if the evidence proved Mark was guilty.

She stared at his words, shoving her heart out of the way until she found the most innocuous reply she could make.

CAITLIN: You're welcome. I'll keep you posted.

She tapped out of the text app, wishing she could shut off her longing just as easily. Her gaze dropped to the phone icon. She'd promised Kidd she'd update Brenda. Maybe that conversation would silence the cry in her heart—since it obviously wasn't listening to her head.

Caitlin took in a deep breath then pulled up Brenda's contact file only to stare at the numbers. Caitlin called her twice a year. Always on the anniversary of Missy's disappearance and again on the date the investigators shelved the case.

Sometimes Brenda would answer, sometimes she wouldn't. The times she did, their conversations were stilted and rife with unfelt emotion. Would she answer this time? Or would Caitlin leave the details on her voicemail, possibly heard, probably deleted unopened? Or maybe this time it would be different. Maybe they might talk, really talk, about—

"Just call her, Fitzhugh. Delaying isn't going to make it any easier." And she really did need to get her heart back under control.

She stabbed the number and held the phone to her ear as rings replaced the silence. *One Mississippi. Two Mississippi. Three Mississippi. Sounds like it's voicemail time.* Caitlin wasn't certain if she was relieved or disappointed. *Four Miss—*

"Caitlin?"

Well, crap. Okay, she'd hoped for voicemail.

"Yeah, hi, Brenda." Caitlin pushed as much brightness into her words as she could muster. "How are things?"

"The same. Gas is up, stocks are down, and Missy is still gone."

Caitlin closed her eyes and willed the guilt away even as she cringed at the truth in Brenda's words. "Yes, about that. There's a new contact at the TBI for Missy's case. Agent Fallon retired, and an Agent Greg Kidd has taken it over." Caitlin swallowed, opting to avoid mentioning Kidd's youth, zeal, and cell number. Not like Brenda would be calling him anyway.

"That's good to know. Thank you."

The air throbbed with tense silence as unanswerable questions warred with unspoken condemnation.

"Was there something else?" Brenda's words were clipped, irritable, and sliced through Caitlin with the ease of a stiletto knife.

"Ah, no. I guess not. Brenda, you have to know I've never giv—"

The call dropped. Caitlin closed her eyes. Why had she thought this conversation might be different? She clicked off the screen, tossed the phone on the bed, and gazed at her briefcase.

The morning after Missy's disappearance, the local police's interviews finished, Caitlin had decided to do her own search, harnessing all her memories of conversations with Daddy around the dinner table about his cases and detective methods. She knew Missy as well as herself. Surely, she would spot something the investigators missed.

On the off-chance Missy had hidden her true feelings, Caitlin had started with their room, scouring Missy's notes and papers for any clues indicating she might have run off willingly. Unfortunately, but thankfully, she found nothing. She skipped her classes that day to search the practice rooms and retrace Missy's steps. Steps Caitlin had taken with her for weeks after their practice sessions.

She'd combed the hallways of the performing arts building, cleared out Missy's music locker, even scoured her preferred practice room searching for clues. Then she'd climbed under the magnolias that sheltered the building, poured over the gazebo out front, even walked every possible route from the back exit.

But no. There was nothing. As the days turned into a week, and finally graduation and summer, Caitlin had forced herself to admit defeat. At least until she could get her own hands on the case file. Certain she'd find Missy, she'd turned down an internship at the Nashville Opera and submitted her application to the ASDI Trooper Trainee program.

More than a decade later, all of Caitlin's devotion, training, and heart still amounted to nothing. Like Brenda said, Missy was still gone. The deep, welling cavern of ache and loss lay open like an abyss in her heart. Caitlin closed her eyes allowing the pain to wrap around her, hoping it would swallow her parallel ache for Dax.

She reached for her pendants, sliding them together along the delicate chain. A cross and a treble clef. The cross, given to her at her confirmation, and the treble clef at her acceptance to Belmont's music program.

Tears clustered in the corners of her eyes. She should have taken the charms off years ago. They served as nothing but constant reminders of lost faith and vanished dreams. But call it a child's longing for simpler times or even her own form of self-flagellation, they tethered her to a past that once held so much promise. A life that she once had no doubt God had set for her.

But despite the call to Brenda and the reminder of Caitlin's own futile search for Missy, her thoughts still returned to Dax. What was he doing tonight? How did he handle being with his dad?

She glanced at her phone, longing to text him again and find out, and yet knowing it was the last thing she should do. Instead, she grabbed her food and forced it down past the bitter tang of loss. When she finished, she tossed the takeout trays with a huff and snagged the print outs of her new PT exercises from her briefcase.

Maybe physical pain would be a better distractor than the emotional at this point. She lurched into the first exercise and gasped as she pushed too far. But there was finally sweet silence in her mind and heart. She repeated the move. And did it again. Even if it only worked for a little while, she'd take whatever reprieve she could get.

Chapter Twelve

Tuesday, September 18
Gulf Shores, Alabama

Dax ducked through the hotel's front door and tossed his empty water bottle in the trash. Nodding to the desk clerk, he headed for the elevator. He needed to get dinner, but given he'd already been recognized on the beach, he figured room service would be a better option. No need to risk drawing even more attention to himself.

He tapped on Mom and Pop's door, and Mom opened it, greeting him with a tired, but welcoming smile. Dax winced. "Going to get room service for dinner. Y'all hungry?"

Mom nodded. "We were just talking options." Her eyes dropped to his clothes, and Dax could feel the sweat slicking his back.

"I'll just get a shower and change and be back in about thirty minutes. Will you order me something?"

"Sure. Any preferences?"

Dax shrugged. "Just something to fill the hole."

Mom winced, then placed a soft hand against his cheek. "I love you, son."

Dax covered her hand with his and nodded. "Love you too."

Twenty minutes later, showered and changed, Dax did a quick check of his email. As promised, Gene seemed to be holding off the higher-ups, but that couldn't last much longer. He glanced at his laptop and decided to hit the assignment again after dinner. He'd wait to tell Gene the rest until he knew what the "rest" was.

The phone rang and Zebedee Reeves's grinning face appeared beneath the name "Preacher." Zeb had been tagged with the nickname after a couple of years of leading the pre-game prayer and praying over any player who'd gotten hurt during a game.

Dax tapped the green button. "Preach. How's it going?"

"Aw man, I'm soaked with probably half the water from the bathtub. Jayden decided to dive in—I swear that kid's gotta be part-fish, even though I can't think of a single swimmer in the family."

Jayden was Zeb and Gina's middle child, and from what Dax could remember, the five-year-old had all the makings of a handful on a good day.

"How are Marco and Trey?"

"Marco got picked for quarterback in pee-wee ball this season. Boy's got an arm you wouldn't believe. And Trey just started walking. Oh, and if that don't beat all, Gina's pregnant again. It's a girl. Can't tell you how excited she is. Says she'll still be outnumbered, but at least there'll be more estrogen in the house to balance out all of the testosterone."

Dax grinned. "A girl? Poor thing. With you as her dad and three older brothers, she isn't going to date until she's twenty."

Zeb's booming laugh pounded through the speaker. "Thirty if I have any say in it. What's up with you? Haven't heard from you in a month of Sundays. I thought for sure when you moved to Atlanta, we'd see more of each other not less."

Dax shook his head. That had been his hope too. Zeb had finished out his NFL career there after the Titans traded him to the Falcons, and he was one of the reasons why Dax opted for the SEC Network post in Atlanta after Caitlin broke up with him. "Well, you've got a wife and kids along with work. I just have work."

"You know, Gina's got a friend she's been dying for you to meet."

"Don't start, Preach." Dax chuckled. "I've still got nightmares from the last time Gina set me up, and that was two years ago."

"Ah, yeah, Diana. Sorry 'bout that one, man. That was totally our bad. No clue she had a crazy ex-boyfriend."

The line fell silent with a comfortable pause. A moment later, Zeb said, "So what's going on? Really."

Dax collapsed on the bed and threw his arm over his eyes, a long slow breath huffing between his lips. "It's not good. And I know I don't have to say this, but keep it to yourself—well, you and Gina. I mean it. I haven't told my producer yet. I know I'm going to have to, but I want to wait until I know more."

Zeb's tone sobered. "I got you, buddy. You know that."

Dax did, and he was grateful. As the words spilled from him, he didn't bother to smother the tears. There was too much history between him and Zeb, too deep of a friendship despite the gulf of months between talks. By the time he'd reached the end of his update, his arm was damp and his emotions were spent.

"Caitlin, huh?" A knowing tone laced Zeb's words.

Dax sighed. "Yeah. I know. Mom already gave me down the road about it. But it's the only thing I could think of doing."

"Mmmhmmm. I get that." Zeb's soft reply eased Dax's lingering concern that he'd done the wrong thing in contacting her. Zeb's voice warmed. "Never will forget that Iron Bowl, man. Auburn might've won the game, but you represented Alabama well that night. Pretending you lost your keys so you could get her business card. Now, that was smooth."

Dax shook his head and chuckled at the memory. "I've never had any game with women, but soon as I saw her, I had to meet her."

"Never would've figured you'd go for a woman in uniform, bro."

"The uniform didn't do it. The woman in it—that was the attraction." Caitlin had been part of Coach's security detail and since Dax was specially invited to the game, he'd been included in the surveillance.

Newly retired from football and waiting for the next door to open, he'd been visiting his parents when Coach called with the offer of sideline access at that year's Iron Bowl. Zeb was still playing in Nashville and jumped at the chance to hang out and reminisce their college ball days—even if he was on Alabama's sideline instead of Auburn's.

"I still can't believe she fell for that line about losing your car keys."

Dax grinned. "She didn't. I think she played along because she was just as interested in me."

While the game raged on the field, Dax and Caitlin had traded glimpses and even a few smiles. But any time he tried for conversation, she brushed him off, all business and intent on her duties. Dax appreciated her focus and his respect for her rose until it equaled his attraction.

"Besides I had to get her number some way. It was the end of the fourth quarter." With suspicion in her eyes and a wry twist of her lips, she gave him her card, saying to call if he wanted to file a stolen item report.

Zeb chuckled. "Like I said, man. Smooth play."

When Dax had called first thing Monday morning, she'd run with the fib, offering to take his statement and fill out the report.

Caught in his white lie, he'd laughed and admitted the ruse. He wasn't sure how, but he convinced her to meet him for coffee, and they'd hit it off.

Then came the break up six months later. When the SEC Network offered him a job as a commentator in Atlanta, he'd headed out, trying not to look back. And now here he was, not only glimpsing back, but allowing himself to hope that door hadn't been completely closed.

Which brought him back to the reason for the call. Dax scrubbed his face. "I don't know what to do."

"About your dad, Caitlin, or both?"

Dax groaned. "I—don't—yeah. Both."

Zeb's reassuring tones slipped between them. "We'll be praying for you, brother."

Dax wiped his eyes and nodded. If anyone could get God's ear, it would be Zeb. "Thanks, Preacher."

"Anytime. And hey, let's not go so long without catching up again."

"You got it."

Chapter Thirteen

Wednesday, September 19
Gulf Shores, Alabama

Caitlin smoothed a glob of foundation onto her face and under her chin. The cream added a hint of rose to her natural alabaster. She uncapped her blush, blending it across her cheekbones until the pink hinted at color rather than screamed it. She gave her efforts a satisfied look, then tucked the products and brushes back in her bag. Though she'd left the music and theater world for law enforcement, she still savored playing with makeup. It was an art all its own—and one she still allowed herself to indulge in despite her career.

Her cell phone dinged, and the screen glowed from the sink counter. *Luke, finally.* She read the time—6:02 a.m. Which meant it was four in Tacoma. "Are you getting up or calling before going to sleep, Fluke?" Deciding she didn't want to know, she clicked off the bathroom light and grabbed the phone, tapping to the text. He'd agreed to the sibling meeting and set eight o'clock her time that night for the call.

She sent a thumbs-up emoji, certain Ethan would agree. She clicked off the phone and headed to the precinct. *Time to take that ball into the end zone.* Caitlin rolled her eyes as the football reference replayed in her mind.

What would it take to get Dax Carpenter out of her head and heart? Maybe when all was said and done and Mark was likely arrested? She couldn't imagine Dax wanting to stick around after she'd been instrumental in getting his dad formally charged.

So why did her heart clench at the thought of never seeing him again?

Caitlin grabbed her wandering emotions and stuffed them away. She had no time for regrets. Mark's guilt couldn't be denied. Dax would leave her life forever. And besides, she wanted both outcomes.

Grabbing her briefcase and room key, she slipped out the hotel room door. She pulled it shut with a definite thud, clinging to the barest flicker of hope she could one day do the same on her feelings for Dax.

Dax, Mom, and Pop followed the receptionist down a long hallway toward Peter Broussard's office. Photos of the Augusta National Golf Club, golf tee flags, and even a framed Masters jacket lined the walls. His shoulders loosened. Football would likely not be a topic of conversation, general or specific, today.

He paused as his thoughts drifted back to the family at the beach. Maybe Caitlin had a point about the fame. He studied the grinning faces of Jack Nicklaus and Tiger Woods. But was fame —and specifically his fame—a good reason for her to end their relationship? Plenty of couples made it work. Why couldn't they have, even with her law enforcement career?

"Mr. Broussard is just in there."

Dax jerked his drifting thoughts back and followed Mom and Pop into the office. Degree certificates from Louisiana State University and Tulane hung on the wall above a credenza filled with photos of a wide age range of people. Peter Broussard looked up from behind his TV screen sized computer monitor and waved them to the seats in front of his desk.

Broussard tugged the rolled sleeves of his dress shirt down his thin forearms and slipped ebony cuff links back into their slots. Then he tapped his gold-rimmed glasses further up his nose and leveled an inquisitive blue gaze on them. When he spoke, the rolling lilt of Louisiana's French Quarter slathered his words.

No, there would definitely be no talk of Alabama or Titans football here.

"Y'all come on in and get situated."

Pop and Mom took the chairs closest to the desk, while Dax opted for the loveseat against the back wall. Peter chattered about the weather and his weekend playing *grand-père*. With a glance to the receptionist, he said, "*Cher*, why don't you get them some cold drinks?"

Mom shook her head and flashed a warm smile to them both. "No thank you, we're fine."

The receptionist nodded then slipped out as Peter flipped through a file on his desk.

"And thank you, Peter, for taking Mark's case."

Peter tapped the file as his head bobbed in an agreeable nod. "Happy to be of service. But before we go any further. I do need to tell ya', Mark, it would best for us to meet privately." Peter shot a pointed look at Dax and Mom. "Attorney-client privilege only applies to you and me. Anything we say in front of Susan and Dax—even though they are your immediate family—is not privileged."

Pop shrugged. "There's nothing to tell they can't hear. I already told you at the police station. I didn't do this."

Peter's eyes narrowed as if weighing Pop's words.

Dax's gut churned while he absorbed the scene. Did Peter suspect Pop was lying? What had he seen or heard to make him question Pop's word? Was it something Dax should have picked up on yesterday?

Dax shook off the feeling of foreboding. No, Peter was a criminal attorney. He simply expected Pop to lie because that's what criminal clients often did. *Right?*

A moment passed, and Peter rested his elbows on the desk, steepling his fingers in front of him. He gave a slow nod, but the look in his eyes didn't change. "Okay, then. I need to know what the state can prove. Did ya' ever live in Gulf Shores? Did ya' ever go to The Broken Flip-Flop around the time of the robbery and murder?"

Pop rubbed his forehead and glanced around the office as if the answers lay somewhere within its walls. "I lived in Orange Beach doing odd jobs for a while after my parents died. Did I go to The Broken Flip-Flop? I have no idea. I didn't have a lot of money, and I ate at a lot of dives, so it's possible."

"Who is this witness anyway?" Mom asked as she gripped Pop's hand.

"I don't know," Peter said. "And I won't know until there's been an arrest. The police don't share information with defense attorneys 'til they have to."

Mom's outraged gasp cracked the air between them. "Mark can't even deny the allegations?" She glanced to Pop, then back over her shoulder to Dax.

Dax winced, but tried for a reassuring smile.

"Right now, no." Peter's brows lifted. "But, Mark, what do ya' think this witness said?"

Pop shook his head and glanced to Mom as if needing to reassure her as much as himself. "I don't know."

Peter laced his fingers together as he searched Pop's face. His easy accent suddenly sharpened. "Why would he name you —identify you—in the crime if you weren't part of it?"

Pop spread his hands wide and shrugged. "Again. I don't know."

Peter remained silent. As the air in the room tensed to just this side of uncomfortable, he released a slow breath and nodded. "Okay then."

Dax leaned forward on the loveseat and lifted a hand. "When can Pop go home?"

Peter shifted in his chair, experience soaking his words. "Maybe in a week? Longer? It all depends on how the witness's information pans out. As a person of interest, you're really in limbo until then."

Mom flashed Dax a worried frown. "You'll need to get back to work—back to your life. You can't be here indefinitely."

Dax reached forward and squeezed her shoulder. "I'm here until this is resolved, Mom. Everything else can wait."

But even as he said the words, how true were they? If this investigation dragged on much longer, Gene and the Network would need a better explanation than a family emergency. What would he say then? *"I'm sorry, but my father's been accused of committing a crime forty years ago he swears he didn't do?"*

Pop took Mom's hand and gave it a long squeeze. "Okay, what now?"

Peter leaned back in his chair. "Go back to the hotel. Go sit on the beach. Try not to look like you're on vacation, but try not to look guilty either." The practical advice cut the air, sliding slivers of concern through Dax. What would make Pop look guilty if he was innocent? And why did Peter still seem unconvinced?

The Lodge's gym was better than hotel average with a good selection of free weights and benches to go along with the usual assortment of cardio equipment. Dax dropped his room key, phone, and water bottle next to a bench and mentally cycled through his list of routines as he scanned the equipment options.

Arms and shoulders it is.

He picked out his weights and began with some easy bicep curls. The workout plan superset them with tricep extensions before adding in the rest of the routine. The pattern would keep his body moving and should distract him from the emotional whirl. Ten minutes in, though, and no such luck. And really, he did need to come up with an explanation for Gene.

With a sigh, Dax allowed decades of muscle memory to take over as he searched for a plausible excuse. Pop said he was innocent, and Dax believed him. But suspicion often equaled conviction—especially in the dog-eat-dog world of the media where wrecking lives only fed the ravenous beast they called *News*.

Dax needed to shut off the speculation and quickly, but how, when there was so much unknown? Peter had said it could be a week before they knew anything for sure. Gene had warned him ditching out during a show was the only hiccup his career could afford. But if this dragged on, the story could only grow more salacious.

What would the Network do then? Would they distance themselves from him and let him go? Would they pass the ESPN job on to someone else?

What would that family from the beach say? Would they have sought him out, recounted his stats so gleefully? Or would they have jeered and snubbed him?

Sports stars were everyone's heroes until they mis-stepped or their actions were too heinous for their fame and talent to overcome. And then it was a free-for-all of coverage that crumbled a career in days that took a lifetime to build. His thoughts stuttered, and a chill skimmed over his heated skin. His entire life revolved around football.

The weights thudded to the floor, and he stared at himself in the mirror. Sweat dripped from his forehead, and his cheeks glowed a deep pink. His arms and shoulders burned with lactic acid buildup. Behind him stood two guys, jaws dropped. He glanced down at the weights and then back at their slim builds.

Ignoring the men's stares, he re-racked the weights, giving the bench an automatic wipe-down, before heading for the door. Football was all he'd known since he'd first pulled on a pee-wee ball jersey. He'd gone to college and graduated with a degree in business, but that meant nothing really. It was a piece of paper that didn't even hang on a wall. Football had done more than build him physically—the sport had been his identity ever since he'd first picked up a ball. Who would he be without it? Fear skittered over his heart as he ran a hand over his shaved head.

I honestly don't know.

Chapter Fourteen

Wednesday, September 19
Gulf Shores, Alabama

Caitlin sat at the Gulf Shores P.D.'s conference table and stared at the evidence board she'd created the day before. Photos and handwritten notes glared at her from under the harsh fluorescent light. She took a swig of regulation police department coffee, grimacing as the burnt taste of over-brewed swill hit her tongue.

"That stuff'll give you an ulcer." Ty leaned into the conference room with a smirk, surveying the suspect and evidence boards. He lifted his own mug as Caitlin set her cup on the conference table and waved him in to join her.

He propped a hip on the edge of the table and took a long sip of his coffee, wincing as he swallowed. "After you left yesterday, I called the Prescott family—well, what's left of them anyway—to let them know we've had a break in the case."

Caitlin's heart twisted. *How many years have you been responsible for calling them?*

Ty's dark gaze said, *Too many.*

She flinched, but she had her own list of families, starting with Brenda. The twin memories of Kidd's call and her non-conversation with Brenda whispered through her.

Forty years had passed before the Prescotts could have closure. How long would it be before Caitlin and Brenda could have the same? And if a resolution did one day come, would they ever be able to talk, really talk, about the girl they both loved? Or would their conversations forever remain stilted, guilt-ridden, and filled with more silence than words?

Ty lifted his coffee cup to Mic's picture on the evidence wall, drawing Caitlin's gaze, and she pulled her thoughts back to the Prescott case. Time to work the case that had actual movement.

"Mic's two brothers lived out of state when the robbery happened, and they've been dead for several years now. His son ran away when he was sixteen and hasn't been heard of since, near as I can figure. His daughter, Jackie, still lives in the area. Married with grown children. Nice lady."

Caitlin studied the photo of the victim, trying to picture the remaining family. Would Jackie be happy or thrown back into the emotional upheaval? It was always fifty-fifty in Caitlin's experience, but personally she preferred calls with news over the canned, *"I'm sorry, but there's been no movement. How are you doing?"*

She glanced back to Ty. "How'd she take the news?"

He tilted his head. "Shaken, obviously—especially after I had to tell her we let Carpenter go."

Caitlin winced but nodded. "Shock is to be expected. But hopefully we can find more than a new witness to make sure the case is closed this time."

"She wants to come in and talk soon, and I told her we'd be available whenever she wanted."

Caitlin's estimation of Ty rose yet again. Family members of the victims were often overlooked in the process of investigating and prosecuting cases.

His cheek lifted in a one-sided smirk. "I did tell her about you working the case. Let her know you're a specialist and your solve record. That gave her some comfort."

No pressure. Thanks, Ty. Caitlin squelched her automatic retort. He was right to tell Jackie. Every family member needed hope to get them through—especially when movement on a case could end in more heartbreak.

"Oh, and speaking of that." She turned to scan the evidence board. "Most of the original file is intact, oddly enough, and I found something interesting." She pointed toward a photo of a palm print taped up next to one of three fingerprints. "Based on the notes, those prints were a late addition to the file, but I can't find where they were run. Do you know anything about them?"

Ty studied the photos, then scanned the evidence log. "The only thing I see is they were found near the bar but outside the main crime scene."

"Yeah, on the door jamb leading to the kitchen."

"Okay, they're an artifact, not evidence. What's the problem? They probably belong to an employee."

Caitlin stared at the prints, her mind churning back through the evidence. "That's just it. According to the detective's notes, all of the staff were fingerprinted to rule them out as the robber who took the cash. None of them match this set. And they don't match Mic's prints from the autopsy."

Ty's eyes narrowed as he studied them. "So whose are they then?"

Caitlin nodded once, then grinned. Thrill shot up her spine. "Exactly. I'm thinking they belonged to the robber who killed Mic. Doug Bewley."

Ty shifted his hip against the table and fixed her with a considering look.

Caitlin spread her hands wide. "That whole thing took place off-camera. What's to say, he didn't grab the door jamb after he pushed Prescott? Ricky said in his statement they were pretty freaked out."

Ty took a swig of his coffee, then cleared his throat. "Before we brought Carpenter in for questioning, we got a court order for his prints. You know, just in case he hightailed it. We can run them against these no problem. That would confirm Ricky's claim Doug Bewley is Mark Carpenter. No need for a confession then."

Guilt twisted her heart, but her mouth dropped open, as the rush of the hunt shot through her. "Did you run Mark's prints against the database to check Ricky's story about the other robberies?"

"We did a basic search, but with the cases being more than forty years old, we didn't expect much and found even less." Ty pushed off the table with a shrug. He ran his fingers over the prints. "Some of the records were uploaded to the precincts' databases, but the prints weren't added into the main fingerprint system. Cold cases don't get much attention unfortunately."

Caitlin nodded. Missing evidence and incomplete data transfers were part and parcel of her investigations. *Time to get creative.*

She scanned the evidence board. "We'll have to request the hard copies of the case files for the robberies Ricky confessed to, and see if we can match these prints to them."

Ty's gaze settled heavily on her. "It'll take forever to get them, what with the number and districts he confessed to hitting."

A slow smile crept up Caitlin's lips as she grabbed her phone.

Ty's eyes narrowed as he studied her. "What are you thinking?"

"That it's very handy to have a hacker in the family."

He snorted. "Do what you need to do. I need to check in with the desk sergeant. Got a witness on another case coming in for a meeting in a few minutes." He slipped out of the room, closing the door behind him.

Caitlin tapped Shannon's number and waited. Shannon picked up on the fourth ring.

"Good timing, SIL." Shannon sounded distracted, and the clicking echoing across the line told Caitlin she was multitasking as usual. A moment later, though, the clicking stopped, and Shan's voice gained focus. "Found Douglas 'Doug' Bewley. He was a foster kid who aged out of the system then dropped off the map."

Caitlin thumped her pen against the conference table, reorienting her thoughts to Shannon's news. "Foster care? That's interesting. Any information on that?"

"Yeah, his father was in jail for being the getaway driver in a bank robbery. The guys who actually did the robbery cut deals and got twenty years. Bewley's dad got life. But it turned out to be a shorter sentence because he was killed in prison ten years in. Some dispute with another inmate over lunch. Sad."

Caitlin cringed. Sometimes she hated the justice system. "What about his mother?"

Shannon's voice again grew distant, and Caitlin could hear more clicking. "In and out of rehab so often she couldn't keep him. No clue what happened to her. But I'm sure you can make an educated guess."

His father's murder in prison explained Doug's disappearance after the accidental killing of Mic Prescott. With prison a done-deal for him, running would have seemed like the life-saving option.

But was Doug Bewley also Mark Carpenter? She didn't know much about Mark even though she'd met him a few times. He'd retired from his electrician's business, liked to work on cars, and encouraged Dax's interest in football. But could he also have been a foster kid who turned petty thief and murderer?

Shannon's voice cut through Caitlin's ruminations. "There's more. Found out Mark Carpenter's Social Security number belonged to a child who drowned when he was five."

Well, that's certainly not a plus in Mark's favor.
"That's morbid."

Shannon hmphed her agreement. "But effective. Nobody looks at kids' Socials until they're old enough to open credit cards. I've seen a few cases where the child had abysmal credit and no idea. In one of them, the poor kid had his identity stolen when he was in middle school. Took forever to get everything fixed."

Caitlin pinched her nose. "My faith in humanity just dropped a bit lower."

"SIL, with everything you've seen, I'd be surprised if you had any left at all." Shannon sighed, as if realizing she was close to poking the wound Caitlin's heart carried around daily. "But that's not why you called. You got another bone for me?"

Caitlin pulled the phone from her ear and tapped the speaker button. "Yeah, texting it to you now. I need you to find out if any of these police departments have cold case robberies at these locations going back to before the time of The Broken Flip-Flop robbery and murder. The witness gave us the basics, and we've found some prints outside of the crime scene at the restaurant. I'm thinking they could be Doug Bewley's."

"Which mean they could be Mark's."

Caitlin's shoulders sagged as the evidence against Dax's dad continued to line up. "Yeah. We're going to run them against the ones the P.D. took when they brought Mark in for questioning, but it would be good to have others to match."

"And since of course I'm going to find case files, what's next?"

Caitlin chuckled at Shannon's confidence. "Dig around and see if they have prints in the files, and then let me know. That'll help narrow down which ones to request first and should speed up the process of linking Mark to them."

Shannon was quiet.

"What?"

Shannon's soft tone firmed. "You know what, Caitie."

Caitlin shot a quick glance through the window cut into the back wall, finding Ty at his desk clicking away at the computer. The door between her and the bullpen was still closed, but she took the phone off speaker anyway, and lowered her voice. "Yeah. This is going to kill Dax and Susan. But there's nothing to be done. If Mark is involved, and killed the restaurant manager, he needs to be held accountable. And Dax understands that."

"Just as long as you're ready for the fallout."

A pang clenched Caitlin's heart. That fallout would include Dax leaving her life for good. But that was what she really wanted.

Wasn't it?

Chapter Fifteen

Wednesday, September 19
Gulf Shores, Alabama

Caitlin poured ice into the plastic bag from the nearly full hotel room ice bucket. She'd asked the housekeeper for a stack of them as she made her way back to her room, knowing she'd need more than one before the week was out.

Her jaw clenched and she flinched as the ice and water mix hit her bare shoulder. Sucking in a hissing breath, she wrapped a hand towel from the bathroom around the bag, hoping to soften the shock. Glancing at the printed exercise routine, she stuck out her tongue at the figures and directions. The new exercises helped her range of motion, but not so much with the aching when she finished.

She gulped down a couple of Ibuprofen pills and checked the room clock. *Ten 'til eight.* Ethan would dial both her and Luke for the sibling call. Surely the three of them could come up with some sort of plan for Daddy.

She dumped the bag of melted ice down the bathroom sink just as her phone rang. Ethan quickly conferenced in Luke as she settled back on the loveseat. Luke's familiar, easy-going tone laced his greeting, easing Caitlin's concern about the drought of contact from him.

After they exchanged basic details, Ethan's voice turned teasing. "So, Caitie, how's it going with Dax? Y'all back together yet? Shannon's thinking there may be wedding bells for y'all yet."

Caitlin rolled her eyes. *Ugh, Shannon talked. Of course, she did.*

"Dax, huh?" Luke asked. "Thought you kicked him and his pretty face to the curb, Sis. Something about being too famous for you?" Luke had been on temporary duty in Japan when she and Dax had dated, but he'd met him once on a video call toward the end of the relationship.

Shaking her head, Caitlin cobbled together an explanation that would hopefully divert their attention. "Yeah, well, he came to me for help on a case. And it's not like I could say no. It's about his dad, and there are no hard feelings."

Ethan's wry snort over the phone line told her she hadn't succeeded. "They may not be hard, Caitie, but there are definitely still feelings—at least on your side. Shannon knows things."

Caitlin blew out a harsh breath. "That is not the point of this call, Ethan. And my love life or lack thereof is nobody's business but mine."

"And Dax," Ethan said.

"Y'all …" Luke dove into his customary role of family diplomat.

Between Caitlin's frustrated growl and Luke's soothing, Ethan sobered. "But you are right about the call."

"What's going on?" Luke asked. "I haven't talked to Mom much, but whenever I do, she's been up and peppy and Dad is fine—well, fine for the diagnosis he has."

With her frustration still bubbling over Ethan's ribbing, Caitlin swallowed her ire and focused on Daddy. "He almost burned down the house." At Luke's gasp, her stomach clenched. She ran her fingers through her hair, ruffling it into a spiky mess. She hadn't meant to scare him. Fluke might be in special forces, but he was still the baby of the family and devoted to their parents.

A quick huff of breath shot between her lips. "No—it wasn't that bad. But he did forget to put soup in the pot he was using. And according to Mom, it smoked up the kitchen enough to set off the smoke detectors, and the neighbors called the fire department."

Caitlin rocketed off the loveseat and paced the length of the room.

"She says she was home before they arrived and got everything back under control. But Daddy's not safe to leave by himself anymore, and he's not really even safe to go with her. Mom said the last time he did, they got separated, and it was a nightmare tracking him down."

The line went silent until Luke's exhale broke through. "Well, what about bringing in someone part of the day to give her a break? One of the guys in my unit had to do that with his mother-in-law. Seems like it's working out okay."

Caitlin flopped back down on the loveseat as helpless frustration twisted her insides. "That's an option for now, but what about long-term? The dementia will only get worse. What happens when Daddy can't walk and has to be in a wheelchair? Mom is all of a hundred pounds soaking wet, Luke. Can you see her maneuvering a wheelchair around—or worse, even *getting* him into it?"

Luke's sigh heaved over the air. "Yeah, there's that."

The line went silent again, and Caitlin realized Ethan hadn't said a word. "Eth—what do you think?"

Ethan released a long, low breath, not a comforting sound. Caitlin braced herself for his next words. "I wasn't going to mention this, Caitie, but there's more to all this."

Stunned, Caitlin sat forward. Ethan was holding out on her? Why? And since when? They'd always been close. When issues came up, they were each other's first confidants. Well, second now to Shannon.

Then again, neither Ethan nor Shannon knew the real reason she'd broken up with Dax.

Okay, so we don't share everything. But Dax was truly no one else's business. Daddy's decline demanded full disclosure.

"What's the 'more?'" she bit out.

"Okay, first off, Mom doesn't even know, and neither of you can tell her."

"Ethan?" A dangerous edge sharpened Caitlin's tone.

Ethan sniffed and Caitlin could picture him staring off into space, searching for the right and most diplomatic words to explain whatever had happened. He wouldn't say anything before he found them, so Caitlin clamped a fist around her impatience and settled in to wait, wishing Ethan had opted for a video call so she could at least read his face. It wouldn't be much, but it would at least offer some preparation for the words when he did find them.

A couple of heartbeats later, he said, "About a month ago, I went over to hang out with him while Mom had a girls' day out with some friends from church. Traffic was a nightmare because of a wreck on Vaughn Road, so I texted her to go ahead. Dad would be okay to stay by himself for a little while then."

Caitlin tightened her mental fist around her irritation as he spun his story with all the skill of a true southerner. *Like mother. Like son.*

"When I got there, I used my key and went in the back door, just like we always do. I opened the door and called inside. The TV was muted, which I thought was odd, but just as I closed the door behind me, Dad grabbed me and ... put me in a chokehold."

"Ethan!" Luke's concerned outburst beat Caitlin's, but hers was no less passionate.

"Once he saw my face, he knew me, and I got him calmed down quick enough. Reminded him Mom was spending the day out, and I came to watch the game with him. It wasn't a big deal. I didn't even have a bruise—his grip isn't that strong anymore."

Caitlin sprang from the loveseat and stalked toward the door. Bile bubbled in the back of her throat. Her fingers gripped the bridge of her nose—a poor replacement for Ethan's ear lobe. "That's not the point, and you know it."

"Look, he thought someone was breaking in, and his old police habits kicked in. Once he recognized me, we were fine."

Luke jumped on the explanation before Caitlin could open her mouth. "What if he did that to Mom? Y'all, he's getting worse."

"Exactly," Caitlin said. "We have to tell her it's time for him to go to a facility. As much as I hate it, Daddy needs more help, and Mom needs to be safe in her own home."

Tone firming with resolve, Luke upped the ante. "And you have to tell her what happened, Ethan. Since the kitchen incident didn't sway her, maybe this will." He paused and humor seeped into his words. "You are the favorite after all."

Caitlin chuckled despite her ire. "Good one, Fluke."

Luke's hitching laugh echoed across the line, then cut off replaced by sober, but muffled conversation and a distant, "Yes, sir, I'll be right there." A moment later, he returned to the call. "I gotta go. My CO just called a meeting. We're home, but on alert."

"What's up?" Caitlin asked.

A wry tone laced Luke's response. "Sis, you know the answer to that."

"Yeah, yeah, I know." She rolled her eyes at the slip-up. "If you told me, then you'd have to kill me. Be safe, little brother. And don't take so long to reach out again. We miss you."

"Love you both." He dropped off the call, leaving Caitlin and Ethan in silence.

She sighed, hating to put Ethan in a position he didn't want. But they'd reached the last option. "He's right, you know."

"What? About being Mom's favorite?"

A harsh bark of laughter rushed between Caitlin's lips. "That too."

Ethan heaved a long hiccupping groan. "Yeah, I know. I just didn't want to scare her. Dad seems fine with her."

"For now, Ethan. For now." Caitlin's imploring words were wrapped with compassion, and yet based in practicality. "And face it, neither you nor I want to take the call when Daddy changes." She paused. "Please. She'll listen to you."

"Okay, I'll be home from the conference on Saturday. When do you think you'll be back?"

Caitlin dropped back on the loveseat. Her gaze landed on her briefcase. "I have no idea. But this can't wait. And besides, she's more likely to listen if she doesn't feel like we're ganging up on her. It's bad enough we've talked behind her back. Staging a formal intervention would go nowhere."

"Two of us talking to her isn't ganging up, Caitie."

"I've already played my hand, Eth. She didn't listen. But she will listen to you. She always does—or at least has since this all started with Daddy. Talk with her. Please."

Caitlin could feel Ethan's sad acceptance, grateful not to be the oldest. "All right. Sunday after church then."

The phone line tensed with a weighted silence, pricking at Caitlin's heart. Hoping to soften the responsibility, she whispered, "You're the best, Eth."

Ethan's tone warmed, and she could envision the corners of his mouth twitching into the crooked smile that used to be accompanied by a noogie to the top of her head. "Yeah, back at ya', Caitie." He paused. "I wish we didn't have to do this."

Caitlin shook her head. "Unfortunately, we're at the end of the options now. And if you don't say something, nothing is going to change and Mom could end up getting hurt." She hated stating the truth in such a blunt way, but they couldn't ignore the facts.

Caitlin ended the call, wishing Luke's boots on the ground were closer to home for times like these. But at least Ethan would now do the heavy-lifting, and she could hopefully have some peace—at least on the home front.

Chapter Sixteen

Thursday, September 20
Gulf Shores, Alabama

Caitlin watched Jackie Gonzalez and her husband, Roberto, through the one-way mirror as they sat side-by-side on the gray leather loveseat. Jackie rested her head on Roberto's shoulder with their hands clasped together. Mic Prescott's daughter was the spitting image of him, minus her wan face and dark circles beneath her eyes. Her frizzed blond curls spoke of restless nights and a resurgence of old, painful memories. Ty was right. Jackie had been knocked off-kilter by the news of a new witness and possible perpetrator identification. Caitlin's heart clenched with guilt and empathy. It might be a typical reaction but witnessing it first-hand hurt on multiple levels.

Memories of Brenda overlaid Jackie's sallow features, and Caitlin gave them rein. When Missy's mom had arrived at the dorms in the days after Missy's disappearance, her face had borne much the same darkness and light—until her ex-husband and Missy's father, Donald, had arrived to clear out Missy's belongings.

Brenda's pale cheeks had reddened with ire. Her sorrow-rimmed eyes flashed with fire. And then the former husband and wife had laid into each other. Their raised voices, personal insults, and four-letter epithets sliced and diced with surgical skill.

Caitlin had rushed from the room, heartbroken for both Missy and her parents. She'd curled up on a bench outside the dorm until they'd each gotten in their cars and driven away. When she'd finally returned to the room, Missy's side was bare, but the verbal sparring still rang in her ears.

Caitlin forced her thoughts from the past and focused on Jackie sitting with her husband, Roberto. Thankfully, this couple appeared devoted to each other. Jackie lifted her head from his shoulder and cast a dull gaze toward the door while Roberto watched with patient care, his free arm draping around her shoulders. A relieved breath slipped between Caitlin's lips. Jackie Gonzalez was a woman loved.

But a moment later, Caitlin's lungs hitched, the steadiness in Roberto's eyes hitting her full force with different memories. Dax had looked at her the same way, that calm, confident gaze of a lifetime love. Caitlin's heart twisted. She had been a woman loved as well. *And you threw it away.*

She squared her shoulders and shoved aside all of the memories. *Focus, Fitzhugh.*

Rapping the door once, she pushed through it, drawing Jackie and Roberto's eyes. "Mr. and Mrs. Gonzalez, I'm Caitlin Fitzhugh, with Alabama State Division of Investigations." Her words eased into the room in the soft, approachable tone she'd perfected over years of meeting family members of cold case victims. When they said nothing, she flashed a slight smile and took the seat across from them. "I'm sure you have a lot of questions. But let me start. First off, how are you feeling?"

Jackie shuddered and clasped Roberto's hand tighter. "I would say about as good as you'd expect, but I'm not sure what anyone would expect to feel right now."

Caitlin nodded. "I imagine there are a lot of mixed emotions. In my experience, every case is different. Sometimes the amount of time that's passed helps the family. Sometimes it doesn't. But the most important thing is to allow yourself to feel whatever emotions hit you, when they hit you."

Jackie's eyes unfocused as she stared back into the past. "You know, I was only ten when Daddy was killed, but I can still remember him. He had this booming laugh and gave the best hugs. My brother and I lived with him after my parents' divorce when I was five."

A small smile flickered over her lips.

"Even though he worked these crazy hours at the restaurant, he seemed to always be there. He'd make these elaborate breakfasts in the morning before we went to school and talk about what was going on with us even though he probably had gotten home only a few hours before."

Caitlin waited for Jackie to share as much or as little as she needed. It didn't matter that none of this would add to the case. She needed to begin the healing process again. Jackie's eyes welled with tears, and Caitlin offered Roberto a sympathetic smile. His dark gaze softened, melting under the helpless inability to fix his wife's pain.

"After Daddy was killed, Billy and I went to Mom." Jackie sighed and shook her head. "Looking back, I almost wonder if it would have been better for us to have gone to one of Daddy's brothers out of state or even foster care." She flicked a worried glance between Roberto and Caitlin. "She wasn't abusive or anything. Just absent—always so wrapped up in her work. And even when she was home, she still hated Dad and how their marriage ended. All she did was bash him. Billy and I were drowning in our grief, and she only piled on more."

Roberto's arm dropped from Jackie's shoulders to rub soothing circles along her back. Grateful for his patience and care, Caitlin gave him an encouraging nod.

Jackie leaned into his touch, closing her eyes as history fell from her lips. "Billy ran away when he was sixteen, and I haven't seen him since. I got pregnant in high school and dropped out, then got into drugs and alcohol. Pregnant again when I was eighteen. The day social services knocked on the door of the flea trap I was living in, I realized I could lose my kids. It was like I'd been dunked in the Gulf in January. I looked at my life, thought back to Daddy and how different it was when he was alive, and I wanted to do better. Needed to do better—to honor him and his love for me and Billy."

She shifted in Roberto's embrace as her lips lifted in a full, warm smile. "That was when I got into AA. I started a job at the local gas station and worked on getting my GED and associate's degree. My AA group met at Roberto's church, so I started attending services there with the kids. He and I met in an adult Sunday school class."

Roberto placed a quick kiss against her temple, still giving her space to talk.

"We got married three years later. And we now have four wonderful adult children. But this ..."

She fell silent and searched the room, shoulders sagging under the obvious weight of reality. "It's like I'm that devastated little girl all over again."

Caitlin leaned forward, catching Jackie's gaze. "That's completely to be expected. It doesn't matter how much you feel you've worked through and healed. News of developments in a case this old will bring up past emotions. I do want to prepare you, though. We are going to do everything we can to bring you closure. But if that doesn't happen or doesn't happen as quickly as we hope, don't be surprised if you start feeling some of the same frustration and grief from the first months after he was killed. That is normal." Caitlin pulled a business card out of her wallet. "This is the number for Victim's Services. I encourage you to talk with someone as these feelings continue to be uncovered."

Roberto took the card, giving it a quick read. "I'll be here for her as will our children. She won't go through this alone."

Caitlin gave him a warm, supportive smile. "That is wonderful. She's going to need family support. But she'll also need to have someone to talk with who is a trained counselor." She turned her gaze to Jackie. "Don't feel pushed or obligated. Just know help is available if you want it."

Roberto slid his thumb across the back of Jackie's hand. "We understand you had to let this man you were questioning go, yes?"

Caitlin winced. "Yes. As can happen in cases this old, we don't have enough corroborating evidence to arrest him. But that doesn't mean we've stopped looking. In fact, Detective Osgood and I are following up on some of the other information the new witness gave us. We're hoping that will link back to whomever robbed and killed your father."

Roberto's gaze warmed with hope and certainty. "We will keep the faith, Agent Fitzhugh. And we will pray for you and Detective Osgood as you search."

Caitlin swallowed hard. Maybe God would listen to them, since he obviously didn't listen to her.

Dax ended the recording and scrolled back to the beginning, running through the three-minute spot twice more, while listening for any inconsistencies. No hotel room AC background noise. All stats were correct. Insights were pithy with the right amount of snark to capture the limited attention spans of the video viewer. Nodding, he opened his email and attached the file figuring it should be small enough to send rather than using his

Dropbox. Gene notoriously missed uploads, but he was a fiend about checking his email.

Before he clicked send, his cell phone rang. *Ah, speak of the devil.*

Dax answered before Gene could get a word in edgewise. "Just about to send you my spot on the Alabama-Texas A & M match-up. Keyshawn Owens looks to put in a good performance —maybe even get some personal records."

"Chuck it." The words rushed over the phone, crashing into him like a defense line diving for a fumble.

"What?"

"Owens just got a DUI. He's benched for the game—if not for the rest of the season."

Dax's groaned. It wasn't unheard for college players to get pulled over, but mostly the local cops gave them a pass— especially if it was a first offense and the officer was a fan. As far as Dax knew, Owens wasn't a regular partier.

"Nearly hit a pedestrian. So there's no glad-handing it. They're putting in M.J. Peavy."

Dax's mouth dropped open. "The red shirt freshman who's had less playing time than the kicker?" He threw back his head and closed his eyes. What stats that kid would have could fit on a postage stamp.

"That's the one. Sorry, buddy. Oh, and I'm still gonna need it by Friday. But at least your old coach is probably scrambling more than you are."

Dax ended the call and dropped onto the bed with a growl. Heaving a frustrated sigh, he stared at his laptop. He should be jumping on the new assignment. Pulling stats and searching for video clips on Peavy. But he had to get out of his hotel room.

His gaze drifted out the window and to the welcoming sand and surf as his stomach rumbled. Glancing at the clock on his phone, his cheek lifted in a one-sided smile. Maybe there was someone else who could use a break too. He tapped open his text app and thumbed an invitation.

Chapter Seventeen

Thursday, September 20
Gulf Shores, Alabama

D*ing.* Caitlin pulled her gaze from the computer screen and checked her phone. *Dax Carpenter* glowed in the banner, followed by a text invitation to lunch. She flicked a furtive glance around the Gulf Shores P.D. bullpen. The other two detectives were out on a case. The sergeant sat at the desk, typing away on reports. Ty had just returned from filling his second cup of coffee and was eye-deep in case notes.

Shaking her head, she flipped the phone upside down. No. She would not mix personal with business. That was a ground rule. Or would have been if she'd ever voiced it. She forced her attention back to her emails from Montgomery. When she'd reached the last one, a department memo about vehicle requisitions, her stomach grumbled.

She glanced at the clock, then bit her lip as she looked over at Ty. She did have to eat. And it had been years since she'd had lunch on the beach. Resolve weakening, she tried one last excuse. "Any word on those case file requests?"

Ty shook his head as his eyes remained fixed on his screen. "Nah, they all said it'll be this afternoon at the earliest."

With no other distractions, she narrowed her eyes and grabbed her phone, reading the text again.

DAX: You free for lunch on the beach? Noon?

She caught Ty's curious gaze out of the corner of her eye as she typed her reply.

CAITLIN: Nothing about your father's case.

Dax's response was immediate.

DAX: No problem.

With all excuses removed, Caitlin shook her head. "Okay. I'm going to get out of here for a bit then. Maybe grab some lunch and walk on the beach. It's been a while since I've been this way."

"It's a nice day. Might as well," Ty said. "I'll text you if anything comes in while you're out."

Swallowing her sigh, Caitlin tugged her keys out of her briefcase and headed out.

Caitlin reached The Lodge's beach access and lifted her hand above her sunglasses, scanning the expanse of white sand. Dark-blue beach chair sets clustered near the stairway, and a few sat scattered off toward the far end of the park. But no sign of Dax. Reluctant to add more texts to the conversation, she still pulled out her phone.

CAITLIN: I'm here. Where are you?

DAX: On the beach. Umbrella and chairs off to the left.

Caitlin turned to the far side of the beach and found him as he moved out from under the umbrella and waved ... was he wearing a beach hat? The wide brim and straw looked almost goofy on a head more accustomed to helmets and ballcaps. But she had to admit, it was kind of cute. Her lips lifted—*Lock it down, Caitlin. Do not let him get under your skin any more than he has already.*

With a firm nod, she slipped off her shoes, rolled up her pants, and sank into the sand, heading his way. She reached the beach chairs, and she ducked under the canvas umbrella. "Never would've pictured you in a beach hat, Dax."

Dax's cheeks actually reddened in a sheepish acknowledgement. Caitlin's lips twitched around a smile.

"Yeah, well, trying to keep a low profile. Got spotted on the beach yesterday, and I remember you weren't too fond of the fame. So …"

Guilt gripped her. Desperate to hide the truth, she'd used his fame as a lame excuse for the breakup and stuck to it, pointing out all the times it had interfered with their dates and the potential impact on her career in law enforcement.

She winced and turned her attention to the food. But the offerings made her eyes widen. "You brought a low country boil?"

Dax flashed a one-sided grin. "Remembered how much you liked it when we had it for Mom's birthday." The light in his eyes warmed with memory, inviting her to travel back down that road with him. Unable to fight it, she let her thoughts drift.

They'd been together almost six months when he'd asked her to go with him to Susan's birthday party. They'd made day trip visits in the past, but this time, the entire neighborhood and their church would be there. The underlying meaning of the invitation was not lost on her. They would be seen as serious. While she wasn't sure she was ready for that label, all she could say was yes.

The party ended up being a blow-out event with not only neighbors and church members attending, but also many of Susan's former students and coworkers at the elementary school where she'd taught for thirty years. And while no one asked outright about Caitlin and Dax, his arm around her shoulders and the way he'd watch her from time to time pretty well said it all.

As she'd met his gaze, she'd realized she didn't mind. She'd fallen for him. Hard. And when she looked around the gathering, she could even picture the life they might share together.

As the sun began to set and the party broke up, Dax had grabbed her hand and pulled her into a meandering walk down the street toward the pond a few yards down from Susan and Mark's house. He'd tugged her into his arms, bear hugging her from behind. They watched the ducks skim the water and waited for the sun to drop behind the trees. Just before it reached the top branches, he fanned two tickets in front of her. To the Montgomery Symphony.

Stunned, she'd turned in his arms. "But you don't like classical music."

He'd looked her in the eyes, heart on full display. "No, but you do."

Then he'd picked her up, closing the foot gap in their heights, and kissed her. As the sunlight deepened to an orangey glow, Caitlin had never felt more loved. Never been more ready to spend the rest of her life with anyone.

But then they'd actually gone to the symphony.

Caitlin blinked and scooted back in her beach chair, the cold dash of history quelling all dreams of them together. Grabbing her Diet Coke, she took a long sip, grasping for any change of subject she could find. Her gaze landed on the SEC Network logo on his t-shirt.

"So ... um ... how's work going? You're still doing TV, right?"

She stabbed a sausage round with her fork, then popped it in her mouth as Dax's easy smile turned down.

"Yeah, well, for now anyway."

Caitlin's brow creased as she chewed. "Why 'for now?'"

Dax relayed how he'd rushed out of the studio before his spot after Susan's call and the resulting fallout. "I don't know what'll happen when they find out the real reason why I left."

Caitlin was silent. Any answer would approach the line she'd established when she agreed to meet him—if not completely cross it. But the worry flickering in his eyes still wrapped around her heart. She reached over and finally allowed herself to touch him again, laying her hand on his forearm and running her thumb against the sinewy muscle. She steeled herself against the shimmer of sensation.

Dax's gaze jerked to hers, eyes widening in recognition, but at least the worry eased. His lips thinned as they pulled back into a resigned smile. Caitlin answered it with her own before returning her hand to shucking her shrimp.

He slipped a few more shrimp from their shells then stirred them in a side of cocktail sauce before popping them in his mouth. They watched the waves in silence, and the soul-soothing comfort of being with him slipped over her heart.

Caitlin forced her gaze away and blinked rapidly. Grabbing her Diet Coke, she took another long sip. Meeting him here was the worst idea she'd ever had. She hauled in a deep breath. No, actually the worst idea was agreeing to take the case. But this meeting ratcheted right up there with it.

As if sensing her agitation, Dax reopened their conversation, keeping his voice light, but interested. "But enough about me. How's your family?"

Caitlin turned back and searched his eyes. His tone might be non-threatening, but his gaze remained filled with memory—and fondness. *Yeah, he and Daddy really hit it off.*

Sorrow sliced through her, but she shook it off and focused on the facts. "Daddy was diagnosed with dementia a few years back. He's still at home, but it's getting harder for Mom to care for him. We had a sibling phone meeting last night, and my older brother is going to talk with her about where to go from here."

"Ethan, right? How are he and ... Shannon?"

Caitlin's lips lifted in a real smile, then she nodded. They'd only met a handful of times, but she was pleased he remembered her favorite people's names. "They're okay. Went through a rough patch in their marriage and business a couple of years ago. And now they're having trouble getting, well, staying pregnant."

Dax's brows lifted as concern shaded his eyes. He'd never made any secret that family and children were important to him.

Caitlin poked another sausage round, but only stirred it in the bowl. Sadness eased through her words. "Two miscarriages in a year. She's handling it well, better than I probably would be." Her mouth dropped as the words replayed through her head. "Um ... not that I ... thought ... think ..."

Dax's lips widened in a teasing grin. Heat flushed up Caitlin's neck, and she dropped her eyes back to her food.

"And what about your younger brother? Still in the military?"

Caitlin latched onto Dax's question with all the joy of a stranded swimmer finding a piece of flotsam. "Yes. Luke's currently stationed in Washington state, but he's deployed everywhere—not that he can tell us where that 'everywhere' is. He loves it." She gazed out at the Gulf, wistfulness creeping into her tone. "But it'd be nice if he'd settle back closer to home one day."

Dax laid his hand on her shoulder, giving it a comforting squeeze.

Caitlin bit her lip and closed her eyes as she fought the urge to lean into his comfort, his strength. *Stop it. You cannot do this. Not now. Not ever. Not if you want your heart to survive.*

Desperate to regain control of her emotions and the situation, she tossed her fork in the plastic bowl and grabbed the lid. "Thanks for lunch. But I need to get back to the precinct."

Dax lifted wounded eyes to her, but he nodded. "Thanks for coming. This was nice. I miss—"

"Bye, Dax." Caitlin rose, grabbing her shoes and beating a hasty, albeit less-than-graceful retreat toward the beach access. Climbing the steps, she swallowed the tears of regret. "You will not do that again."

Chapter Eighteen

Thursday, September 20
College Station, Texas

Ricky Adams pushed through the doors of his lawyer's office. The baking Texas air hit him full in the face. He studied the thick, white envelope clutched in his hand. The *Last Will and Testament of Richard Vernon Adams* now existed. All of his final wishes had been laid out, approved.

On his death, Antoine would inherit the Sliver Shooters, and Jill, his restored brick-nosed 1980 Ford F150 parked in the law office's lot. The two things he owned of any value would go to the people who mattered most to him. Perfect. He just had to take his last breath, and that would come soon enough.

Now he needed to finish clearing his conscience, which would happen when he gave his deposition and later testimony. Thanks to the surgery, as long as the trial didn't drag out, he'd be around long enough to see the whole elephant eaten. Ricky nodded, satisfaction rolling through him. He glanced to the sky and smiled. "Well, Big Guy, guess you are looking out for me after all."

Ricky pulled his keys out of his pocket and climbed into the truck. Tugging open the glovebox, he tossed the copy of his will inside, then turned on the engine. Cold air rushed into the cab, smothering the heat to a tolerable level.

His gaze landed on the clock. Antoine would be unlocking the Silver Shooters right now—and he'd be worried when Ricky wasn't already there. But this had been the lawyer's only available time to meet. And Antoine would be doing the unlocking by himself soon enough anyway.

Ricky reached to put the truck in gear as his cell phone rang. He read the caller ID. The hospital. Good timing.

"May I speak with Ricky Adams?"

"You got 'em. Guessing this is about tomorrow, right?"

The woman's voice warmed with sympathy. "Yes. I wanted to pass along the pre-operation protocol." She reviewed the no-eating-no-drinking policy.

Again, pretty much what he had expected. It wouldn't be much of a hardship. Over the last few weeks, he'd had little interest in food anyway.

"For your recovery, I see we have you discharging to a skilled nursing facility instead of home. Is that correct?"

Ricky cringed. He wasn't an old fart, even though sixty pounded on his door. But he wouldn't live to see that number anyway, so going to place filled with people decades older didn't matter much in the long run. "Not my first choice, but it's the only one I've got."

The nurse sounded concerned. "You don't have anyone you can stay with or who can provide home care?"

Ricky scrubbed his forehead. His gaze landed on the glovebox. He did have family, but he wouldn't ask Antoine or Jill. They would do whatever he needed in a heartbeat. He'd stood on his own two feet for the last forty years. He wasn't about to burden anyone during his last weeks and months. "Nope. Not a soul."

"I'm sorry."

He shrugged. "Don't be. I made my choices. It's my bed to lie in."

The line was silent. But really, what could she say that meant anything? He'd had his share of flings with barflies, but never anyone he'd consider long-term material. And Jill, much as he cared for her, was more like a sister, though she could pass for his daughter. All in all, he'd lived a better life than he deserved—and certainly, a longer one than Mic.

"All right then. We'll see you at the surgery check-in at six tomorrow morning."

"It's a date."

Ricky turned into the parking lot at the Silver Shooters and cut the engine. He sat until sweat beaded across his forehead, then climbed out and headed to the wide front porch. He smiled to the three groups of customers seated on one side and skirted between the tables, choosing an empty table near the porch railing. Jill and Whitney split the porch on Thursdays. With no one seated on this side, one or the other had to be running late.

Probably Whitney. Girl needs a minder most days.

As he settled in a chair, the front door thumped open. Jill pushed through it backwards with a tray laden with draft beers and a heaping basket of wings. She glanced over her shoulder, and her brow wrinkled as he caught her eye. Setting down the drinks and wings, she confirmed the customers were satisfied then made a beeline for Ricky.

"You okay?"

Ricky's cheek wrinkled with a one-sided smile. "Good as I can be."

Jill's eyes narrowed, perhaps judging his truthfulness and concerned about his tardiness. But she wouldn't call him on either.

Ricky wouldn't tell her anyway. On the drive over, he'd decided to let everything be a surprise. The bar. The truck. A final and heartfelt act of love that would kill him to show while he was on this side of the ground. Besides, they already knew how much they meant to him.

If he'd learned anything from Mic's death, it was how to be a stand-up guy. Not just for himself. But for Mic. To honor him— maybe even live out the life he should've lived. Ricky ran a hand over his face. He hoped to God he'd done well by Mic. And if not, he prayed these final days and weeks would give him the opportunity to do so.

Jill laid a concerned hand on Ricky's arm, drawing his attention back to her. "Hey, what time do you have to be at the hospital?"

Ricky hmphed. "Six. Only clear liquids tonight and nothing after midnight so don't be forcing food on me like you usually do." He smiled to soften the sharpness of the words.

Jill glanced over at her tables. The customers drank, ate, laughed, and in general, enjoyed their lives. Ricky wished them well.

"I'll be at your apartment at five-thirty."

Ricky jerked his gaze back to Jill. She'd have at most three hours of sleep after her shift. "I'll get a cab."

Jill's lips firmed. "You'll do no such thing. You've been too good to me. This is the least I can do."

Ricky opened his mouth to argue, then closed it, reading the steel in her eyes. "Thanks."

Jill smiled, then turned as Whitney's car swerved into the parking lot. The girl barely put it in park and cut the engine before she rushed to the porch, waving her hand. "I know. I know."

Ricky snorted. "Can't wait to hear this excuse."

Jill heaved a sigh, then smiled. "Gonna be a doozy. I'll tell Antoine you're out here. Come in whenever you're ready."

Chapter Nineteen

Thursday, September 20
Gulf Shores, Alabama

Caitlin tugged open the door to the Gulf Shores Police Department and checked the clock on the waiting room's wall. Only an hour had passed since she'd left for lunch, so there was little chance the other precincts had sent over the case files.

Caitlin huffed. Why had she agreed to lunch with Dax? Why had she not recognized a casual meal would turn more serious? Distance. She needed distance. And to solve this case. Then they would go back to normal, she could rebandage her heart, and forget the life it longed to live with Dax.

She slipped into the bullpen, stopping short. Ty's chair shrieked a protesting whine as he swiveled to greet her. Delighted, he slapped his desk. "Zoom! Zoom! Zoom! We got 'em, Fitzhugh."

Brows lifting with a silent question, Caitlin tossed her briefcase on her chair and joined him on his side of the desks.

Ty pointed to his computer monitor. A pair of fingerprints covered in red lines filled the screen, highlighting whorls and loops. "Mark Carpenter's prints match the artifact ones you caught. He was there. And he's Doug Bewley."

Caitlin shoulders sagged as the first inklings of dread washed through her, curling her stomach. *Well, you wanted distance. This will do it.*

She shook her head. "Doesn't nail him as Prescott's killer. But with the scar and the injury that likely caused it on the video, it's more than enough circumstantial evidence for an arrest. I think a jury will believe it—especially if the district attorney is any good."

Caitlin's phone dinged with a text. She tugged it from her pocket and read the banner. "It's Shannon."

SHANNON: Call me ASAP.

Caitlin pressed the phone icon, and Shannon answered before the first ring ended. "Well, good news and bad. I confirmed the six robberies occurred based on the case files I found. But only three of them had uploaded the original documents. Pensacola. Tallahassee. Mobile. Which makes sense given those departments are larger."

Caitlin pushed aside her roiling emotions and managed to smile at Ty. "Great work, Shan. I'll get those case files requested today."

"Oh, that was the bad news."

Caitlin blinked, but shook her head. She should know by now that Shannon didn't send ASAP texts without juicy insights. "And the good?"

Shannon's voice filled with self-satisfaction. "All three of those departments uploaded the fingerprints found at the crime scene along with the case files. Sending them to you now."

Caitlin's lips widened into a grin, despite the foreboding pricking the back of her neck. "I'd tell you you're the best, but you already know that and I don't want your head to get any bigger than it already is."

Shannon's wry snort cracked in Caitlin's ear. "Love you too."

Caitlin ended the call and relayed Shannon's information to Ty.

His grin grew wider than she'd ever seen. His dark eyes danced with glee. "I'll start running the prints and requesting files now. And I'll call the judge for an arrest warrant." He leaned back in his chair with another squeak. His gaze grew contemplative. "Imagine. Closing seven cases."

And Dax's father is the culprit in every one of them. Caitlin's eyes dropped to the open case file, and Mark Carpenter stared up at her from the attached photo. Her stomach burned. *Dax knew this could happen.* But somehow the truth did little to sweeten the sour taste in her mouth.

Ty picked up the phone and tapped in a few numbers. "Judge Reynolds's office, please. This is Detective Tyrone Osgood. I'm needing an arrest warrant." He tucked the phone's receiver against his chin. Admiration lit his dark eyes. "You sure live up to your street cred, Agent Fitzhugh."

Caitlin forced a smile. Maybe so, but this time she wished to God she hadn't.

Caitlin trailed Ty and two uniformed officers down the hall at the Lodge, counting the room numbers like a T-minus clock. But instead of thrill and elation of an impending lift off, dread and remorse dogged her steps. In less than five minutes, Dax's life would be forever changed, and she was the culprit.

Well, me, Ty, and the two uniforms. Shannon's earlier caution filtered through the darkening thoughts. *Mark Carpenter is responsible for ruining Dax's view of him, not you.*

But Shan's words, no matter how truthful, couldn't ease the constriction around Caitlin's heart. Even reminding herself again she'd warned Dax this could be the outcome held little relief.

Ty and the uniforms paused in front of Room 413. As Ty raised his clenched fist, Caitlin hated her job.

Three bangs were followed by an authoritative, "Police. Open up!"

Caitlin counted again. But this time it was seconds. Anything above twenty would warrant breaking in the door. Four-star hotel or not.

Ten. Eleven. Twelve.

A door opened further down the hall. Caitlin raised a hand, ready to wave the person back inside. But it wasn't a tourist. Or even a hotel employee. It was Dax.

The air around her thickened, slowing time and action.

His eyes widened, zeroing in on the scene. His face drained of color. His mouth dropped open.

Caitlin felt his shocked gasp rather than heard it. And a heartbeat later, his gaze met hers.

She sucked in a hitching breath, his devastation hitting her like a gut punch. She'd known this would be his reaction. Had prepared her head for it. But nothing could have prepared her heart. The heart that still belonged to him no matter what she tried to tell it.

Mark and Susan's door opened in her peripheral vision. The uniforms cuffed Mark. Ty read the Miranda Rights. But all Caitlin could do was stare at Dax, her heart shattering for him.

Three bangs echoed from the hall followed by a muffled, but ominous command. Dax's heart dropped. His brain froze. He'd seen the scenario on cop shows often enough.

No. She would've told me at the beach.

He held his breath, straining to hear. But silence reigned. He rolled his shoulders, trying to dislodge the odd sensation pricking him. He must have imagined the noise. Maybe the housekeeper dropped something. Yes, that had to be it.

But there was one way to be sure. Dax forced himself to move. He gripped the door handle and closed his eyes, lifting a desperate prayer toward heaven. *Let me be wrong.*

He scanned up one end of the hall. No housekeeper. Maybe she'd already left? The odd prickling sensation returned, urging him to turn around. Two uniformed police officers and Detective Osgood clustered around Mom and Pop's room door. Just beyond them was ... Caitlin.

Cold reality rushed through him. She stood, lips parted and one hand extended. But as she seemed to register his presence, her face softened. Her hand dropped.

Caitlin.

She'd warned him this could happen. But he hadn't believed her. Not really. Dax knew Pop. Believed him. And Caitlin would prove his innocence not his guilt.

Had she known at the beach? Was that why she'd left so fast? Could she have lied—at least by omission—to his face?

Her cheeks paled, and her lips parted on his name. She stepped toward him, hand once again extending. He read the pain in her face. No, she hadn't known at the beach. It was small comfort as the Miranda speech reverberated down the hall, but he'd take whatever solace he could find.

The officers pushed Pop out of the room, and Dax's gaze locked with his. Lips parted, eyes unfocused, Pop shook his head.

Disbelief or resignation? Despite his protests, his explanations, Pop was being arrested. So did Dax actually know anything about the man who raised him?

Pop and the officers disappeared down the hallway. The detective trailed behind them. Mom hurried from their room, purse and keys in hand. Her gaze flicked from Pop to Caitlin and then to Dax. She opened her mouth to say something, then shook her head and followed Pop and the officers, leaving Dax alone in the hallway with Caitlin.

Silence wrapped them like a cocoon as they stared at each other. He took a step toward her, then another. He needed her in his arms. Her eyes said she needed to be there too. But still they stood apart.

She lifted her hand and cupped his cheek, allowing them both at least that touch. "I'm sorry, Dax." Her words were a whisper, a breath. And then she turned and was gone.

Dax fell back against the wall, closing his eyes. *What on earth do I do now?*

Chapter Twenty

Thursday, September 20
Gulf Shores, Alabama

Dax threw himself on the bed and rolled to his side, staring out the window to the waves beyond. Their easy cadence, tumbling one over another, couldn't quell the roiling inside him. Pop had been arrested. Mom had gone after him. And Caitlin had said she was sorry.

He'd love to call Caitlin. He should call Mom. He needed to call Gene. Instead, he called Zeb. Preacher answered on the second ring, and the events spewed from Dax's lips like a bursting dam.

"Dax. Man."

"Yeah. I don't know what to do. What to think."

"First thing is give yourself some time. This is an awful shock." He paused, then took in a quick breath. "Tell you what. Why don't I come down? I've got vacation days I'm due."

"But Gina, the kids. You can't leave them."

"She'll understand. Her mom's been wanting to come up from Orlando to spend some time with them."

"Thanks, buddy. But she needs you more right now. The boys plus the baby on the way. There's nothing you can do here anyway. It's just ... really good to hear your voice."

"Call me anytime—day or night. I've got you, buddy."

"Thanks. I will." Dax ended the call and slung his arm over his face, covering his eyes as the horror of the day washed through him. What was he going to tell Gene? Pop was arrested, but an arrest wasn't a conviction. He could still be innocent. And with nothing definitive, anything he'd tell Gene would still be supposition and stir a pot that bubbled enough already. No, he'd hold off until he knew facts. Until then, he had a spot to record. And if it was his last one, he wanted it to be the best.

Caitlin stood arms crossed and stared through the one-way mirror while Ty paced the small interrogation room. Mark and his lawyer sat across from him. She flipped on the intercom and listened.

Ty planted his hands on the table. "Fingerprints don't lie. We've got you at The Broken Flip-Flop, Carpenter. Or should I say, Bewley? So why don't you just tell me your side?" Ty pushed off the table and spread his hands wide as if a thought just occurred to him. "Maybe Ricky talked you into doing these jobs. No one had ever caught you in the act before. You got scared when Prescott showed up. You pushed him harder than you thought and didn't intend to kill him. Just admit what you did, and the DA will go much easier on you."

Mark's eyes remained fixed on his cuffed hands. Broussard weaved a pen between his fingers. Neither seemed impressed with the case Ty made, despite the immutable evidence.

She flicked off the intercom and headed back to the bullpen. As a consultant, she could sit in on the interview, could ask her own questions. But Ty hadn't asked, and she hadn't volunteered. She didn't think her heart could take it. Logging into the computer, she clicked the email icon and read through her inbox, hoping for a distraction.

A familiar voice called from the desk sergeant's window. Susan. Caitlin's stomach knotted. Like their first encounter in the waiting area, there was no avoiding Dax's mom, and Caitlin didn't want to. None of this was Susan's fault. Caitlin waved to the desk sergeant, then pointed to the breakroom.

Susan joined her a few minutes later, escorted by the desk sergeant. Caitlin gestured to the coffee pot and Coke machine, but Susan shook her head. They each pulled out a metal chair that had seen better days, then sat across from each other at the small table.

Caitlin studied Susan in the silence. Had she had known all along about Mark? Dax was thirty-seven. So that meant Mark and Susan had met not long after Mic Prescott was killed. Had Mark told her what he'd done?

With Broussard still in the interrogation with Mark, she'd have to tread carefully with her questions. Even though Susan couldn't be compelled to testify against her husband, part of Caitlin needed to know how deep the secrets in the Carpenter family ran.

Susan worried her wedding band as she lifted a watery gaze toward Caitlin. "It's bad, isn't it?"

Unwilling to overplay her hand, Caitlin simply nodded.

"How bad?" The words were a squeak, choked with unshed tears.

Caitlin gave Susan's hands a long squeeze, hoping to still their tremble, but her next words would only shake Susan more. "Very. There's direct evidence linking him not only to the robbery and murder here but also to several unsolved robberies in Florida."

Susan paled whiter than the walls around them.

A relieved breath slipped between Caitlin's lips. Susan hadn't known. But that truth would make the next words Caitlin said even more devastating.

She gripped Susan's hands harder and marshalled every ounce of her resolve, hating the role, but caring too much to leave the duty to Ty. She lowered her voice to a steady, soothing murmur. "But that evidence also means Mark isn't who he says he is. His real name is Douglas Bewley. I'm so sorry, Susan, but Mark's been living a lie for forty years."

Susan's hitching gasp bounced off the cinderblock walls. She lifted her eyes to the ceiling, tears slipping down her cheeks and slicing Caitlin's heart. Caitlin braced herself to see hatred, loathing, or even anger when Susan turned her gaze back. She had to know Caitlin played a large role in getting them to this point. But when their eyes met, only anguish and a heartrending despair lurked in their depths. Caitlin almost wished for anger.

"How could I not have known? Caitlin, we were married. We talked. Really talked. About our lives, our dreams. We had a child together, raised him together. We went to church. We had a life."

Caitlin remained silent, allowing Susan whatever time she needed to process through her new reality. Questions, doubts, and disbelief would be her new normal for weeks, if not months or years—especially as Mark went through the trial and sentencing.

The life Susan knew was as dead as Mic Prescott.

An hour later, Caitlin sat at her temporary desk, cradling her head in her hands. Susan had left a few minutes prior with a sheriff's escort to ensure she reached The Lodge safely. Ty sat across from her, typing up the interrogation report and readying the file to meet with the ADA.

"This is a win, Fitzhugh. For Jackie. For the owners of the places he robbed."

Caitlin lifted her head to flash him a wan smile. "Yeah, I know. It's just ..."

"Hard. I get it. But I've gotta give you major points for seeing this through."

Caitlin shrugged. "Think I'm going to take a walk."

Ty's lips pulled back in a sympathetic smile. "Go on and take off the rest of the day. I've got this covered."

She lifted her brows in a silent question, and Ty nodded. She logged off her computer and grabbed her briefcase. "I'll see you in the morning. And I'd like to be there when you tell Jackie."

"I'll give her a call and set something up for tomorrow. Get outta here. Go get a drink. Ice cream. Walk on the beach. Whatever."

Caitlin's cheeks flinched. *All of the above?* But all she did was nod.

Dax hit *send* on the video as a knock sounded on his door. He leaned down to check the peephole and found Mom standing in the hallway, head bowed, and fingers gripping her purse straps like a life preserver. He opened the door and watched her face crumple.

Without a word, he pulled her inside and eased her on the bench of his kitchenette table. He grabbed a Coke from the fridge, popped the top, and handed it to her.

She traced the silver letters on the can in silence. Her finger slid along the giant E as she whispered, "It's really real, Dax. Your dad's been arrested."

"It could still be mistaken identity, Mom."

She lifted a pain-filled gaze to him. "Honey. It's not. Caitlin told me. Probably more than she should have. They have fingerprints. They match your dad's. He did it. The robbery. The murder. And more."

Dax closed his eyes, but the truth of her words couldn't be ignored. *Now what?*

Unable to stomach the idea of food, Caitlin set her GPS for the Gulf Shores pier. Although within throwing distance of Dax's hotel, she couldn't think of anywhere else she could clear her mind. She meandered her way along the boardwalk, smiling at fishermen and fisherwomen and pausing to watch as they reeled in catches.

Life. Normal life. Their worlds might not be perfect, but at least she hadn't been responsible for destroying them. Her gaze caught of the outline of The Lodge. What were Dax and Susan doing now? What was Dax thinking? Susan might not hate her, but did he? Caitlin closed her eyes against the thought and focused on the breeze hitting her face and the surf crashing against the pylons.

Her phone blared from her back pocket. She could ignore it. Should ignore it. She was in no shape to talk to anyone. But it could be Mom. And if something else had happened with Daddy—

Caitlin swallowed her pain, heaving a relieved sigh as she read the caller ID. "Hey, Shan."

"What happened?" Shannon's normal, easy Alabama accent sharpened with wary concern.

Tears clogged Caitlin's huff. "What didn't happen? The fingerprints you found matched Mark's. We arrested him. Ethan is going to talk with Mom about either getting more help at home or putting Daddy in a facility ..."

And Dax probably hates me. Again. Her voice trailed off. Her greatest concern staying silent.

"Oh, honey. I'm so sorry. Ethan told me about the sibling call when we talked last night, and I figured the prints would match up. You're too good at your job not to find the truth." She paused, and her voice softened. "How are you doing with all this?"

"I knew it was coming with Mark—it's even what I warned Dax might happen. And Daddy's decline is unavoidable ..."

"That doesn't answer my question, Caitie."

Caitlin ran a hand across her forehead as the guilt she'd held at bay suddenly burst through its wall. "Does me standing here on the Gulf Shores Pier, contemplating jumping off and swimming away give you a good answer?" She grimaced as the words came out sharper than she intended.

Shannon's sympathetic hmph told Caitlin she took no offense. "Yeah, that's pretty much how I thought you were doing. I'm coming down in the morning."

Caitlin blinked hard, willing away the tears even as she savored Shan's immediate support. "Ethan's still at the conference. What about your clients?"

Shannon's tone firmed. "I'll bring my laptop—it's got everything I'll need, but you are not going through this alone."

Caitlin sagged against the railing. Her voice cracked around her reply. "If you don't know it already, Shan, I love you."

"Love you back, SIL. Text me your hotel information, and I'll be there before lunch. Try and get some sleep tonight."

Telling Shannon she'd leave a second keycard with the front desk, Caitlin ended the call, her gaze settling on the breathtaking scene surrounding her. An intrepid paddleboarder skimmed through the breaking waves. On the horizon, a barge inched across the edge of the Gulf. She watched them both until the sun began its nightly dip into the water, searing the sky with oranges and reds.

As the fishermen and women snapped coolers closed and snugged lines and hooks into the reels, Caitlin joined them in their trek from the pier, wishing she could simply enjoy her own catch of the day. Hers, however, came not as tasty meal, but marinated in the pain she'd caused the man she loved.

Chapter Twenty-One

Friday, September 21
College Station, Texas

A knock sounded on Ricky's apartment door at five-thirty on the dot. Swallowing his wry chuckle, he shook his head. He'd been hoping he could duck Jill's offer of the ride to the hospital. She'd be better off sleeping, especially after last night's craziness.

Groups from two rival fraternities had gotten into a fight around the pool tables after one claimed the other had cheated during a game. Jill got sideswiped by a random elbow trying to escape the dust-up. He'd called the police, and they'd filed an assault charge on the frat boy who'd hit her. She'd for sure be nursing a black eye by now.

He opened the door and winced. Yeah, that elbow definitely left a mark. But then he groaned. Jill wasn't alone. Antoine towered behind her, looking beat-up tired.

Antoine lifted his brows. "You think I'm gonna let her drive with that shiner? Or even let you head to the hospital by yourself?"

A rueful chuckle slipped between Ricky's lips. No matter all the bad he'd done before he'd come to Texas, he'd definitely managed to do good since.

Mic, I hope I did you proud. Guess I'll find out when I get upstairs. A shiver skirted across the back of his neck. He rubbed the skin, pushing the hairs back down, but doing little to soothe the unsettled feeling inside him. Opting for a distraction, he took a quick look around the living room. Couch, TV, a couple of concert posters on the wall. Nothing he'd really miss despite the number of years he'd lived there.

With a nod, he picked up his suitcase. "All right then, you two. Have it your way."

Antoine slipped the suitcase handle from Ricky's grip. He gave his head a wry shake, locked the door, and held the key ring in front of Jill. They stared at it, the keys clinking together. One for his apartment, his mailbox, the Silver Shooters, and two for the truck. His whole life on a keychain.

Jill's eyes widened. "Why are you giving me these?"

Ricky opened her hand and dropped the key ring in it. He tilted his head toward the truck. "No telling how long I'll be laid up in the home after the surgery. Need someone to water my plants and take the truck for a spin."

Jill's eyes narrowed. "You don't have any plants."

Ricky snorted. "True enough. Then at least make sure the truck gets some road time now and then."

Again, she looked as if she weighed his words, curious if he knew something she didn't.

Ricky kept his face neutral. It was the truth anyway. The doc said the surgery would buy him some time above the six-month window. But Ricky had the distinct feeling that window would all be spent away from here. "Need to get going now."

Jill tucked the keys in her purse, eyes bright and watery under the exterior lights.

They climbed into Antoine's Jeep Cherokee and headed for the hospital. A few minutes later, Antoine pulled to a stop at the surgery entrance. Ricky opened the door of the front passenger seat, then turned and leveled a serious look on them. "Best thing for you both is to go home and get some shut-eye. Ain't a thing you can do pacing around here. And I don't want to see hide nor hair of you when I wake up."

Antoine opened his mouth to object, but Jill got there first. "Ricky, you're—"

"I mean it. Both of ya'. You want to do something for me? Take care of the Silver Shooters. Open up just like usual. Heck, even run a special in my honor if you want. I'll let you know where I end up after all's said and done. Come and see me then."

Antoine looked like he wanted to say something, but instead nodded as he draped his hands across the steering wheel. Ricky pierced Jill with a determined look. She grimaced, but gave her own nod.

"You two and that bar are the best family a body could ask for." Ricky climbed out of the Jeep and grabbed his suitcase. "All right, then. I'll see ya' on the flip side."

He patted the door and headed into the hospital without a look back, trusting them to do as he asked. A moment later, the Jeep's horn beeped twice, bringing a smile to his lips. "Love y'all, too."

At 9:00 a.m., Ricky still lay in a hospital bed, watching the clock on the wall tick the time away. *So much for a six a.m. call time.* He shivered and adjusted the warmed blanket over his thin hospital gown.

The nurse had been in twice to update him. Once to tell him it wouldn't be long before they'd start the anesthesia. The next to say the surgery ahead of his had some complications and would run long. It was all good, though, really. He couldn't do anything else anyway. They'd get to him when they got to him.

His phone buzzed from where it sat next to his wallet atop the rolling side table. Ricky reached for it, wincing at the tug of the IV needle in his forearm. "Hello?" He kept his voice low, uncertain if he could take calls without blowing up one of the machines.

"Ricky. Detective Ty Osgood. Wanted to give you an update on the case."

Ricky glanced at the equipment. Nothing had exploded or even fritzed. *Guess it's safe enough.*

"You've got good timing, Detective. I'm at the hospital for that surgery I told you about. Should be coming to get me any time now."

"I'll keep this brief. But it is good news, thanks to you and the consultant from the State Division of Investigations. Mark Carpenter, uh, Doug Bewley, has been arrested and will be arraigned later this morning for the robbery and murder of Michael Prescott."

Relief washed through Ricky. Tears pricked the corners of his eyes. The next big chunk of the elephant had been eaten. "Yes, sir. That is good news." His voice cracked, and he swallowed hard. His gaze latched onto the empty hospital mug, longing for more than the barest saliva to wet his throat. "What happens next?"

"Now that Carpenter is being charged, the DA's office will send one of the ADAs to you for the deposition. Their office should be calling you later today, but from what I hear, they want to see you Monday, if at all possible."

Ricky scratched at his hospital ID bracelet. "Monday works for me, but I'm guessing they'll have to clear it with my doctor."

Osgood's voice filled with concern. "Do you have that contact information? I'll pass it along to the ADA so they can get everything approved."

Ricky relayed the details he knew as the door pushed open. He caught the flash of irritation in the nurse's eyes and figured he'd been right about cell phone use. *Better to ask forgiveness than permission sometimes.* "Hey, Detective, the nurse just came in. Looks like they're ready for me."

The nurse's eyes widened as she absorbed Ricky's reason for violating the rules. She gave a brisk nod, then pushed a few buttons on his monitor before giving him a pointed look.

Ricky ignored her. "Thanks for everything, Detective."

"I'm the one who should be thanking you."

He shook his head, savoring the odd sensation of peace whispering through him. "You know what they say, 'Confession is good for the soul.' Catch ya' later." He ended the call and watched the nurse as she adjusted the IV bags.

Another scrubbed-up person pushed through the door. Between the surgical cap and mask, Ricky couldn't tell if they were a man or a woman until they spoke.

"I'm your nurse anesthetist, Miguel. Doctor Chen will meet us in the surgery bay, but I'm going to start your pre-surgery sedative here." Miguel explained what Ricky could expect as the anesthesia took hold and how he would likely feel as it wore off in post-op. "Now, I want you to count backwards from one-hundred."

As the numbers left Ricky's lips and the sedative started to take hold, he heard another voice. Deeper, more melodic. "You did good, Ricky. I'll take it from here."

Figuring it was just the nurses talking to each other, Ricky smiled, closed his eyes, and let everything go.

Chapter Twenty-Two

Friday, September 21
Gulf Shores, Alabama

Peter Broussard greeted Dax and Mom at the courtroom door. He gave them a soft, sympathetic smile, but his eyes held the resignation of a seasoned lawyer.

Dax's lungs hitched on a breath. How had Peter known about Pop's guilt within a few minutes of meeting him when Dax had known him all his life and been so utterly wrong? Had Dax really never known Pop at all?

Peter patted Mom's arm. "This will be quick, *cher.* Basically, the assistant district attorney will introduce the charges, then he and I will present our arguments about bail." He looked over his shoulder at another suited man in the hallway and lowered his voice. "I'm going to warn ya' now. I'm not fully confident we can get it with the evidence they have. But if we do, how much money can you easily put up?"

Dax calculated his bank account balance. Decent. Add in his stock portfolio and he could put down a hefty amount.

Peter's gaze shifted to Dax. A question lurked in its blue depths. *Are you willing to pay anything at all?*

Dax cringed. How much should he spend to free a seemingly guilty man? Yet, this was Pop. "Whatever it takes."

Mom shook her head. "No, Dax. I'll put up the house, but …" Doubt tinged her words.

Dax's eyes shot to her. Would she prefer Pop remained in jail until the trial? She did believe the evidence and Caitlin's read of it.

A bailiff pushed open the courtroom door and glanced around the hallway. "Lookin' for Mark Carpenter's lawyer?"

"That would be me." Peter gestured for Mom and Dax to follow him.

Dax scanned the courtroom as they walked toward a bench on the left side. A smattering of people sat scattered throughout the room. Near the judge's bench, the court reporter hunched over her transcription device. But neither the detective who arrested Pop nor Caitlin were present. Not that Dax really expected them.

Why were all the other people there? Were they other attorneys and family members waiting their turn?

Feeling exposed, Dax ran a hand over his shaved head, missing the beach hat Caitlin had teased him for wearing. The sun hat had been effective that day, making him just another beach bum out enjoying the sand and surf. But what about now? Thankfully, Carpenter was a common last name. Maybe no one here would make a connection.

Except you are in the courtroom audience, doofus.

Maybe it would be better if he left. Just to be safe. He shot a glance to Mom. Cheeks pale, eyes dull, she sat a shadow of herself. His stomach dropped. No, he couldn't let her face this alone.

Dax scoped out the gallery again. A man in a suit pawed through his briefcase. A couple near the back had a furious conversation in hushed tones. A woman two rows up scrolled through her phone. Even the kid in the back had his eyes closed and head leaned against the bench, earbuds poking out from under his skater haircut. No, no one was paying them any attention.

Dax shrugged off the worry. He was just being paranoid. He knew one thing for sure; he now had to call Gene.

A door on the left of the courtroom opened, revealing a man in a gray pinstripe suit with a thin, blue tie and dark hair brushed back from his face. Dax did a double take as a bailiff followed behind him. The man in the suit. That was ... Pop?

Dax wracked his brain for the last time—or really even the first time—he'd seen Pop in a suit, but nothing came to mind. The closest he could recall was Grandpa and Grandma's funerals. Pop had worn black twill pants and a black plaid dress shirt to both. Even on Sundays, the dressiest clothes he'd wear would be khakis and a button-down shirt.

"All rise. Court is now in session. The Honorable Judge Carol Wimbley presiding."

"Sit, please." Dax heard the gallery obey, but kept his eyes trained on Pop. He still looked like the man who had raised him. Still wore that same expression of innocence. Could he really be that good at lying?

He's had forty years of practice.

Judge Wimbley leaned forward and stared down at her courtroom audience. "Counselors, I'll hear your arguments."

The lawyers rose, and Peter gestured for Pop to stand as well, then whispered something in his ear. Pop looked over his shoulder at Dax and Mom, giving both an encouraging smile. Dax wished it had worked.

"Ya' Honor," Peter said. "My client, Mark Carpenter, has been accused of a forty-year-old robbery and murder by his so-called partner. Mr. Carpenter vigorously disputes this claim and has been an upstanding member of the Elba community for almost that same amount of time. He's a retired business owner, and his wife is a retired teacher. They live on a fixed income after a modest, middle-class life. We ask that he be released on his own recognizance."

The ADA dropped his legal pad to the table and propped his hands on his hips. "Judge, Mr. Carpenter, who the state will prove has been living under an assumed name, may have lived a clean life after his crimes, but that isn't the issue. He is a man who has dodged his culpability in those crimes for forty years and must be held accountable for them. His financial means, or lack thereof, and his having no ties to the Gulf Shores community actually could lead to him running well before his trial date. We ask he be remanded without bail to ensure he stands trial."

Judge Wimbley studied Pop, then leveled her considering gaze on Mom and Dax. After a long moment of silence, she said, "I'm not taking any chances, Mr. Carpenter. I'm remanding you without bail. Trial is set for four months from today."

"Ya' Honor!" Peter called as he gestured to Mom.

But Judge Wimbley shook her head. "That's my ruling, Counselor. Next case."

Two court bailiffs escorted Pop back through the doors he'd entered. Dax wrapped Mom up in a side hug. Peter turned a resigned grimace on them and slipped his files back in his briefcase. The ADA's smug grin grew as another attorney took Peter's place at the defense table.

Four months. Pop would be in jail for four months until the trial. Dax now had specifics to tell Gene. But as he absorbed Mom's trembling shoulders, he once again pushed all thought of the phone call aside. Family came first. Especially what little family he had left.

Caitlin stepped into the interview room and studied Jackie Gonzalez. The shock of a few days ago had faded, and the dark circles had lessened. Hope brimmed in her eyes. Caitlin offered a comforting smile and pulled out the chair across from her. "Is Roberto not coming?"

Jackie shook her head. "He's with our grandkids. They're on fall break and Michelle, my oldest, and her husband are working."

Caitlin laced her fingers together. "I have good news for you."

"Yes, Ty mentioned that on the phone, but he said he couldn't go into details."

"We've formally arrested the person of interest after finding fingerprint evidence linking him to the robbery and murder at your father's restaurant. They also connect him to other robberies along the Gulf Coast."

"Praise God."

Caitlin flinched, uncertain if any praise was warranted in the situation. "He was arraigned this morning and is being held without bail as a potential flight risk. The trial is four months away, but the assistant district attorney thinks the case is strong. He's flying out to Texas on Monday to do the formal deposition of the witness."

Jackie reached across the table and squeezed Caitlin's hands. "Thank you, Agent Fitzhugh. Thank you for closing this awful chapter of my life." Her gaze grew distant. "I only wish my brother could know."

Sympathy wafted through her. Jackie had lost so much through the course of all this. "You have no idea where he is?"

Jackie shook her head. "I don't even know if he's still alive." She sighed, but pulled a smile across her lips. "At least I can put Daddy completely to rest. That's a huge blessing."

Caitlin rose, escorting Jackie back through the bullpen. Jackie paused when they reached Caitlin's desk. "I can't thank you enough. It was a long time in coming, but the peace is worth it." She squeezed Caitlin's forearm and headed out.

Caitlin watched her go. Closure. Jackie had closure for her loss. But it came with a painful price, wounding Dax and Susan. What type of closure would they find, and when would they find it? Would she be there to witness it? Did she even want to be?

On the heels of those thoughts came unbidden ones that were even worse, laden with jealousy and past personal heartbreak. Would she and Brenda ever have closure for Missy? Or would they live forever in the limbo of the unknown, unable to move forward but equally unable to go back?

The questions whirled through her, buffeting and swirling her emotions. Caitlin dropped the file on her desk, then leaned against it as Ty passed by with yet another mug of swill.

He took a long sip, surprise wreathing his face. "Hey, you should get some of this. It's not half-bad."

"New front desk lady made it," the desk sergeant called across the room. "Thinking she's a keeper."

Ty chuckled as he set the mug on his desk. "How'd it go with Jackie?"

"Good. She's pleased, as you might expect."

His thick shoulders eased. "I talked with Ricky Adams earlier this morning and let him know about the arrest and arraignment. He's pleased, as you'd expect." Ty glanced at his watch then back to Caitlin. "He's got to be in surgery by now. The nurse came in while I was on the call. Thinking we'll know how it went by the end of the day—tomorrow at the latest. The ADA's got his tickets booked for Monday morning with a deposition scheduled for Tuesday. We'll have everything we need then for trial."

Caitlin swallowed hard. These were all good things, but somehow, they wrenched the knife in her heart tighter. "Hey, I'm expecting Shannon any time, so I'm going to head to the hotel and meet her. Text me if anything comes up, will you?"

Ty studied her, his cop's eyes weighing her words and reading her face. Caitlin hoped she had enough wherewithal remaining to hide her emotions, but judging by the empathy that seeped into his gaze, she'd failed. He dipped his head. "Take whatever time you need."

Chapter Twenty-Three

Friday, September 21
Gulf Shores, Alabama

Dax twirled his chopsticks through the Chinese takeout he and Mom had grabbed on the way back to the hotel. Mom fiddled with her share of the lo mein, the bulk of her portion cooling untouched on her plate. He'd already reheated it once for her. It wouldn't be long before it'd need another good nuking.

He wasn't surprised by her absent appetite. Not when he'd lost his own an hour before they stopped for the food. But she would have to eat at some point. Dax opened his mouth to ask her about yet another round in the microwave when his phone vibrated in his back pocket. Tugging it out, he cringed as he read the name on the screen. "It's my producer."

He walked toward the balcony, staring at the phone. With Pop officially arrested, charged, and now awaiting trial, he finally had a story to tell. He just wished he'd a better idea of how to share it. The buzzing stopped. His voicemail picked up. But he couldn't put the conversation off any longer.

A moment later, the phone vibrated again. Dax took in a deep breath, marshalled a beginning explanation, and tapped the green button.

Gene's expletive-laden tirade started before Dax could even say, "Hello." Four letter words bounced off hard-bitten questions. "You've gone viral. And I had to find out from a pre-pubescent, pimple-faced intern."

Dax blinked. His skin chilled. *Viral? How?* He clicked over to his Twitter account and let his own curses fly. He trended with his own hashtag. Flashing an apologetic look to Mom for the vulgarity, he tapped back to the phone app but Gene's tirade had regained steam.

How had he been linked with Pop? Dax had watched everyone in the courtroom. No one looked like a reporter, and there were no cameras allowed in the courthouse—at least according to the sign displayed in the lobby. Guilt flushed through him. "I don't know how this happened, Gene."

"I'll tell you how it happened, Dax. Someone snapped a picture of you in a courtroom with your mom and dad, then tweeted it, saying your dad was charged with robbery and murder. That post got picked up by a group of sports bloggers and wanna-be armchair commentators on Reddit. The rest blew up from there."

Dax smothered another string of curses. Clenching his fist, he punched the air, uncertain who was the bigger target for his anger, the fans, Pop, or himself.

Gene's rant continued, with barely a breath between his words. "Now the Network's switchboard is lit up like a Christmas tree with calls from all the news outlets wanting a statement. And we're all sitting here sucking our thumbs wondering what's going on. How could you keep this from me? I'm your producer."

Dax opened his mouth, hoping to slide in a few words as Gene's ire seemed to fade. But Gene found another verbal gear, playing the last and worst card in the pile. "You're finished. At least at ESPN. They're not going to touch you—even if it wasn't you and it was forty years ago. There's talk of invoking the morals clause of your contract here. But so far, Legal hasn't found a loophole to force you out."

Dax scrubbed a hand over his face and pulled out the only explanation he had. "Gene. I'm sorry. I didn't believe my dad could do this. I was sure they had the wrong man, and I didn't want to say anything until it was certain. You won't believe me, but I was planning to call you today after the arraignment."

The air between them fell silent, although charged with resigned acceptance. Gene's family history yet again apparently afforded Dax breathing room and sympathy. "Okay, look, maybe I can understand that. I guess if I were in your place I'd be shocked too. But if you have any dream of saving your career, you need to jump on this. I know a good PR guy. He can spin it for all its worth. You need to distance yourself from your dad. Get back to Atlanta today."

"Today?" Dax turned on his heel and found Mom watching him, concern mingling with tears in her copper eyes. She'd already been through the wringer with Pop. He couldn't be responsible for making it worse. "But my mom—"

Gene's voice firmed. No excuse would be enough. "She's gonna have to understand. You need to save yourself here."

Dax shook his head. "I-I'll let you know." He jabbed the End button and tossed the phone on the bed running a hand over his head. Stubble bit his palm.

"What's wrong?" Mom's quiet question lashed at his rising guilt. Once again, his fame had hurt, rather than helped.

"Someone took a picture of me and you with Pop in the courtroom and posted it on Twitter. It went viral, and Gene just tore me a new one."

Mom rose and pulled Dax into a hug. "I'm so sorry, honey."

Dax closed his eyes as he tucked her into his chest, wishing he was young enough to feel her chin on his head rather than the opposite. "That's not the worst of it."

A long sigh rumbled between them. He could see Gene's point, but could he really do as he said?

"He wants me back in Atlanta now to start damage control. He says my shot at ESPN is gone. I might be able to save my career at the SEC Network, but only if I distance myself from Pop ... and you."

Mom eased back and looked at him with patient love radiating from her gaze.

Dax gave her a long squeeze. "I don't want to do any of that. As much as I hate Pop for lying and living a lie, he's still my dad. And I can't leave you to handle all of this by yourself."

Mom stepped out of his arms. Steel infused her tone and her gaze sharpened. "Dax, I love you for wanting to protect me, but I can take care of myself. Yes, this has been a blow. No, I haven't fully come to terms with it. But I will with enough time."

He turned and stared out the window as his shoulders hunched under an invisible weight.

"I know a good PR guy. He can spin it for all its worth."

Dax flinched. "Pop lived a lie for forty years. If go back to Atlanta and hire this PR guy to spin this—basically to lie for me —how is that any different than what Pop did? But if I don't do what Gene says, I could lose everything I've worked for. Football is all I've ever known, all I've ever been good at. If I don't have football, then what do I have? Who am I?"

Mom tugged on his arm, pulling him back around to look at her. Truth and love gleamed in her eyes. "Son, who you are isn't football. It's just a *part* of who you are. And while you may think it's the biggest part, it's really not. It's an activity that harnessed a talent and led to a career."

Placing her hands on his shoulders, she leveled a blunt southern mama look on him. "Hear me, son. Football is not your identity. You are first, last, and always a child of God. Ever since you walked down the church aisle when you were eight years old and asked Pastor Ben to baptize you."

Dax snorted and glanced away, but she tapped his arm, drawing his attention back. This time her eyes softened with a deep, unconditional love. "Your daddy brought this on all of us. He killed someone—whether he meant to or not—and took that person away from his family. That's on him. Not you. You do what you need to do to make sure everyone understands that. And if that includes hiring some quick-talking person, you do so with my blessing. Don't let your daddy steal any more from you than he already has."

A long, heavy breath spewed from her lips as the heartfelt lecture seemed to deflate her. She eased down on the edge of the bed. "I'm worn out. I think I need a nap and some quiet time. And you need to get your head together."

Dax leaned down to kiss Mom's forehead. "Get some rest." He stuck the food cartons in the fridge and gave one last look to her as she climbed fully dressed into the bed. Maybe things would look better tomorrow. "I'll check in with you later tonight, Mom."

A muffled hum was her only response. Dax slipped out the door, shutting it softly behind him. Could Mom be right? Could his life be more than football? Or was Gene right? And was it okay to lie to save what remained of his career?

He shook off the questions and headed toward his room. Mom was right about one thing. He had to get his head together.

Caitlin pushed through the door of her hotel room and walked straight into Shannon's waiting hug. As her cheek met Shan's shoulder, the torrent of tears she'd managed to stuff since yesterday afternoon fell unchecked, drenching Shannon's

Alabama t-shirt and darkening the crimson to a color closer to purple.

Shannon said nothing. Instead, she waited, hugging Caitlin tighter. Caitlin soaked up the reality she wasn't alone. She pulled back and looked at Shannon through tear-puffed eyes. Caitlin had no words, but Shannon didn't need them. She tugged Caitlin to the loveseat. Grabbing the box of tissues on the way, she sat with one leg tucked up under her and waited some more.

Caitlin took a handful of tissues, dried her cheeks, then blew her nose. The tissues dropped from her hand to the floor, and she slumped against the loveseat. They sat in silence, punctuated by the whine of the wall AC unit and the occasional voice in the hallway.

At length, Caitlin cleared the remaining tears clogging her throat. "I met with the victim's family, or what's left of the family, today. His daughter. She's waited forty years for closure. And now it's here."

Shannon squeezed her hand, but still said nothing.

"And all I could think of was, what if it takes forty years for there to be closure for Missy? Am I an awful person for thinking that? For being jealous?"

"Absolutely not." Shannon tugged at Caitlin's hand and leaned toward her. "It's actually reassuring."

Caitlin huffed.

Shannon continued, "It means you really are human, Caitie. I'd honestly be worried if you hadn't had some sort of reaction."

Caitlin bit her lip. Her eyes unfocused as she voiced one of her deepest fears. "What if we never find out what happened to Missy?"

"Then you never do. And I'm sorry for that. But there are some things we won't know until we get on the other side." Shannon let the silence fall again. Then a few moments later, she patted Caitlin's arm. "I'm sorry about your dad."

Caitlin swallowed hard. "It has to be done, Shan. I hate it

with everything in me, but I can't sit back and wait for Daddy to do something to Mom or himself. But it's going to kill her. Like losing Daddy all over again."

Shannon shook her head as her lips firmed. "She's strong, Caitie. She's where you get your strength. It may take time, but she'll work through the pain and see the blessings behind the decision. I just hate all of this has fallen on you at the same time." She paused. "Have you talked to Dax since the arrest?"

Caitlin's heart twisted. "I'm probably the last person he wants to see right now."

Shannon's cheeks twitched around a small smile. "Oh, I'm not so sure. I remember the way he looked at you, Caitie. Dax was a man in love. In the kind of love that lasts a lifetime—no matter what."

Caitlin picked at the couch's fabric, eyes darting to Shannon's engagement ring and wedding band. How many times would she have to say it until she convinced Shannon? "It won't work, Shan."

"You mean because of Missy?" The question was soft, gentle, but sliced deep nonetheless.

Caitlin's eyes widened. How did Shannon know?

Shannon gaze warmed. "You forget how well I know you—and I was there when she disappeared. I admit, I didn't put two and two together right off. But it's pretty clear now, seeing you with Dax back in your life and knowing your original reasons for ending the relationship. You pushed him away because he scared you. Your love for him scared you. But, Caitie, a love like you two had doesn't happen by chance. It's a gift you have to embrace, cherish, and fight for."

Caitlin grimaced as memories of Shannon's own fight flickered through her. "Like you did with Ethan?"

Shannon nodded as her lips lifted in a fond, encouraging smile. "Trust me. Love is worth the effort."

Questions, doubts, and worries swirled in Caitlin's heart. She jumped off the loveseat and paced the room, finally collapsing on her bed. Was Shan right? Or was her fear? God help her, she didn't know.

Shannon patted Caitlin's foot. "I'm going to grab some food at the restaurant up the street. Meet me at the pool in twenty?"

Caitlin's tired brain registered Shannon's plans and the bikini straps peeking out from under her loose top. "This is a work trip. I didn't bring a suit."

A smirk creeped up Shannon's cheeks. "Well, guess who brought two?" She tugged open the zipper on her suitcase and tossed a green one-piece at Caitlin. The suit landed half on her face, drawing a reluctant chuckle from her lips.

"Get changed," Shannon said. "You need to get out of this room and think about something else. And I need some sun and chlorine before I tackle the emails in my inbox."

Caitlin moved to the edge of her bed. "You really are the best."

"Back at ya', SIL." Shannon winked at her as she grabbed her purse and room key. "Twenty minutes, or I'm coming back up here and dragging you down."

Chapter Twenty-Four

Saturday, September 22
Gulf Shores, Alabama

The *Law & Order* theme song jerked Caitlin out of a fitful sleep. She and Shannon had lounged by the pool for the rest of the afternoon, allowing the sun to ease her aching heart. But when they'd turned in for the night, Caitlin had tossed and turned as questions circled in her head.

Was she being wise or foolhardy by closing the door on a relationship with Dax? She had valid and long-standing fears. She couldn't risk her heart again. But Shannon's words tempted something deep inside her. A yearning that sleep allowed to run rampant through her mind, whispering possibilities, creating dreams, and nurturing banished longings.

Grateful for the reprieve, Caitlin snagged the phone and hit the green button without looking at her caller ID. In the next bed, Shannon still racked the z's. Groggy, but mindful of Shan, Caitlin threw off the covers and padded toward the hotel room's narrow entry. "Caitlin Fitzhugh."

Ty's voice reverberated in her ear. "Sorry, did I wake you?"

Caitlin rubbed her eyes and forced her fuzzy brain to concentrate. "No problem. What's up?"

Ty's usual easy tone turned somber. "Just got a call from the hospital about Ricky Adams."

Closing her eyes, she pinched her nose. "I'm guessing it's not good."

"It's worse. He's dead."

Her eyes popped open as the words ricocheted through her. "I'm sorry, what?"

"Yeah, nurse said he threw a clot during the surgery, stroked out, and he's gone as of a few hours ago." Ty heaved a resigned sigh. "Look, I know you were heading back this morning, but we're gonna need to meet with the DA to talk gameplan."

Caitlin's mind spun with ramifications. Ricky had died before his formal deposition. Which meant their case against Mark just lost its most credible evidence. And Mark could walk. "What time is it anyway?"

"A little after seven."

Caitlin's lips dropped open as she confirmed his time on her phone. She never slept that late. She shook her head. "Okay, let me throw on some clothes, get about a gallon of coffee in me, and I'll meet you at the precinct."

"Make it the DA's office. I'll text you the address." Ty ended the call.

Caitlin gripped the door jamb desperate for stability in the latest emotional whirlwind.

Shannon padded into view. She crossed her arms and leaned against the wall. Her eyes gleamed with sympathy. "I heard. It's not over, huh?"

Caitlin slammed through the bathroom door. "Not by a long shot."

Caitlin pulled into a parking space on the town square of Bay Minette, the county seat of Baldwin County a little over an hour north of Gulf Shores. The square itself was like an aging southern belle, having seen better days, but still knowing how to dress for occasions.

The courthouse radiated pristine authority from its position of prominence in the square's center. Bordered by a manicured lawn, the granite building peered out from behind mature live oaks in full leaf. Historic store fronts boasting local shopping and legal services ringed it like attentive beaus at a debutante's ball. But only one sweetheart drew her gaze. Decked out with window awnings and stenciled lettering the DA's office waited a block away on one corner.

A light breeze jostled a grouping of crepe myrtle bloom shells onto Caitlin's windshield. She climbed out of her car and brushed at them as she scanned the pull-in parking spots. Having no idea what Ty would drive, she snagged her briefcase and headed off.

Despite the fancier exterior, the office had a lived-in feel punctuated by the receptionist's tired, but welcoming smile. Her thick Alabama drawl rolled into the air like humidity in August. "May I hep, ya'?"

Caitlin managed her own answering smile. "Special Agent Caitlin Fitzhugh with the Alabama State Division of Investigations. Detective Tyrone Osgood and the DA are expecting me."

The receptionist's smile gained warmth. "Yes, they are. Can I get you some coffee, a donut?"

Caitlin shook her head. Her stomach already churned with the acrid blend of hotel room coffee and infuriating frustration. "Maybe later."

"All right, then. Just this way."

The receptionist knocked twice on the half-glass door, which bore the name Grady Ross.

"Come on in."

She pushed open the door, then stepped back. Caitlin absorbed the stacks of files, ten-year-old computer, and faded degrees hanging on the wall. Grady Ross sat behind the battered wood and metal desk. His long face was half-covered by a full auburn beard an odd genetic match to his ash-blond hair. Blue eyes that had undoubtedly seen too much over his years gave her a sad once-over. He tilted his head toward the empty chair next to Ty.

Ty nodded his greeting then made the introductions, adding a brief summary of Caitlin's role in the case. "We wouldn't have a suspect at all if not for her."

Grady hmphed and flicked his weary gaze from Ty to Caitlin. "That's all well and good, but with no witness, you don't have a case. Broussard can't cross-examine a dead man, and he will for sure point that out to the judge."

Ty tapped Grady's desk, drawing his attention. "But we've got fingerprints proving Mark Carpenter, or Doug Bewley, was at all of the locations. Plus, there's the video of the suspect wiping blood from the same place Mark Carpenter now has a scar."

Grady snorted and tossed the case file back toward Ty. "Fingerprints that could have been left at any time. And the scar could've come from anywhere. At least, that's what Broussard's gonna say."

He leaned back in his chair and fixed an irritated look on them. "And anything Ricky Adams said, even in a police interview, would be considered hearsay since no formal deposition was done before he died."

Well, if you hadn't been so stingy and let the ADA fly out there before we got you all the evidence you had to have, then you'd have your deposition. Caitlin bit her tongue and flashed a speaking look toward Ty.

Grady lifted his hands in a helpless gesture. "I've got nothing of substance to present to a jury about a robbery and murder that happened forty years ago. Which means we don't stand a snowball's chance in summer of getting a conviction."

Caitlin spread her arms wide. Disbelief washed through her. She'd reopened too many doors to have this one slammed in her face. "So what? You're not even going to try? I thought we were here to talk strategy not defeat."

Grady leveled a darkening glare. "Look, Agent Fitzhugh, I don't go to court with cases I don't have a chance of winning. Find me something else that puts Mark Carpenter in those locations at the times of the robberies, and we'll look at it again. Until then, release him. I'm not risking my record. It's an election year. And you can think what you like about my decision."

Caitlin swallowed her curse. Grady was right about the lack of evidence, but he still was a coward for not at least trying. She slipped out of the office with Ty on her heels. Balling her hands into fists, she relished the biting sting of her fingernails against her palms, wishing she could take out her frustration on the One who caused it.

Thanks a lot, God. Didn't I ask you to not leave me hanging again? I get that we're not really on speaking terms, but couldn't you have answered at least that prayer?

A heavy hand fell on her shoulder, and Caitlin turned to see Ty's disappointed gaze. "This happens."

Caitlin groaned. "We've got to break the news to Jackie and Roberto."

Caitlin and Ty pulled in front of a well-kept ranch style home in Foley, Alabama. When he'd called Jackie from the parking lot outside the DA's office, Ty offered to stop at her home rather than having her drive once again to Gulf Shores. Jackie had agreed, saying her youngest grandchildren were spending the day with them.

Caitlin put her car in park and watched three boys under the age of ten chase each other through a sprinkler in the front yard. Roberto held a hose with a spray nozzle and tagged the boys as they tried to escape. Jackie stood against the railing, a glass of tea in hand, and watched the antics with a grin. The sweet, contented expression faded as she registered Caitlin and Ty's somber faces.

Roberto lifted his finger from the sprayer and shot a questioning look toward Jackie. The boys clustered around him, curious but wary about the new arrivals.

Jackie shook her head. "Y'all keep playing. Gran's just going to talk to these nice people for a bit." Her face paled as she waved Caitlin and Ty up the front walk.

She led them into the homey living room cluttered with discarded trucks and action figures. Pulling Iron Man and Captain America off the couch, she gestured for Caitlin and Ty to sit. "I take it this isn't good news."

"I am so sorry, Jackie." Ty rested his elbows on his knees. "It's probably the worst thing that could happen." He explained Ricky's death and the DA's refusal as gently as possible. But Caitlin's heart still tightened as the reality glistened in Jackie's eyes.

Jackie cradled the action figures to her chest. Tears dripped to her cheeks. "He did the crime, but he's going to get away with it."

Caitlin curled her hands in her lap. There were no words, no touches to ease the news. "Yes. He is. For now. Obviously, the file will remain open. And I'm going to keep it active on my caseload."

"Why would God allow him to be identified if he wasn't going to be punished?"

Ty twisted his fraternity ring. "I'm sorry, Jackie."

Caitlin smothered her own complaints about God and his ways of working. Was it better to know the truth and experience the unfairness of not having justice, or live with the mystery like she and Brenda did with Missy?

Slowly, Jackie reopened her eyes and stared at the action figures in her arms. Her gaze drifted around the room, lingering on family photos wedged along the mantle. In the silence, her fingers stroked the well-used toys.

"He took my daddy from me and my brother. And I made choices I may never have made because of Daddy's death. But I also would never have met my husband. Had my children. Or have this life that has turned out to be better than I ever could have imagined. God has brought good out of something awful." Jackie's cheeks wrinkled in a sad, but oddly peaceful smile. "Maybe that's enough."

Caitlin's mouth fell open with a soft gasp. This woman who had lost so much also recognized how much she had gained. And gave God the credit. Something tickled Caitlin's memory. What was it? Something about restoration, years, and locusts?

If God did restore, did bring good from bad, why had he done so for Jackie, but not for Caitlin and Brenda? Was it because Caitlin had pushed him away, certain he didn't care, while Jackie seemed to have clung to him? A feeling slipped through Caitlin's heart, like a whisper or a near-kiss. She shook off the sensation and wrapped an invisible band around her heart.

Chapter Twenty-Five

Saturday, September 22
Gulf Shores, Alabama

Mentally and emotionally spent, Dax sprawled in the Adirondack chair on his porch. Vacationers dotted the beach below like ants around a sand colony. A few yards toward the state park, two people constructed and decorated a canopy. White gauzy fabric that looked like curtains wove around the tall wooden beams. Two more people, towing a dolly filled with white chairs, joined them, and they began unloading and placing them near the canopy.

Dax's phone dinged with a text notification, drawing his attention from the beach. He tore his eyes from the scene and thumbed open the message.

PREACHER: Man, Gina just opened her Twitter feed. You know you're viral, right?

Dax shuddered. At least it was Preacher. He tapped a reply, asking Zeb to call if he had a minute. The phone rang a heartbeat later.

"So, buddy."

"Yeah." Dax scrubbed his bristly head and scratched at the

stubble joining it on his cheeks. He needed a shave, but maybe a beard and hair would give him the anonymity he desperately craved. He snorted. *Too late now, Carpenter.*

Dax rolled his eyes. "Gene's livid, and he has every right to be. I should have told him sooner, but there was nothing to tell. Pop claimed he was innocent. There was nothing to prove he wasn't—until yesterday."

"How are you doing?"

"Gene wants me to hire a PR guy to spin this for damage control—"

"No, man. How are *you* doing?"

Dax closed his eyes. "Stunned? Betrayed? This was my dad. I thought I knew him. When he first was taken in for questioning, Mom asked me what else he could be lying about. At the time, I told her not to borrow trouble, but now it's all I can think about. If he lied about this, what else did he lie about?"

"I think you need to take your own advice. Everything's going to come out over the next few months. And there's no way to prepare yourself for it. Take it as it comes. Just like the next play on the field."

"Gene wants me back in Atlanta today, putting space between me and Pop. But that leaves Mom here handling everything on her own."

"What's left to do there anyway?"

"Really? Not much. The judge denied bail, so Pop's in jail until the trial, which isn't for four months. I'd like to get Mom home to familiar surroundings, but Elba's a small town. Maybe it would be worse there."

"You could always bring her back with you."

Dax brightened at the suggestion but sobered a heartbeat later. "Gene said I have to put as much distance as possible between me and both of them."

"What's your mom say?"

"She said to do what I need to do. She's a strong woman. But

I can't desert her. If I lie and say I'm estranged from my parents or I hate them for hiding this from me, I'm no better than Pop."

"What happens if you don't spin it?"

"The ESPN desk is already gone. That leaves the SEC Network. I don't think they can fire me outright since I didn't do this, but I can see them kicking me back to the sidelines."

Zeb hummed as he seemed to chew on Dax's words. "Would that be such a bad thing? You could live where you wanted … go back to Alabama full-time … it's not like your personal life has taken off here."

Dax snorted. A reluctant smile twitched his lips. "Well, if y'all would quit setting me up with flakes, maybe that would change."

Zeb's agreeable chuckle boomed through the air. "Naw, man. Gina and I have been fighting a losing battle there. You've been hung up on Caitlin ever since you two first met. Do you honestly see your heart changing?"

Dax stared out at the canopy and the cluster of workers. "Yeah, I don't know. Maybe if the right person comes along."

"I think the right person did. She just got scared for some reason."

"Her reasons for the breakup haven't gone away. In fact, they just got worse."

"Something about your fame, right?"

"Yeah, seemed like every time we went out someone would come up and want to talk football. I'd spend the next thirty minutes or so reviewing games and stats while she sat there and listened. Can't tell you how many times my food got cold. Now this whole viral thing. It'll go away eventually, but it'll happen again—especially when Pop goes to trial."

"I dunno, man. Sounds like a cop-out to me. I mean so she got tired of listening to you talk shop, and your name gets hashtagged. Like you said, that's not going be forever. What about when it was just the two of you?"

Dax closed his eyes and drifted back to his favorite memory of them. Caitlin had swiped one of his Titans jerseys a few days before and came to his house wearing it over a pair of leggings. The short sleeves dangled around her elbows, and the hem hit her mid-thigh. She looked adorable, but the light—no, the love— in her eyes as she teased him while he shaved his head fixed her forever in his heart.

God, I loved her ... and I still do.

Preacher's tone warmed with male insight. "Yeah. I figured as much."

Dax blinked as he realized he'd spoken the thought aloud.

"Look man, you've got everything you need to be a good husband and maybe one day a good father. You just got to walk it out. Take the lead and trust God to be there as you go."

"Okay, Preacher."

"You know I'm right. What are you going to do about it? What do you really want out of your life?"

"Yeah, that's the real question, isn't it? Thanks, Zeb." He ended the call with promises to keep in touch.

Dropping the phone on the table, Dax watched the beach scene continue to play out. The chairs were all placed, and the workers attached flowers to the aisle chairs. A man in a dark suit holding a book joined the two people under the canopy, and the three began a serious discussion.

What did he want out of life? Was it only a career in football? Or did he long for something else? A wife. A family.

And even then, was it an either-or—or a both-and?

Zeb had all three, and while Dax knew there had been years of compromise, especially in the early days when travel games took priority over birthdays and anniversaries, Zeb and Gina not only made it work, they thrived.

And what if football went away? What then? Mom said he was more than the game. But could he really call himself a "child of God" if he had no action to support the label outside of his baptism as a kid?

Years had passed since he'd been to church outside of Christmas and Easter with Mom and Pop. He couldn't remember the last time he'd picked up a Bible. And the only praying he'd done had been with Zeb leading those pre-game prayers.

Dax took in a deep breath and slowly released it. Something inside him shifted, tugging his thoughts back to his walk down the church aisle at eight years old. He'd been sitting with Mom and Pop as the sermon wrapped up. At the end of every service, the pastor would ask if anyone wanted to come to the front and accept Jesus. Dax couldn't remember a soul ever taking him up on his offer, and sometimes wondered why he still asked after all those years. That Sunday, though, the pastor's question hit him hard, and Dax heard a voice inside him answer yes.

Without a word to Mom or Pop, he'd slid out of the pew and into the aisle, walking past people he'd known all his young life. Warm smiles and even a few tears welcomed his progress toward the altar where the pastor stood with a pleased grin wrinkling his cheeks. As Dax followed the pastor's leading through the prayer, his heart seemed to grow wider and bigger. And after his baptism that next week, he'd been happier than ever before.

Not long afterward, he discovered football. Tingling whispered across the back of his neck. Football had come after his baptism. Not before. Could his love of the game and his talent for it be a gift from God? Something given as a reward for accepting him and believing in him? But not his actual identity?

The air around him stilled. The seagulls fell silent. Even the people on the beach seemed to freeze. Peace flooded his heart and mind. A chuckle bubbled up inside him. His heart lurched with the same thrill from his childhood.

Okay. So, yeah. Mom was right. He was a child of God. First and foremost. If football went away, he would still be a child of God.

He huffed as reality crashed around him. Being known and loved by God was all well and good, but he still had to work. He'd invested his NFL salary well, so he had no immediate need. But that money wouldn't last forever. And if football wasn't a career option, what then? Could he trust God to provide something?

A flutter whispered across his heart. God had given him football and a career beyond anything he could ever have imagined since he'd donned his first pee-wee jersey. Yes. He could believe God would continue to provide for him.

Comforted, Dax smothered all thoughts of hiring PR guys and spinning Pop's arrest. He closed his eyes and whispered, "I trust you, God, for whatever the outcome."

He savored the simple quiet for a long moment, then opened his eyes and watched as the world returned to its movement. But still, he remained frozen in his own way. Standing at a crossroads, waiting for the path to be revealed. If his future wasn't necessarily football, then what could it be?

His gaze turned back to the beach. More people had joined the original workers. Couples and young families sat in the chairs as suited men escorted new arrivals to their seats. Could Zeb be right? Did he have what it took to be a husband and a father? Could he really have a future with Caitie? Certainty firmed in his heart.

Yes. He could. But even more, he wanted it. To be Caitie's husband and the father of their children. Could God have used Pop's identification to not only bring closure to a family who'd been hurt, but also to reunite him with Caitie? To give them a second chance?

Dax glanced at his phone, recalling his exploding Twitter feed. Caitie's reasons for ending them, however, were still valid. But something pricked at him. What had Zeb said? Something about her argument sounding more like a cop-out? That she'd just gotten scared for some reason?

Dax thought back to the night of their breakup. They'd been leaving the symphony event when a society reporter jumped in front of them, camera flashing and asking questions about their personal life. Who was she? Were they serious? What was next for his career?

She'd been silent the whole limo ride back to her house, refusing to even hold his hand. When he'd walked her to her door and leaned in to kiss her goodnight, she'd pushed him back saying she couldn't see him anymore. Couldn't deal with the cameras and the questions. Went on about how she was a private person. How her career in law enforcement couldn't withstand his constant fame.

She'd been adamant. No words, gestures, promises, nothing could change her decision. She'd cut him off hard and fast, refusing any phone calls, unfollowing him on social media. When she told him they were over, sadness had filled her eyes. But thinking about it, something else had lurked in them. She wasn't just upset. No, Zeb was right. Something scared her.

So maybe she did have valid reasons for ending their relationship. But she hadn't said any of them that night. An invisible weight shifted off Dax's shoulders. "God, I want a future with Caitie. But I need your help getting it. What am I missing here? What's she hiding?"

Dax shoved out of the chair, wished the bride and groom on the beach a long, happy marriage, and grabbed his truck keys, ready to do whatever it took to claim his own future.

Chapter Twenty-Six

Saturday, September 22
Gulf Shores, Alabama

Dax pushed through the front doors to Gulf Shores's only Hampton Inn and beelined to the front desk. Caitlin had warned him off the Hampton Inn as a hotel for himself and Mom back when they'd met up in the police station's waiting room. She had to be staying here. Unless she'd already checked out and returned to Montgomery. *Please God, let her still be in town.*

The front desk clerk looked up from her computer with a welcoming smile. "May I help you?"

Dax placed his hands on the counter. He flashed the grin that turned pretty much every female head. "Yes, I'm a friend of Caitlin Fitzhugh's, and I believe she's a guest here. Could you tell me her room number?"

The clerk's lips firmed.

So much for the smile.

"I'm sorry, but I can't give out room numbers or confirm her reservation status. It's hotel policy."

Dax glanced over his shoulder. Her car hadn't been in the parking lot, but she could be at the police station. If she'd checked out, would the clerk still be unwilling to give out the information? "Please, it's really important. And I promise, I really do know her."

She shook her head. Steel infused her words. "I'm sorry, sir."

Dax heaved a frustrated sigh and played the card Caitlin hated. "I'm not sure if you recognize me, but I'm Dax Carpenter. I played for Alabama and the Titans."

The clerk's gaze softened as if she appreciated the attempt, but her response was the same. "Sorry, sir. But I don't follow sports. And even if I did, I still can't give you the information."

"Dax? Dax Carpenter?"

Dax spun around and found a woman about his age with long, dark hair and darker eyes standing at the business center's entry. She looked familiar, but he couldn't place her.

She crossed her arms. Her lips lifted in an easy smile as she watched him with interest. "Shannon Fitzhugh. Caitlin's sister-in-law ... we met ..."

Relief flooded Dax and he rushed to her, extending his hand. He wrapped hers almost twice around, but her grip was firm in his grasp. "Of course. It's good to see you again." He glanced back over his shoulder. The desk clerk had returned to her duties.

Shannon released his grip and refolded her arms. Her gaze once again surveyed him with curious appraisal. "Caitie's not here. She got a call about your dad's case and left a while ago."

Relief slipped through him. He wasn't too late—at least to talk with her. "She's still in Gulf Shores?"

Shannon bit her lip, taming a mischievous smile. "Yes, but I think she's planning to head out tomorrow. You seem like you've got something important on your mind."

Dax opened his mouth and turned to scan the lobby. Only the front desk clerk was around, but that could change in a minute.

Shannon tilted her head toward the empty business center. "Come on in. Let's talk." She ambled to the end of the long conference table and shut her laptop. Dax grabbed a seat near the middle of the table. "What's this about, Dax?"

He shrugged, trying to play off his eagerness. Shannon might be Caitie's family, but this was between him and Caitie. "I need to see her."

Shannon smirked and folded her hands in front of her. "Yeah. I got that. But why? It can't be about the case because you'd be at the police precinct rather than here."

Feeling like a boy caught passing love notes in grade school, Dax's cheeks heated. He stared out to the hotel lobby. He wasn't getting out of an explanation. But how much should he tell Shannon? Mom had raised him not to talk out of school when it came to relationships. She'd said nothing good came from venting to anyone except the other person in it with you.

Yet from what he remembered, Caitie and Shannon were tight. Maybe she knew the details he needed. And if she did, getting needed background details was worth crossing a relationship line.

He fixed her with a steady look. "Let's just say I'm not letting her go again."

Shannon's playful expression sobered, but her eyes glittered. "You know, I always thought you two were good together. I know what Caitie says happened. But what's your side?"

Dax scratched at a deep groove in the wooden tabletop, searching for an answer. "I'm not sure I have a side, to tell you the truth. I was falling for her. I thought she felt the same, like we were building toward something. Then she up and breaks it off. Claimed my job and the fans were the issue. But I don't buy that—not now." He shot her a determined look. "Not after seeing her these last few days and thinking back on the time. No, her ending us had to be about something more than my fame … something big."

Shannon narrowed her eyes, studying him.

Dax waited. Hope bubbled in his heart. Shannon knew something. Maybe even everything.

"Did she ever tell you why she went into law enforcement?"

Dax nodded, even as he realized how evasive Caitie's answer had been. Again. "Yeah, said it was kind of like the family business. Her dad being a police captain. Ethan having the consulting business for law enforcement. Luke in special ops."

"Yeah, I figured she'd have side-stepped a real explanation. You need to start back there—that is, if you're really wanting the truth."

Disappointed Shannon didn't give details, he had even more respect for her as trustworthy confidante. "I do want the truth, and I'm not taking anything less this time."

A wide grin spread across her face. "Good man."

He couldn't help his own smile. "You said she got a call from the precinct?"

"Early this morning and hasn't been back. Guessing she's still there."

Dax rose from his chair and tugged out his truck keys. He opened his mouth to say thanks, but Shannon waved him off.

Her gaze sobered. "Don't be afraid to push. She's not going to give in easily."

Concern clenched his stomach. His instincts had been right. Caitie's reasons were much deeper, much more serious. But he had to know the truth. Every option for their future depended on it.

Dax climbed into his truck and checked his GPS, seeing the precinct was only a stone's throw from the hotel. He turned out of the Hampton Inn parking lot, and his phone rang. Tapping the green button, Peter Broussard's rolling accent lolled from the speaker.

"Well, Dax. I've got some good news for your daddy and bad news for the prosecution."

Dax pulled to a stop at the light. His gaze landed on the phone as if he could see Peter. "What's that?"

"The witness that identified Mark as Doug Bewley apparently had some sort of surgery and died the next day."

Dax's lips dropped open. "That's awful."

"For him, maybe. From what I hear, cancer ate him up pretty good, so it might well be a mercy too."

Dax shook his head as he pushed away Peter's rationale. The light changed, and he eased on the gas, paying more attention to Peter's news than the drive. "How is this good news for Pop?"

The air hummed with Peter's melodious accent. "Well, he died before being officially deposed by the ADA, which means none of what he said can be used in court. Not the identification, not the allegations, nothing but the fingerprints the police matched." His voice firmed with pride and confidence. "I can sure spin that circumstantial evidence. Mark could have been all those places for good reason. What's to say he didn't have a legitimate reason for the new name and social security number? Maybe he wanted to start fresh after being a foster kid. Given what happened to his parents, it'd be believable. Plenty of people started over back in the day."

Dax's gut churned. More spin. More twisting of truth. If he couldn't do it for himself, could he let Peter do it for Pop?

Peter continued, oblivious to Dax's discomfort. "I know the DA. He's not one to let his ADAs roll the dice when he isn't sure he can get a conviction."

Dax pulled to a stop at another light. "What does all this mean?"

"The police are releasing Mark and dropping the charges."

Dax froze as Peter's words washed through him. *Dropping the charges. They are dropping the charges.*

A car horn honked behind him, pulling his gaze to his

rearview mirror and then to the light. It was green. Gunning the engine, he blew through the intersection.

Pop was being released. The charges would go away. Dax would have no need to spin anything.

And yet, the truth remained the truth, provable or not. "None of that means Pop is innocent."

Peter huffed. "True dat."

So Pop was a free man, and one who could continue living a lie. A lie both Dax and Mom would have to live with too. Dax pulled into the police department's parking lot and ended the call with Peter. Choosing an open space near the entrance, he cut the engine. His phone rang a second time. He checked the screen. Mom. "Did Peter call you?"

"Yes. He said they'd be releasing your daddy in the morning. Something about not having enough evidence to prosecute him?"

Dax stared at the front door of the police station. Tomorrow. Pop would walk through that door tomorrow a free man. But not an innocent one. A long, slow breath seeped between his lips. "But Caitlin's still sure he did it."

"Yes."

Dax gripped the steering wheel. "What does that mean? What do we do?"

Mom said nothing.

"Yeah. I don't know either." He ended the call and scanned the parking lot. Patrol cars lined one section while a few vacant spots dotted the rest. But Caitie's car wasn't there.

Now what?

Chapter Twenty-Seven

Saturday, September 22
Gulf Shores, Alabama

Caitlin smothered a curse, lurching to a stop at the turn into the parking lot of the Gulf Shores Police Department. Dax's truck swallowed up a space near the entrance. She cast a scathing look toward heaven. "Really, God? I haven't had enough of a day?"

Thankful Ty had gotten caught at the last stoplight; she found a space further down in the lot. Dax stood by his truck with one arm resting against the tailgate.

She sighed. They did need to talk. About the case. And nothing else. Squaring her shoulders, she joined him by his truck as Ty pulled into the lot.

Ty slowed his car. His brows lifted in silent question, but she shook her head and waved him on. With a nod, he found his designated spot, then headed for the side entrance.

She gave Dax a long look. They were not having this discussion in the precinct. But the parking lot wasn't ideal either. The sidewalk seemed to run a decent length though. She pointed to the street. "Let's walk and talk."

Dax fell into step beside her, taking the gentleman's position between her and the road. The perfect southern suitor. Caitlin yanked her thoughts away from that dangerous territory.

Work. The case. Talk only about the case.

"Pop's lawyer called me. You have to let him go."

Caitlin studied his eyes, but found only remorse in their depths. She frowned. "The victim's daughter is devastated."

Dax shook his head as they reached the corner. A dog park opened up ahead of them. By silent agreement, they stopped to watch the handful of owners play with their fur-kids. "I can't imagine what she's feeling. I'm so sorry for her. And for you."

Caitlin glanced away, trying to ignore the guilt and shame creeping through her. Dax's hand wrapped around hers and tugged. She met his gaze and wished she hadn't. The hazel color had warmed to molten golden, and she longed to fall headlong into its depths, wrap herself in its promise.

"Caitie?" Her name was a question and a memory rolled into a whisper. He pulled her into his arms and lowered his lips to hers.

They brushed together for a breath before she jerked away. Swallowing tears, she pushed against his chest, freeing herself from his heartbreakingly familiar embrace. "Dax. We can't. You know that." She stepped back, her gaze landing somewhere around his broad shoulders. He reached for her, fingers just missing her hand as she scrambled to put more distance between them. "There's no going back."

"What if it's not going back? What if it's going forward?" His voice quaked, again so familiar, so heartbreaking. He'd used the same tone when they'd broken up. "Caitie, I'm in lo—"

"No." She had to stop this now. For good. He wasn't. She wasn't. She wouldn't allow either of them to be in— "Dax. You may think you are, but you're not."

She crossed her arms and forced a nonchalance she could never feel around him. "It's the proximity combined with the history. That's all. The case is done, and we're going back to our lives. The past is just the past. Again."

Doubt warred with certainty in his eyes. Memories of their first date, their first kiss, their last date and last kiss flickered through her. Regret twisted her heart. She shoved everything away. Memories. Nothing more.

She watched him watching her, searching her face for chinks in her resolve. He wouldn't find any. Forcing her gaze to hold his, unwavering, unyielding, she stared him and his confession of love down. She would not succumb. It would hurt so much more if she lost him later. And she intended to never feel that pain ever again.

"Is this about why you became a cop?"

Caitlin's breath caught on a stunned gasp. Had he seen through her? And if so, what had he seen? How?

His lips parted on a sigh as if her silence confirmed his suspicions. "That's it, isn't it? Shannon told me I needed to ask you. Really ask you."

Shannon. Of course. Caitlin smothered a curse and looked away, gnawing at her lower lip. Tightening her arms around her stomach, she shook her head.

"I'm asking, Caitie. And I'm not leaving here—leaving you—with anything less than the truth." He reached for her again, and this time, she couldn't avoid his touch. His fingers traced her cheek as his thumb soothed her battered lip. "Because what's between us deserves the whole truth."

Her pulse ricocheted, eyes darting to his. Raw, deep love gleamed in his gaze. She'd seen that look before. Right before he kissed her their first night together. Her lungs seized again. "Co-co-college." She pushed the halting word between them, letting it lay there as if it explained everything but knowing it would only prompt more questions.

Dax, however, stayed silent, waiting.

How long would he wait?

His eyes said, *Forever, if needed.*

Caitlin forced a swallow around her dry tongue. There would be no leaving the words, the truth, unspoken. But maybe if he knew everything, he would understand. Would back away. Would disappear from her life again before her heart took another beating. "Missy was my best friend since seventh grade. We were more like sisters than friends. She disappeared finals week of our senior year of college. She's never been found."

Confusion clouded his gaze. "I'm so sorry, Caitie. But why would that have any impact on us?"

Caitlin marshalled more words, stringing them together like bubbles dancing on a river. "Do you remember our last date? When you took me to the orchestra?"

A smile flicked over his lips, then faded. "Yeah, I thought you'd love hearing that opera singer since you mentioned you'd wanted to be one. What about it?"

"For the last piece of the night, the singer was accompanied by a cellist." Caitlin let the explanation hang. Surely, he would put two and two together.

Dax shook his head, eyes bewildered. "Okay."

"Missy played the cello. We were performing a duet for our finals project."

Dax's mouth parted, empathy softening his eyes.

"And we were going to perform that same song." Caitlin longed to bury herself in his embrace, but forced herself to turn away. A poor, but much safer substitution.

"Caitie."

She shook her head and blinked away the tears that threatened to fall. If he saw them, she would be in his arms. And it would be all over. She would never be able to walk away. "As soon as I heard the opening notes, I knew. I had to break it off with you. I cared about you so much more than Missy, and I knew what her disappearance had done to me. I couldn't risk losing you."

Dax placed a finger under her chin. "Caitie, look at me."

Unable to help herself, she lifted her eyes to his, and once again wanted to dive into their soothing depths.

He licked his lips. "Everyone has lost someone. Recent or way back when. But that doesn't mean you have to let that loss take even more away from you." He released her chin, but feathered his fingers across her neck, his thumb tracing her jaw line. "You said Ethan and Shannon have lost children. But when I talked with Shannon, she still has joy, even hope."

His hand dropped to her shoulder giving it a long squeeze.

Hating her weakness, Caitlin leaned into his touch, garnering a warm smile.

"Your mom is losing your dad to a terrible and terrifying disease. But if I know her, she's out there with her heart wide open. And there's me and my mom. We just lost the father, the husband, we were sure we knew." His thumb soothed the dip in her shoulder. "Missy's disappearance devastated you. I get that. But you can't let fear of losing someone—of losing me—keep you from living life. A life with me."

He cupped both of her cheeks, running his thumbs along the sensitive skin and raising shivers in their wake. His eyes filled with a plea.

"Caitie, let me love you. And let yourself love me. No, there are no guarantees. But life can be rich, and beautiful, and worth living if you open up your heart and hold onto the someone you love—the one who loves you."

Caitlin's heart twisted, yearning to accept his twin offers of love and a future, but instead she pulled away from him. "I can't, Dax. Please just let it be and move on. Go find someone who will love you the way you deserve to be loved."

Dax's eyes clouded with sorrow. "I already have. She just needs to give herself permission."

Caitlin's throat closed around a clog of tears, silencing any response. Unable to speak, or even look at him, she spun around and headed straight for her car.

Caitlin burst through her hotel room door, slamming it back against the door stopper with a dull thud. Pain shot up her shoulder, but it barely registered in the haze of emotion. Outrage and hurt poured through her as her eyes landed on the one person she had trusted above everyone. The person who had pigeonholed her into that devastating conversation with Dax. "I can't believe you, Shannon."

Shannon's gaze flashed up from her book. Surprise lit its dark depths. As she watched Caitlin, the startle faded to resignation. She laid the book aside and sat up on the edge of the bed while Caitlin paced the room.

Caitlin balled her hands into fists, planting them on her hips only to release them in a wide sweep of her arms. "I've told you it wouldn't work with Dax and me—couldn't work with us. But no, you wouldn't accept that. You had to push. Had to tell him what I trusted you to keep to yourself. And for what?"

Shannon remained sitting, hands clenched. "For you, Caitie. Because you're miserable without him. You won't admit it, but you are."

Caitlin stalked back to the door, desperate to ignore Shannon's argument. To dodge the truth hammering at her heart.

"You love Dax. I know it. Ethan knows it. Your mom knows it. But most importantly, you know it. And you're shutting yourself off from something wonderful because of fear."

Caitlin turned back, slicing the air with her hand and cutting off Shannon's argument. "No. Not fear. Reality. Why couldn't you just let it be? I had enough damage control to manage before you sicced him on me." Caitlin ran a hand through her hair, wrecking the pixie cut. "Now he thinks he's still in love with me.

And he thinks he has a case for us." She shook her head as her eyes widened. "How on earth do I fix that?"

Shannon rose and grabbed Caitlin's hand. Empathy filled her eyes. "You face your fear, and then watch God work in your life. That's how you fix this."

Caitlin wrenched away. "God, yeah right. You think he worked in Missy's life?"

Hurt replaced the empathy in Shannon's gaze. "I don't know. But it's not my job to know. It's my job to trust."

Fire licked at Caitlin's heart. How could she trust Someone who had ruined her life? "Trust comes with action. And God has done nothing to prove himself trustworthy to me."

Grimacing, Shannon slipped her laptop in its bag, grabbed her toiletries from the bathroom, and zipped up her suitcase. "Look you need space, so I'm going to head home. Call me when you cool down." She paused at the door a gave Caitlin a pained look.

"I love you, SIL." As the door shut softly behind her, Caitlin burst into sobs, the whirlwind of emotion once again breaking free of her grip. She flung herself on the bed and pounded the mattress, railing against the unfairness of God, his plans, and desperately hoping she could somehow survive them.

Again.

Chapter Twenty-Eight

Sunday, September 23
Montgomery, Alabama

Hung over from yesterday's emotional onslaught, Caitlin had checked out of the hotel and driven the three hours home to Montgomery in a leaden fog. But the blitzkrieg wasn't over. In a few hours, Ethan would sit down with Mom to talk about Daddy.

Her stomach twisted. Practiced and skilled in the art of negotiation, Ethan would choose the right words, tone, and opening. But how would Mom take the conversation? Would she continue to deny the obvious, holding on to hope Daddy might finally stay at a certain point rather than continuing down the long spiral? Or would she admit she could no longer cling to what was, to who he was, and allow for more help than the occasional neighbor sitting with him?

Ethan would call her as soon as he left Mom and Daddy's house. But until then, the minutes would pass with the slow creep of a muddy river. Caitlin checked the clock in her car as she cut the engine. Still too soon. Groaning, she tugged out her suitcase and headed for her front door.

She hung her keys on the rack just inside the door, then stood in the entry and surveyed her living room. The house was a rental, but it was as much home as the one where she'd grown up. Pops of brilliant hues from her collection of modern art glowed from the pure white walls. Dark mahogany stained wood floors anchored the room with an elegance that belied her career in law enforcement. When Dax had first seen her home, he'd actually taken a step back, as if reassessing who he thought her to be. And then those hazel eyes had gleamed with a deeper appreciation.

She dropped her bag and sagged against the door. How would he decorate a home? When they'd been together, he'd lived in a furnished loaner from a friend while he was figuring out post-retirement life. The country French décor was beautifully done, but certainly no match to his personal style.

Caitlin wrenched her thoughts away from him for the hundredth time since she'd left Gulf Shores. She had ended them again. It was over. Forever. But her willful heart didn't agree with her mind's choice. And her tired mind was losing the battle, badly.

"Busy. Keep yourself busy. Too busy to feel." Caitlin pushed the command between her lips and gripped her suitcase handle. First thing, laundry. By then, maybe Ethan would call. After that, she could catch up on her Netflix queue. Tomorrow she'd be back at her desk, which would be buried in more background checks and scut work. Plenty to keep her busy.

At some point, she had to call Shan. Guilt pinged her heart. She'd been worse than awful to her, repaying her unconditional love and support with anger and a tongue lashing. Shan only wanted the best for her, though their views of what that might be were polar opposites. Still, Caitlin had no excuse for the vitriol she'd spewed at Shannon.

I love you, SIL.

Caitlin closed her eyes as Shannon's parting words

whispered through her, easing the guilt. Yes. Shan did love her. And Shan knew Caitlin loved her as well. Their relationship would survive Caitlin's anger.

She heaved a long sigh as she rolled her suitcase into the laundry room. And maybe Shannon was right. Maybe she did belong with Dax. Maybe they could—

Caitlin tore her thoughts away from that dangerous path. No. She would apologize to Shannon, mend the breach she'd created, and life would go on.

She yanked open the zipper on her suitcase, sorting and tossing her clothes in the washer. While the first load swirled, she changed into jeans and a long-sleeved t-shirt, tucking her feet into flip-flops. With one chore started and comfy clothes donned, what else could she do?

Groceries.

Heading to the kitchen, she tugged open the refrigerator door. Although never fully stocked due to her long work hours, the bag of walnuts, jar of grape jelly, and squeeze bottle of ketchup made her life look more pathetic than usual. But refilling the fridge and even the dry goods in her pantry would give her something else to do. Encouraged, she grabbed a pen and pad of paper from the junk drawer and scribbled out a list. Unfortunately, the task took less than ten minutes.

Tucking the list in her purse for later, she poured a glass of water and wandered to her back porch. Dense green Bermuda grass cushioned the small, fenced-in yard. She'd added a wrought iron café patio table and chairs, but rarely used them. A neighbor's dog barked from over the fence. Maybe she should get a dog? It would give the backyard a lived-in feel, and the company would be nice.

Caitlin shook her head, turning back to the kitchen. Again, her odd work hours left little time for such a responsibility. But if she wasn't alone, someone else could let out the dog and make better use of her chef's kitchen.

Dax was a great cook. And he'd loved trying out recipes on my gas stove.

She'd been stunned by his talent. More than one savory pasta dish and elaborate breakfast crêpe had originated there. She'd loved stealing sips of his post-workout smoothies the most. He'd whip up tangy and sweet blends that tantalized her senses. While he cleaned the blender, she'd steal his glass, downing gulps. He'd chase her through the house, grabbing her from behind and tickling her until she cried, uncle. Then, he'd drain the glass in a few swallows and kiss her senseless, the fruity drink made even sweeter by his lips.

Caitlin closed her eyes, savoring the memories in the echoing silence of her empty home.

How much fuller would her life be if she followed Shannon's advice and let Dax back in? He'd said she had his heart. And Caitlin suspected he would always have hers.

Toward the end of their six months together, she'd caught herself imagining what forever would be like with him. Anniversaries, birthdays, holidays. Even the quiet simple moments of sitting and watching the sunset together. Why couldn't she just let everything go and step into a life with him?

Her heart clenched, and her stomach twisted. *No. No. No. Stop it.* If Missy weren't enough of a reason, Mom was. She loved Daddy deeply, and yet, still lost him.

Her phone dinged with an incoming text. Caitlin pushed aside the futile imaginings and padded back through the house to her purse. Ethan's update glowed from the screen.

She clicked it open and winced as she read the words.

ETHAN: It was a hard convo, but Mom understands our view.

Caitlin pursed her lips.

CAITLIN: Did you tell her what happened to you with Daddy?

ETHAN: Yeah. And you were right. It tipped the scales. She's going to talk to his doctors tomorrow.

She hated that Ethan had to lay that bombshell in Mom's lap, but her safety was more important than her feelings. Caitlin cringed. Mom's feelings, however, still needed considering.

CAITLIN: Should I go see her tonight?

Ethan's quick reply eased her guilt.

ETHAN: I think she'd like that.

CAITLIN: Done.

She studied the word and read back through the conversation. Ethan's own feelings had taken a blow.

CAITLIN: And thanks, Eth. I know that wasn't easy.

ETHAN: Love you, Sis.

Caitlin switched over to her ongoing text conversation with Mom. What would she really want to know?

CAITLIN: Hey, Mom. Been out of town for work and just got home. Want me to bring dinner over?

She read the text twice before hitting send. It was enough. She waited for a moment. Mom didn't always keep her phone with her. But maybe after the conversation with Ethan, she'd have it close by?

When no answering dots appeared, Caitlin tucked the phone in her back pocket. Her eyes wandered around her empty house as her heart once again reached for memories of Dax. *No. I'm not thinking about him. Or us. Or what could be.* She grabbed her keys and purse and headed back out to her car. *Groceries. Get the groceries.*

Caitlin parked in the rear of the Publix lot and once again scanned her grocery list. It consisted of a lot of things that either were or could be frozen. She shook her head. Perishables tended to die a quick and uneventful death in her fridge. Her phone rang as she unbuckled her seatbelt. She fished her phone out of her purse and forced a bright tone as she answered. "Hey, Mom. What do you think about dinner?"

"That's perfectly fine. But Caitie, I just heard on the news that Dax's father was arrested for a robbery and murder. Did you know that?"

Caitlin leaned her forehead against the steering wheel, swallowing her groan. Just when she'd gotten her thoughts focused, here he came again, tearing through her resolve. How much should she share with Mom? Learning of any contact between the two of them would surely reopen Mom's heart to a path Caitlin just couldn't walk. But she also couldn't lie to her.

"Actually, that's why I was out of town. I helped get him arrested." The words left her mouth on a frustrated breath.

Please, Mom. Leave it be. It hurts enough as it is.

"You put him away? Caitie. I—I don't know what to say."

How about nothing, Mom? Tears pooled in her eyes as she fought to keep the question silent. If she spoke it aloud, Mom would only have more questions.

"I'm sure that had to be difficult."

Caitlin hmphed into the phone, hoping Mom would take the hint and move on to another topic.

"How was it seeing Dax again? I assume you saw him, right?"

She squeezed her eyes shut, but tears dripped onto her cheeks anyway. "Hard. Good. Somewhere in between?"

"Caitie." Mom's soft reply was soaked with mother's intuition and a wealth of love.

"Mom, I can't right now. I—I just can't." Caitlin swiped her cheeks with the back of her hand. A black smear of mascara stretched across her knuckles.

Great, I'm going to look like a raccoon while I shop.

"What do you want me to bring for dinner?"

Silent reigned for a moment, and Caitlin could picture Mom trying to decide if she should push. *Please don't push.*

"How about the family brisket meal from Duley's?"

Grateful for the reprieve, Caitlin swallowed the pain and guilt. "Perfect. Let me get my groceries home, then I'll be over around five."

"We'll see you then."

Caitlin ended the call and lowered her visor mirror to check her makeup. Sure enough, messy streaks of mascara darkened her undereye areas. Grabbing a tissue from the box in her floorboard, she dampened it with spit and went to work repairing the evidence of her heartbreak. Thankfully, the rest of it was all internal.

Unfortunately, that didn't make it any less convicting.

Chapter Twenty-Nine

Sunday, September 23
Gulf Shores, Alabama

Dax's bare feet sank into the wet sand with every step he sprinted down the beach. The sun had risen only a couple of hours ago. He doubted the seagulls and surf fishermen would recognize him, but he'd still grabbed an old Alabama ballcap out of his truck before starting his drills.

Mom had opted for room service breakfast followed by church at one of the local congregations. He should have gone with her, but after a night of restless sleep, his thoughts continued to spin. He had the truth from Caitie. But it had set neither of them free. Both remained trapped, her by fear, and him by denied love.

Dax blew out a breath and slowed to a jog. But had he really expected her to jump in his arms saying she would be his forever because he made her confess her deepest secret?

He snorted as he wiped his face with his shirttail. *Yeah, I guess I did. Way to go, Carpenter. You got the first down, but you've got no follow-up play. How do you plan to make it to the end zone?*

He stared out at the waves. The water lapped against the sand, kissing it then releasing it, only to return a moment later for another embrace. She had felt so right in his arms, his lips against hers. Like home and forever.

But she had backed away. Again.

Ended them. Again.

What could he do? He wanted a life with her—could see a future with no woman but her. But if she wouldn't fight through her fear and take the risk, then all he had were empty dreams and a broken heart.

Something pricked at him. He'd decided to trust God with his career. Couldn't he also trust his future with Caitie to God? He looked up at the sky. "God, I do want a life with Caitie. Zeb's right. I can't see myself with anyone else. But as much as I want it, as much as I love her, I can't fix this fear she has. You can. So please, help her."

Peace eased through him. Caitie might think she'd ended them, but Dax would choose to believe she was wrong, that God would work them out. After all, why else would they have gotten a second chance, even with Pop's arrest being the reason?

Satisfied with that play, Dax eased down onto the wet sand and let the waves thread between his toes. Sand slipped away, melting and returning under the steady ebb and flow. A cool bite in the light breeze hinted at winter on the coast.

His eyes drifted across the clouds, searching for more than peace. "Now, God, what about Pop? How could the man I've known all my life have robbed and killed someone? Is he truly not the same person he was when that happened? And if he isn't, what then? Shouldn't he still be held accountable—even if there's not enough evidence to do it legally?" A shadow fell across his feet. Tugging off his hat, he focused on the figure above him. "Mom? I thought you went to church."

She shrugged and eased down onto the sand beside him. "I was until I saw the news and figured it might be best to miss it."

"I can see that."

A small, pleased smile curved Mom's cheek. "I couldn't help but overhear your questions. I'm glad you're talking to God, son."

His eyes widened as he thought back through his prayers. How much had Mom heard? Talking with God about his future hopes and dreams with Caitie was one thing, but Mom?

She fiddled with her loose cotton pants and grimaced. "Your questions about your daddy are all valid. And some of the same ones I've been struggling to answer myself."

Dax watched her for a moment. Did he really want to know? But she obviously needed to talk, so he asked, "What are the others?"

Mom picked up a handful of wet sand and mashed it between her fingers before releasing it in the waves. "Well, what I do next, for one. He's your daddy, but he's my husband. You can leave and live your life free and clear. I have vows to consider."

Dax's heart turned over. He hadn't thought about that. Of course, Mom would have that added pressure.

She stared at her wedding ring. "On top of that, I have to wonder if the marriage is even valid."

Dax slung an arm around her shoulder, pulling her into his side, kissing her temple. "I'm so sorry, Mom."

She leaned against his shoulder, and they sat in silence, watching the waves until Dax's phone dinged. He tapped open the text message and held it for Mom to see.

"Peter says Pop's release is being processed now, and he'll be ready to go soon."

"Let's go get him. Maybe then we can figure out where we go from here."

Dax rose and helped Mom to her feet. With another hug, they trudged up through the loose sand, the squawking seagulls and the waves the only break in their silence.

The ride to The Lodge from the police precinct was the longest seven minutes of Dax's life. Not even the last two of the NFL playoff game which had stretched to twenty between time-outs, flags, and commercials had felt longer. By the time they reached Mom and Pop's room, the tension screamed under the weight of fatigue, resignation, and disillusionment.

Pop headed to the bathroom to shower and change while Dax and Mom waited at the kitchenette table. Mom's head lay against the back rest, eyes closed, lips moving in silent prayer.

Dax grabbed her hand and joined his pleas with hers. *God, what do we do now?*

The shower turned off and a few minutes later, Pop appeared, dark, wet hair combed back, cheeks freshly shaven. He slipped onto the bench next to Mom and waited in the silence.

The air conditioner clicked on, pouring more cold air into the already chilly atmosphere. Dax studied Pop, who stared at his hands and the fingerprints that condemned him. Mom twisted her wedding ring.

He should leave. His parents had couple things to discuss. But Dax couldn't bring himself to move. Not when he still needed answers for himself.

Pop would get away with robbery and murder. Not because of a mistaken identity, but because a witness had died. Pop wasn't innocent. He was guilty.

Dax had to say something. But what? *God? Please.*

Dax opened his mouth and spoke the first words that formed. "This isn't right, Pop."

Pop lifted his eyes and spread his hands. "What's not right about it, son? I told you I, Mark Carpenter, didn't do this. And I've said that all along."

"Mark." Mom's low, grieved tone soaked the air between them. She took in a quick breath as if coming to some sort of decision. She linked her fingers with Pop's and turned them over, tracing the pads of his fingertips. "Mark Carpenter may not have done this. But Doug Bewley did. And you can't deny fingerprints, Mark. You were Doug Bewley."

Hurt flickered in Pop's eyes. The air conditioner clicked off, but the condo-sized refrigerator still hummed. He opened his mouth, but no words formed. He watched Mom's fingers. Her engagement ring and wedding band gleamed under the ceiling lights.

"I love you, Suz." The whisper lurched from somewhere deep inside him.

Mom laced their fingers together and squeezed. "I know. And I love you. I have ever since you came to fix that breaker."

She paused, allowing the truth to settle between them. A moment later, in a firm, clear voice, she continued. "But Mark, you need to be the man I love. Honorable. Caring. Honest. Ready to take responsibility. Doug Bewley robbed and killed a man. You … robbed and killed a man. Accidental or not, provable or not, it still happened. That debt still needs to be paid."

"I could spend the rest of my life in prison. Die in prison." A haunted tone skimmed Pop's words sending a shiver across the back of Dax's neck.

Mom nodded. "A family was torn apart, and they need justice. If that family were us, if you had been killed, wouldn't you, Mark Carpenter, the man I love and have been married to for thirty-eight years, want justice for us?"

Lips thinning into a narrow line, Pop glanced between Mom and Dax. He squeezed his eyes shut and gave a quick shake of his head. "Of course I'd want that for you two."

Mom's voice turned pleading. "Then want it for them."

Dax grabbed Pop's free hand, touching him for the first time since the whole debacle began. Pop's skin, darkened and roughened by years of labor, felt more like hard leather. "Pop, denying the truth, lying. This isn't the man I grew up knowing, trusting, admiring. That man is good and honorable. He always did the right thing. But getting away with a crime you know you committed, that's not him. That's not you. And if you truly believe you are a different man, a new man, then do what he would do."

"This is the right thing to do." Mom took in another long breath and finally raised her eyes to Pop's. Love and heartbreak gleamed from their coppery depths. "I won't leave you for doing the right thing."

Pop studied the kitchenette table for a long heartbeat and gave a brief nod. "Maybe Ricky was right. Maybe the only way to really clean the slate is to take responsibility for what happened." Clearing his throat, the words escaped him on a hitching exhale. "I've told you the truth. I am Mark Carpenter and have been for forty years. Mark Carpenter is a good, God-fearing man. But yes, I was once Doug Bewley. I've done my best to atone for that man, but I've also never been able to forget him."

Tears welled in Pop's eyes as he slipped his hand from Mom's to stare at his condemning fingers. "Mom was in and out of rehab when I was a kid, so I lived with my dad. When I was seven, he drove the getaway car during a bank robbery. From what I understand, had no idea what his friends planned. But they cut deals with the District Attorney, leaving him holding the bag. He got a life sentence, and I went into foster care."

Dax tried to swallow around his dry tongue, replaying what little he knew of Pop's parents. None of it matched the real story.

Pop licked his lips as if fortifying himself against the coming pain. "Ten years into serving his time, another inmate shanked him because of a bowl of pudding. Dad got the last serving of chocolate. The other guy had vanilla."

Mom gasped and reached for Pop's hand. Dax shook his head unable to fully comprehend the savagery.

Pop ran a thumb over Mom's hand. "I lived with twelve different foster families until I aged out at eighteen. Ricky

Adams and I met in middle school and started ditching classes together. We hit the road after graduation, doing basic smash and grab robberies for food and beer. We'd sleep on the beach, moving around, living life as it came.

"When Mic Prescott died." Pop's voice faltered, and he swallowed hard. "No. When I, Doug Bewley, killed him, I realized how out of control my life had gotten. But the possibility of ending up like Dad terrified me. I thought if I could bury Doug with Mic, I could start completely over. Make good come from the bad."

He leveled a pleading look on Mom and Dax. "And good has come from it. I started a business, fell in love with the most amazing woman in the world, got married, and we had an incredible son." He squeezed Mom's hand and reached over to pat Dax's arm. "I've lived a good life I didn't deserve." He fell silent for a moment as if coming to a final, life-altering conclusion. "But now, yes, it's time to own up to the past." His gaze filled with a deep certainty. "Will you call Peter, son?"

Chapter Thirty

Sunday, September 23
Pike Road, Alabama

"George, dinner's ready. Caitlin brought your favorite from Duley's. Come join us."

Silence greeted Mom's invitation. Caitlin set the plates and silverware on the table while her pulse kicked up a notch. Was Daddy losing his hearing along with his mind? It had been two weeks since Caitlin had last seen him. She peeked around the corner into the living room and found Daddy glued to the SEC Network channel, watching the highlights of yesterday's Alabama-Texas A & M game. Alabama apparently crushed the Aggies despite losing their wide receiver.

"Daddy?"

"Gimme a minute, Caitiebug. Daddy's just watching the game. That Dax Carpenter really should be heading to the pros. He's got great hands, and he's quick on his feet."

Tears pricked her eyes. She swallowed hard. Daddy was fifteen years in the past. A soft hand patted her shoulder. She turned and found Mom. Sadness wreathed her lips. "Mom." The word quivered with heartbreak.

Mom tugged Caitlin back into the kitchen. "I know, Caitie. Your daddy's not having a good day today. But I know he's glad you're here."

Unconvinced, Caitlin shrugged. Mom slipped back into the living room, knelt to eye level with Daddy, and touched his hand. "George, honey. The game's over. It's time to eat."

Daddy slowly turned his attention from the TV to Mom. "Okay. What's for breakfast?"

Caitlin closed her eyes. The clock had just flipped over to 5:00 p.m.

Mom, however, took his question in stride. "Barbecue. Your favorite." She smiled and brushed her fingers through his thinning gray hair.

"You're so good to me, Laurie." Awe and love wove through his words, and for a brief moment, Daddy was there. Turning away, Caitlin swallowed her sob.

Daddy shuffled into the kitchen with Mom holding his arm and steering him to the table. He half-fell, half-sat into his usual chair, then took a long look at the empty plate in front of him.

A breath later, he scooted around in his seat ready to get up.

"Stay there, George. Caitlin's bringing the food over now."

Caitlin grabbed the dish of barbecue brisket and a bowl of baked beans, hurrying to the table before Daddy could start to leave again. "Here we are." She forced a grin as she spooned food on his plate.

He pinched a thick piece of the brisket between his fingers and shoved it in his mouth. Sauce dripped from the corners of his lips. Caitlin grabbed his napkin and dabbed at the mess, but he jerked his head away. "Go on now. Let me eat."

Her eyes widened, and she cast a helpless look to Mom.

"I'll clean up everything later. Your daddy needs to focus on eating more."

Caitlin absorbed Daddy's thinning shoulders and sagging skin. Yes, he had lost weight, and a lot of it, since she'd seen him last. She sank into her own chair as Mom brought over a mound of cornbread muffins and a bowl of green beans. She placed two muffins on Daddy's plate and hid a spoonful of green beans under the baked beans, flashing a mischievous grin.

Caitlin returned the smile. Daddy never had been much of a green food eater. She could well-imagine that had only gotten worse. As Mom settled in her seat, she bowed her head for a quick, silent blessing, then flashed a pointed look to Caitlin's empty plate and the feast in front of them.

Caitlin took the hint and added a slice of brisket and spoonful of green beans to her plate, but instead of eating, her gaze returned to Daddy. Grease slathered his fingers and barbecue sauce dripped down his chin, but at least half of the brisket was gone. Even a few of the green beans made it past his gag reflex. She glanced at Mom, who looked pleased with his progress.

"This is more than he's eaten in days. It's a good dinner, right, George?"

Daddy grunted and shoved a whole corn muffin in his mouth. He chewed, then coughed hard, spewing bits back on the table.

Mom grabbed a stack of napkins, wiping his mouth while rubbing his back. "Easy, George. That's it. You just took too big a bite."

Caitlin sat watching the scene play out. Slowly, Daddy cleared out the muffin and took a long swallow of water. He ran his forearm under his nose, pushed back in his chair, and lurched to a stand. Mom wet a dish towel and wiped his hands and face then walked him back to the living room. She pulled him toward the couch, halting his progress to their bedroom. "You had a good dinner, George. But let's sit up a while before you go to bed."

Daddy wrenched out of her grip. "No. I'm tired."

Mom placed a soothing hand on his chest. "I know. But you need to sit up a while longer." She picked up the TV remote and held it in front of him. "Why don't you watch some TV? The Alabama game is on. You love watching Dax Carpenter play."

Caitlin's heart melted. Yeah, Daddy had loved watching Dax play. Long before she'd met Dax on the Alabama sideline at the Iron Bowl, she'd known all about him—at least, as a player. Daddy had quoted his stats as proudly as if he were one of his own kids. The first time she'd brought Dax home to meet them, Daddy had talked his ear off, replaying every great catch and touchdown.

Her brow creased. There was no way Daddy could watch Dax play now. But he didn't appear to doubt Mom's word. He eased down onto the couch, and she tapped to the DVR of yesterday's game.

"There you go, sweetheart." She kissed his forehead and returned to the kitchen table.

Caitlin forced a bite of cooling brisket into her mouth. She gave Mom a long assessing look, seeing her with a cop's eyes rather than a daughter's. Daddy wasn't the only one who'd lost weight. "Let me make you a plate, Mom."

Mom waved away the offer. "I'm not that hungry right now. I'll have mine later. I like to try and keep mealtime as normal as possible."

Caitlin speared a green bean while Mom cleared away Daddy's plate and cleaned the table. Mom sat in her chair with a sigh and a mug of coffee. Caitlin studied the fatigue that bracketed Mom's eyes, the pained pinch of her lips, and her drooping shoulders. She hated it, but she had to broach the obvious topic. "Have you heard from Ethan lately?"

Mom lifted a weary gaze. "You know I have. Today after I got home from church. And I assume the three of you talked before that. How is Luke, by the way?"

Heat flooded Caitlin's cheeks. "He's fine. And we only did it because we love you. Mom, getting Daddy help doesn't mean you're not honoring your vows to him. In fact, it's the exact opposite. You're putting his needs above your own. He requires more help than you can provide safely—and it's only going to increase as the dementia progresses." Caitlin sent an imploring look her way. "Getting him settled somewhere is the best way you can love, honor, and cherish him now."

Mom sniffed and flicked her gaze to Daddy, who sat enthralled by the football game. She squeezed Caitlin's hand, releasing a long, watery breath. "I know. And I love all of you for caring. I'm going to call his doctor in the morning and see what our options are."

Caitlin closed her eyes in relief. *Finally, something's going my way.*

An hour later, Mom could no longer keep Daddy from going to bed. Caitlin helped get him into his night clothes. Once he closed his eyes, Caitlin curled onto in the armchair in their room and watched him sleep. But as he drifted peacefully, her thoughts reeled.

Caitie, let me love you. And let yourself love me.

You're shutting yourself off from something wonderful because of fear.

Dax's plea mingled with Shannon's assessment. Could she? Was she?

Or was she like Mom, trying to protect someone who had disappeared—trying to keep them from disappearing forever?

Caitlin closed her eyes as reality refused to be silenced. She loved Dax. And fear did rule her actions when it came to them. But she had lost Missy, and her disappearance altered her life forever. If she lost Dax, a man she loved more and deeper than Missy, what then? Would her wounded and broken heart even survive?

Daddy turned on his side. The blanket fell away from his

shoulders. She eased over and snugged it back into place. Sinking onto the bed, she watched his dreams play out across his face. "I wish you could tell me what to do, Daddy."

Feet scuffed the tile floor, and Mom murmured, "I can tell you what you need to do. You need to grieve, Caitiebug."

Caitlin smothered her gasp. Rubbing her forehead, she glanced over her shoulder at Mom standing in the doorway. "Grieve? Grieve what?"

Mom stepped into the room and placed her hands on Caitlin's shoulders, drawing her away from Daddy's bedside. Wrapping Caitlin in a hug, she continued in a whisper. "Not what. Who. You need to grieve for Missy."

Heat rushed up Caitlin's neck. Smothering her angry retort, she slipped from Mom's grip. "I cried for two weeks straight after they closed her case."

"Yes, but Caitie you're stuck. It's as if you put a lid on all your pain and struck some sort of bargain with God, thinking maybe if you found answers for others then one day your payback would be information about Missy." Mom's eyes softened with unshed tears. "Yes, her disappearance is awful. But you have to accept what happened and let her go. That's the only way you can move forward."

She fixed Caitlin with a worried look. "You do want to move forward, don't you? Or do you feel guilty you weren't the one taken?"

Caitlin blinked. Was it love or was it survivor's guilt? She let the question roll through her, but it found no place to land. So maybe not survivor's guilt, but she definitely could have been taken instead. How many times had she stayed late at the rehearsal rooms? Walked home still focused on a piece without a thought for her safety?

There was always that twinge in the pit of her stomach whenever she'd call Brenda. Always the hint of condemnation undercutting their conversation about Missy and the case. Caitlin shrugged off the thought. "I don't know."

"Grieving Missy doesn't make her disappear forever, Caitie. It honors her memory and allows you to heal. Missy would want that. You should want the same thing."

Caitlin walked out of the bedroom. "I'll talk to you later, Mom. Tell Daddy I love him." Grabbing her purse, she headed for the door and the blessed relief of solitude.

But solitude only allowed Caitlin's thoughts free rein. They swirled in her head, blending together in a mish-mash of doubt, fear, and weariness, leaving her edgy and jittery by the time she pulled into her driveway. She headed into her house, ignoring the neighbor's friendly wave. She'd peopled enough today.

But she couldn't squelch the impulse to climb into her attic. She'd packed away her college memorabilia and stored it in the hot confines. Out of sight, but safe. Maybe revisiting the past could settle her heart, convince it once again she'd made the correct decision all those years ago.

The box marked *college* sat under a pile of Christmas decorations, labeled in large letters so she'd never be surprised if she opened it. Caitlin swiped her arm over her brow, brushing away the sweat beading on her forehead. She huffed. There would be no quick flicking through the memories up here. The box would either have to come with her or remain untouched.

"Fine." The word carried all the vitriol of more questionable four-letter varieties. She lugged the box down the attic ladder, steeling herself against her shoulder's screaming protests.

A few minutes later, she sat at her kitchen table, ice bag strapped to her shoulder, and opened the lid. Caitlin choked on a gasp. The program from their senior performance lay face up.

The Belmont School of Music welcomes you to a night of performances by our graduating seniors.

Printed the week before Missy's disappearance, the program announced their duet would close out the evening. Caitlin had no idea how the dean had explained the cancelation the night of the show. And she had no memory of how she'd ended up with a copy of the program.

Her fingers traced Missy's name, her own, and then the title. Jules Massenet's "Elegie." The original French lyrics followed their English translation.

> *O sweet springtimes of old verdant seasons*
> *You have fled forever*
> *I no longer see the blue sky*
> *I no longer hear the bird's joyful singing*
> *And, taking my happiness with you*
> *You have gone on your way my love!*
> *In vain Spring returns*
> *Yes, never to return*
> *The bright sun has gone with you*
> *The days of happiness have fled*
> *How gloomy and cold is my heart*
> *All is withered*
> *Forever*

A chill rippled through her heart. Had either of them known, even suspected, the words would bear out almost as prophecy?

But that was exactly what had happened. At least for Caitlin.

Until Dax slipped under her guard at the Iron Bowl, returning spring to her life—if only for a short season. But could it truly return again if Missy never did?

Mom thought so. So did Shannon. And Dax certainly did.

What had he said? She had to "give herself permission" to love him? Would grieving Missy allow her to do that? Could

Mom be right too? Would grieving her best friend and soul sister allow Caitlin to move forward?

The ice bag slid off her shoulder and landed with a watery plop on the tile. Caitlin stared at it, savoring the numbness in her shoulder and wishing she could do the same to her heart. But ignoring it was the only option. Shoving the program back in the box, she snapped the plastic lid in place and headed to bed, swallowing a muscle relaxer on the way in the vain hope of sleeping off her emotions and the memories tied to them.

Chapter Thirty-One

Monday, September 24
Gulf Shores, Alabama

Peter Broussard sat behind his wide desk, mouth slack and brow wrinkled, and stared at Pop. "I'm sorry, I don't believe I heard you correctly. Would you please repeat that?"

Dax shifted on the loveseat. Mom grabbed Pop's hand and flashed an encouraging smile. Pop rubbed his free hand against his jeans and took in a quick breath. "Everything Ricky Adams said was true, and I want to confess. To the murder. The robberies. All of it."

Peter's shock faded to amazement. "Well, then. I will need to contact the DA and see what he'll offer."

Dax leaned forward and raised his hand, gaining Peter's attention. "What do you think that'll be?"

"Well, there's no telling at this point. While it's helpful you're coming forward on your own volition, all the time you denied the charges probably won't play in your favor."

Mom shook her head. "But he could have walked away a free man."

Peter released his twined fingers. "And I'll make sure to

emphasize that. Of course, the judge will have the final say. The DA and I can only make a recommendation for the plea deal. I can push for a cap of twenty years, given your age and your willingness to plead guilty. And I'll negotiate hard for something well under it."

"Twenty years." The words fell from Dax's lips unbidden. Pop was sixty-two. He could very well die in prison.

Pop turned in his chair, eyes filling with patient acceptance. "I've lived a good life—like I said, much better than I deserved. I'll do whatever time is required. I have a debt to pay."

Reality landed like an elbow to the solar plexus. Breath left Dax's lungs in a whoosh. It was the right thing to do, but Pop's life really was over.

Peter peered at Pop with somber eyes. "Before I call the DA, I need to know everything. It has to be the whole truth this time, Mark."

"I understand." Pop shifted in his seat, rolling his shoulders, as if adjusting to a new weight. "Ricky and I were school buddies with no real drive for anything but drinking beer and sleeping on the beach. We'd made our way from Apalachicola west along the Florida panhandle doing smash and grabs and getting out of town as fast as possible.

"We'd been in Gulf Shores about a week when I discovered I had a knack for fixing things. I'd been watching this wannabe mechanic fiddle with his car at this dive where Ricky and I were hanging out when the day got too hot." Pop shook his head as amazement seemed to wash over him. "Somehow, I just knew what the problem was, so I offered to fix it."

Dax thought back to the years of Pop's tinkering on the Mustang and other cars. He did have a talent that seemed to defy logic and got cars up and running when other guys had written them off.

"I got it repaired and, over the next little while, I'd go around offering my help. Gave us a break from liquor and convenience store robberies. And made more money. That's how we ended up at The Broken Flip-Flop. Mic's oven blew a breaker, and he'd heard I did work off the books. He had issues with his ex and didn't want her learning something was wrong at the restaurant. So, Ricky and I agreed to fix it."

Peter's gaze sharpened as he weighed Pop's words. "Why rob him?"

Pop huffed, shaking his head as if still trying to understand it for himself. "I honestly don't know why—just seemed like the thing to do at the time. It was summer, and I saw how busy he was, figured out how much money he would rake in. It could be one big score and then we'd move on. Take a break from everything for a while.

"I decided to hit him after hours on July Fourth. Ricky was against doing the job—he thought a lot of Mic. But I hammered away at him. Telling him how easy we could get the money. How no one would get hurt. Mic had the rest of summer to make up the night. Stuff like that until he finally agreed."

Pop cast a pleading look at Mom. "And I really did plan to wait until well after the restaurant closed. Mic wasn't supposed to be there. He saw us, recognized us, and my first thought was, 'I can't go to prison. I'll die there like Dad.' So I shoved him. He punched me—that's how I got this scar over my eye. I shoved him again. I only wanted to buy us enough time to get out of the restaurant and away. But Mic hit his head against the edge of the bar, and just like that he was dead."

Pop swallowed hard, his arms widening in a helpless gesture. "We panicked. Ricky wanted to report it, but I knew we were done if he did. So, I convinced him we had to run and disappear. No one in Gulf Shores really knew us. We had no family to speak of, so there was no one to miss us. It was the easiest thing in the world to start over.

"I had no idea where Ricky went after that night, but I headed north. Found someone who could get me a new ID, and I used my share of the take that night to start over. I got into electrician school, studied hard, worked even harder."

Pop lifted his eyes to Peter. Certainty settled over Pop's shoulders. "I have been a business owner until I retired two years ago. I'm a member of our church. And I've kept every law, not even a speeding ticket, ever since then. Peter, my fingerprints might convict me as Doug Bewley, but I can tell you with all assurance, Doug Bewley died the same night as Mic Prescott. I am not that man. But I will accept my role in his crimes."

Peter pursed his lips. "All right, then. I believe you."

Mom placed her free hand on Peter's desk, drawing his gaze. "What now?"

"Well, *cher*, I'll contact the DA and tell him Mark wants to turn himself in and plead guilty."

Mom flicked a glance between Pop and Dax. Worry shaded the copper depths. "I hate to ask this. But Dax's career is already taking a beating."

Pop's brow wrinkled as he turned to confirm her words with Dax.

"I've got a lot of damage control to do." He recapped the social media firestorm for Peter.

Pop dropped his head, gaze falling to the floor. "I am so sorry, son."

Peter cleared his throat. "I'll push for a special plea day, but, even then, the soonest we could get on the docket would be thirty days. The DA will likely agree to that if I release control of the press conference to him. He's up for re-election, so that's a pretty sweet treat to toss him. While it might not sound like good news, there is an upside. The DA's a cradle Alabama fan, goes to every game he can, so he'll likely keep Dax's name out of it as much as possible and focus on solving a forty-year-old case."

Mom's shoulders eased. "Is it time to the make the call?"

Pop flashed a reassuring smile. "Let's get this moving. I'm not going to change my mind, but I'd rather begin the process."

Peter picked up his desk phone and tapped a series of numbers. He greeted the receptionist, identified himself, then explained the reason for his call. A moment later, he pressed the speaker button, and a thick Alabama accent drawled through the air around them.

"Broussard. I'm glad to take your call."

Peter's lips flattened in a wry smile. "Yes, I'm here with Mark Carpenter, his wife, Susan, and their son, Dax, on speaker. If you have a few minutes, we'd like to discuss the offer Mark just presented to me."

"Go ahead."

"Mark is ready to turn himself in as Doug Bewley and plead guilty to the robbery of The Broken Flip-Flop and the murder of its owner, Michael Prescott. But there are a few requirements for this plea to go through."

"I'm listening."

"I know you're an Alabama fan, so I'm certain you recognized his son's name."

The DA's voice warmed. "I did. Quite the player and great career."

"Yes, indeed. And that is the biggest requirement. Dax's current career has taken a beating in social media since a picture of him with Mark and Susan at the original arraignment was posted online. The longer this drags out, the more likelihood of its negative impact on Dax, and possibly Alabama football."

"I can appreciate your concern, and I would want to minimize any disparagement to such an auspicious institution. What are you thinking?"

"We'd like for the plea and sentencing to happen in thirty days. Less would be even more ideal."

A choking sound hacked the air. "I'm sorry, Peter, can you run that by me again?"

"Thirty days, Grady. It's for the good of everyone. The damage to Dax's career is minimized, you get your conviction in time for the election, and Mark doesn't have to live without a timeframe for his life to completely change."

The DA took in a long slow breath. A squeak broke the silence as if he'd leaned back in his chair. "I'll want more than an ankle monitor, given he's been running from his crimes for forty years. He needs to agree to jail time until the sentencing. Sure, he's feeling remorseful now, but no telling what he'll be feeling thirty days from now."

Lifting his eyebrows in a silent question, Peter looked at Pop.

Pop mouthed the word, *Okay*.

"All right then. Thirty days until sentencing, Mark turns himself in today, and remains in the Gulf Shores jail. Now, about the time he serves."

"Well, the statute allows for up to twenty years."

"I understand. But Mark told me his side and based on his explanation, the death of Michael Prescott scared him straight. He's lived a clean life for the last forty years, not even a speeding ticket. And Prescott's death was a complete accident. Mark pushed him away, Prescott hit his head against the bar counter, and died instantly. No weapons were involved. Just panic and chance."

The DA fell silent again. "There is the family's loss to consider as well."

"I understand, as I'm sure Mark does."

Pop lifted a hand, garnering Peter's attention. "I'd like to say something about the family, if I may?"

Peter's lips pinched, but he nodded. "Grady, my client would like to speak to that question about the victim's family."

"Go ahead then."

"I remember Mic had an ex-wife, and a child—maybe even two. I don't know for sure. I do know I can't bring him back. I've seen the pain and suffering my actions and living a lie have caused my own family, so I can only imagine what Mic's family felt and probably still feel. And I am tremendously sorry for my actions."

The DA cleared his throat, and his accent sharpened. "What are you looking for, Peter?"

"Given Mark's age, his forty years of law-abiding life, and his voluntary confession, I think ten years is reasonable. And I'll cede all press conference duties to your office."

Dax held his breath as cold sweat slicked his hands. Ten years? Could it be possible? Pop would pay his debt but had the opportunity to return to a normal life afterward. *God? Can you make this happen?*

"All right, then. But he turns himself in at the Gulf Shores Police Department in two hours, and he tells his story in court with a formal allocution."

Peter leveled another long look at Pop, who nodded again. "Agreed. We'll be there."

Chapter Thirty-Two

Monday, September 24
Pike Road, Alabama

Caitlin sat on the mat table, grimacing as her physical therapist took her through the last round of exercises. After thirty minutes of range of motion and weighted activities, her shoulder ached, and so did her head.

"And rest." The PT's soothing directive eased between them. Concern lit her eyes.

Caitlin released the yellow Thera-Band with a grateful sigh, the taut plastic flapping loose against her forearm.

"You overdid it this week."

Caitlin shrugged. "Couldn't be helped."

"It had better be, or you'll be on desk duty for a while longer."

Maybe that wouldn't be such a bad thing.

The PT pulled the e-stim machine over and fixed the electrodes to Caitlin's shoulder, then added a cushioned ice pack. "Can I get you anything else?"

Caitlin glanced at the clock. Nine a.m. "Yeah, would you

mind grabbing my phone out of my purse? I need to check in at the office."

And with Shannon.

The PT smiled and, after confirming the e-stim intensity with Caitlin, brought her purse from the locker area. Caitlin dug out her phone and checked her text messages. Nothing.

Not that she expected anything, considering how she'd laid into Shannon at the hotel. Shan always followed through on her word, and she'd allow Caitlin whatever time she needed to cool down. Caitlin sighed and clicked on Shannon's name. She held tightly to Shan's soft profession of sisterly love as she tapped her message.

CAITLIN: I'm sorry. Forgive me?

She closed her eyes and set the phone down, hoping the apology and request were enough. A moment later, the phone dinged. Caitlin took in a quick steadying breath.

SHANNON: Already have. How are you today?

Her wounded heart warmed at the words. *I don't deserve you.*

CAITLIN: Finishing up my Pain & Torture session. Can we meet to talk?

A laughing emoji accompanied by a hugging face appeared on her screen followed by another text.

SHANNON: Come to the office when you're done?

Ethan should be back, so she could check in with him too. Caitlin thumbed her acceptance, then called her boss. "Bill, it's Caitlin."

"Fitzhugh. I heard about the Carpenter case and the witness. That hurts. You back in town?"

The ice pack slipped on her shoulder. She cringed at the icy slide down her arm. The PT hurried over and readjusted the pack. "Caitlin, five more minutes."

She bobbed her head and returned to the call. "Got in yesterday afternoon. Finishing up PT now, but I need to swing by

Ethan's. Get the final details from Shannon's work on the case and her service invoice. I'll be in the office after that."

"Sounds good. Just left another stack of files on your desk to keep you occupied."

Caitlin rolled her eyes. "Um, thanks?"

Bill's chortle reverberated in her ear, drawing a brief smile from her. "See you when you get here."

She ended the call. Day organized, she checked the e-stim timer and settled in for the remaining minutes.

Thirty minutes later, Caitlin tapped on Shannon's door. Muffled tones echoed through the wood. Wendy had said to go on in, so Caitlin slipped inside. She set her purse on the floor and took a seat while Shannon continued her phone consult.

"Yes, I'll start on the server malware patch today. Should have it in place by the end of tomorrow. For now, make sure no one on your staff opens any email attachments from anyone. Doesn't matter if they know them personally." She clicked through a series of screens on her computer. "All right. I'll keep you posted." She hung up the phone and studied Caitlin with a long, but loving look. "Hey."

Caitlin's lips twitched into a wan smile. "Hey, yourself. I'm sorry."

Shannon nodded. "I know. I forgive you. And for what it's worth, everything I did, I meant for your good."

Caitlin glanced out the window before returning her gaze to Shan. "Yeah, I know. That's what makes this so hard."

Shannon's shoulders sagged. Her eyes narrowed as if she were weighing how much further she could take the conversation. The bouncing, jovial *Leverage* theme song from her phone stalled anything she might have said. Slipping the phone from her purse, she read the caller ID. Her cheeks paled and her mouth dropped open. "It's my OBGYN's office."

Caitlin's eyes widened, and she reached for her purse. "Do you want me to leave?"

Shannon bit her lip, then shook her head. "No, Ethan is in a meeting. It'd be nice to have someone here."

Caitlin reached across the desk and squeezed Shannon's hand. "Always."

Shannon smiled then turned her attention back to the call. "This is Shannon Fitzhugh."

Caitlin watched her, cop's eyes assessing the microexpressions flickering over Shannon's features. Her brows curved then lifted. Lips parted. Finally, her hand clutched her throat as she closed her eyes. Dread seeped into Caitlin's gut. Whatever the results, they weren't good.

"Thank you, Doctor. I'll talk with Ethan." Shannon ended the call and leaned her head back against her chair. A tear dripped down her cheek.

"Shan," Caitlin whispered.

Shannon swiped her hands across her cheeks and stared at the ceiling. Grief radiated off her in waves.

Caitlin sat, allowing Shannon the same grace she had shown her on Saturday. After several minutes, Caitlin stretched her hand across the desk and tapped lightly, drawing Shannon's red-rimmed gaze. "Want me to get Ethan?"

Taking a deep breath, Shannon cleared the tears from her throat. "No, he'll be out of the meeting soon enough. And we need this contract to go through."

Caitlin nodded, then waited for Shannon to say whatever words she might have.

"There's no fixing it. We're genetically incompatible."

"Oh, Shan, I'm so sorry."

Shannon flashed a watery smile, then bobbed her head. "God must just have a different plan for us. And it's going to be okay."

Caitlin blinked. She shook her head in awe. She and Shannon were the same age. They had similar faith upbringings. And yet Shannon's faith ran deeper than Caitlin's belief ever thought of being.

Had Missy's disappearance crippled not only Caitlin's heart but also her faith? It had to have. Rather than leaning into God like Shannon was doing now, Caitlin had backed away, doubting his love and cursing his plan. Would her faith be as strong as Shannon's if she'd trusted him back then?

But then, maybe this news would rock Shannon's faith like hers had been by Missy. Maybe this is what it would take to make her doubt the loving care of an almighty God. "This is devasting, Shan. How can you believe this is God's plan for you and Ethan and everything will be okay?"

A long, hiccupping sigh sputtered between Shannon's lips. "Bad things happen all the time, Caitie. Yes, this one hurts. And hurts bad. But I can't, and I won't let it define me."

She set her elbows on her desk. Lacing her fingers together, she leveled a tear-filled, but firm gaze on Caitlin. "What I will do is trust God's plan and purpose. I know he loves me and Ethan, and he put us together. I know he gave us the desire to be parents. And I'm choosing to trust that even if the obvious way isn't how he's going to do it, we will be parents one day. God is faithful and trustworthy. And he does make everything work together for good."

Disbelief whirled with anger, twisting Caitlin's heart into a pained eddy. Missy had disappeared, Ricky Adams's died before he could testify, and Daddy continued the downward slide into dementia. None of those situations had good outcomes. Caitlin couldn't see anything positive in Shannon's news.

Yet Shan said she would choose to trust God would make good happen at some point. Could that be it? Could time be a factor? After all, Shan didn't seem to expect immediate results.

Missy had disappeared fourteen years ago. Did God need more time to bring Caitlin and Brenda a good ending?

But then again, it had taken forty years for Ricky and the Prescott family to have movement on their case. Which was good. But Ricky dying in a surgery that was supposed to extend his life? And Mark Carpenter walking on the charges? Where was God's good in that?

And Daddy had no hope of recovering what he'd lost.

No. God wasn't good. He didn't care. If he had, none of this would have happened. Good would have already come for all of them.

Behind her, Shannon's office door clicked open.

Ethan walked through the door. "Hey, babe, landed another one."

Caitlin looked over her shoulder.

Recognition lit his eyes. "Caitie? What are you doing here?"

When neither she nor Shannon replied, he stopped midstride. His eyes landed on Shannon, concern flickering in their brown depths.

She flashed him a sad smile. "Got the test results. We're not having kids the old-fashioned way."

Ethan pulled Shannon into his arms, tucking her head under his chin and skimming his fingers along her spine.

Caitlin looked away from their embrace, an angry lump clogging her throat. She rose and slipped toward the door, leaving them to their grief and comfort. "Call me. Anytime."

She paused at Wendy's desk on her way through the lobby. Unwilling to divulge the news, she said, "You might hold Shannon and Ethan's calls for a while. They need some time."

Wendy's brow furrowed as she glanced to the closed door marked Private, but said nothing. Caitlin opened the exit to the bright jangle of the company's phone. Wendy answered with her customary greeting, then said without a pause, "I'm sorry, but he's in a meeting right now. Let me take a message, and I'll get it to him as soon as he's finished."

Heart and mind roiling with the unfairness of life and loss, Caitlin yanked open her car door and plopped into the front seat. Throwing her purse on top of her briefcase in the passenger seat, she pounded the steering wheel. "Really, God? Haven't they been through enough? Hasn't our family been through enough?"

When no answer came, she wrenched the car into reverse, gunning it out of Starline Security's parking lot and onto the main street. The traffic light switched from yellow to red, and she slammed on the brakes, earning her a loud, complaining honk from the driver behind her. Her purse flew into the passenger footwell, the briefcase following. She grabbed at it, but a file slipped out, spilling onto the floorboard. She glanced over. Missy's smiling face peered at her.

Caitlin's heart plummeted. A curse launched from her lips. She stared at the photo. Memories flickered through her. The driver behind her leaned on his horn again. She checked her rearview mirror, resisting the urge to flip him off, then stomped on the gas pedal, and squealed through the now green light. She forced herself to to focus on the road, but Missy's face grinned up at her from the photo.

Unable to ignore the unblinking stare, Caitlin swerved into a restaurant parking lot and slammed the car into park. She unbuckled her seatbelt and grabbed the papers, intent on shoving the whole file back in her briefcase.

But Mom's words whispered through her. *You need to grieve for Missy.*

Caitlin's breath caught. Her hand trembled. She leaned back in the seat and, closing her eyes, she swallowed hard as the words echoed again.

You need to grieve for Missy.

Could Mom be right? Had she buried her loss in the job, making that unspoken bargain with God?

Caitlin thought back over her career. How many times had she held her breath at the successful end of a missing person's case and waited for her phone to ring with information about Missy? How often had she railed at God when that call never came?

Memories of Missy floated in front of her. Laughing, smiling. Focused rapture as she put bow to strings and lost herself in the simple beauty of music. Stunned with joy at the offer to join the Nashville Symphony.

Tears streamed down Caitlin's cheeks as her throat tightened. Slowly, the darkest hidden questions bubbled up within her, gaining a voice after years of silent torment. Was it her fault she disappeared? She could have waited for Missy. It wasn't like she'd done anything earth-shattering when she'd gotten back to the dorm. "Why didn't I wait for her? If we'd been together, would she have disappeared?"

Sobs wracked her body. Caitlin grabbed the steering wheel, desperate for something, anything, to hold onto under the tormenting guilt. "I miss her so much. I miss hearing her laugh. I miss sharing secrets, and crushes, and dreams. I want her back. Please give her back. Please."

But another darker truth rose out of her guilt. Missy was not only missing, but likely dead. And no amount of Caitlin's holding onto her could alter that.

Something inside Caitlin broke open and a gushing river of pain, guilt, and loss poured through the gaping crack unchecked, unstoppable. "Why her? Why not me? Why not someone else? Why anyone at all?"

The wails deepened as a fresh perspective hit Caitlin hard. Missy's disappearance was more than physical. More than emotional. It was spiritual. The hole she'd left in Caitlin's heart had never healed. Instead, it felt more like a broken branch still clinging to the trunk, not growing or giving in return, but instead, draining the tree of life. Draining Caitlin of life.

If she didn't do something, she would continue to bleed until nothing remained but the shell of pain and unresolved grief. "Mom's right, I can't keep holding on to Missy's memory. It really is killing me. But I can't seem to do anything else. She was too much a part of me."

Something deep inside her, more felt than heard, whispered through the torrent of pain. *Peace. Be still.*

Her sobs eased to quivering exhales. The storm inside her calmed, leaving new questions in its wake. "God, you're supposed to have all the answers, so help me understand. Help me make sense of this. Why did Missy have to leave?" Her voice faltered. "Why did you?"

In the stillness, she heard another whisper across her heart.

I'm here. I didn't leave you. And I never will.

"Was it my fault Missy was kidnapped?"

No. Evil made a choice you couldn't have stopped.

Warmth seeped through her, blanketing the pain, absorbing it until all that remained was the sweetest sensation of love. She wasn't to blame. Caitlin closed her eyes, allowing the truth to engulf her and soak into all the dry areas of her soul.

"I don't want to live like this anymore, God. Terrified of losing someone I love again. I want my life back. I want my heart back." She paused and allowed the greatest truth of all to slip from her lips. "And yes, I want Dax. I want a life with him. But what do I do? How do I let her go so I can have that life?"

Missy's face returned, floating, smiling, but this time, her eyes lit with understanding and peace. Caitlin reached out as if she could touch her. "I love you, Missy. But I have to face reality. You're gone, and I have to say goodbye. For you. For me." As Caitlin whispered one last goodbye, Missy's image smiled then faded away, leaving Caitlin with a soul-deep peace.

It melted through her heart, mind, and soul like a summer breeze, wrapping her in a comfort unlike anything she'd ever experienced. It was a hug from Mom, a smile from Daddy, and a kiss from heaven all rolled into one, and then even more than all of that.

Caitlin savored the sensation, the overwhelming, all-consuming peace. Could this be what Shannon felt? What empowered her to trust God's plan, setting aside secular wisdom and her emotions? What she'd clung to when she and Ethan fought for their marriage?

"God?"

I am here. Trust me.

But could Caitlin really trust him? Yes, she'd said goodbye to Missy, but there were still no answers about her disappearance. Ethan and Shannon still couldn't have children despite their hearts' desire for them. Daddy still continued to suffer with his mental decline. She could still lose Dax, no matter how much she wanted a future with him.

I make all things work together for good.

But how did Missy's disappearance result in good?

Faces and cases from Caitlin's past flashed through her. Families who had closure. People who had been found alive and reunited with loved ones. All because Missy had disappeared, and Caitlin had changed her career from the theater to law enforcement.

Ethan and Shannon might not be able to have biological children, but they could still be parents. There was adoption, foster care, even opening their home to the kids in their neighborhood.

But what of Mom and Daddy? Yes, they'd had a long, loving life together, yet he couldn't escape his downward spiral.

But they did have a long, loving life together.

What about losing Dax?

What if you don't lose him?

Air rushed from her lungs as her long-held thoughts and fears shifted. She'd been so focused on sparing herself from the potential loss she'd never considered another option. Was it possible? Could she have a long, full life with Dax?

Only believe, Caitlin.

She closed her eyes as the words soaked into her heart and soul. Those words, God's words, felt more right and truer than any arguments she had created for herself. Scrubbing her face and drying the last of the tears, she took in a deep breath. "Okay, God. I'll believe."

Chapter Thirty-Three

Monday, September 24
Montgomery, Alabama

Three hours later, Caitlin tossed a completed background check in her outbox and sighed as she grabbed the next file from the inbox. Bill hadn't been kidding about the stacks of case files he'd added to her desk. She would definitely follow the PT's advice and be more mindful of her shoulder. She had to get back in the field away from the busy work. But at least she was chipping away at it at a decent pace.

After her earlier meltdown and reconciliation with God, a renewed sense of purpose and interest had buoyed her through the morning. She glanced at her clock and contemplated a refill of her coffee as her cell phone rang.

Ty Osgood's number gleamed from her phone screen. Curious, she tapped the green button. "Ty, didn't expect to hear from you for a while. What's up?"

Ty's voice boomed into her ear with a nervy edge of excitement. "You sitting down?"

"Uh. Yeah. Why?"

"Mark Carpenter turned himself in. He's going to plead guilty."

Caitlin's mouth dropped open. "Mark had a get-out-of-jail-free card. Why on earth would he give that up?"

"Apparently, he had a change of heart. Thanks to you, we're closing the Prescott case. I'm sure once sentencing is done, the other jurisdictions will want their turn. Seven cases after all."

Her stomach clenched. *Oh, Dax.*

"Wow. That's ... great."

"The DA agreed to the defense's offer of ten years, but this is a solid win for a lot of people. Starting with Jackie Gonzalez."

"Yes. Yes, it is. Please pass my well wishes along to her and Roberto."

Ty ended the call and Caitlin studied the screen. God had brought good out of Mic Prescott's case in spite of Ricky's death. Wow. And yet, while Jackie would see it as a huge win, how would Dax and Susan feel? This couldn't be good for them, could it?

Without a second thought, she tapped Dax's contact number. She had to know. Her voice was low, soothing as she cupped the phone, wishing it could be his cheek. "Ty told me about your dad. How are you?" Concern flooded her heart.

Dax's relaxed tone filled her ear. "You know, I'm actually good. Even though he's going to jail, Pop really is the man I knew him to be."

Caitlin's heart warmed. Relief seeped through her. Yes, Dax did sound good. Happy even. *Score one for you, God.*

"Dax, I'm so glad. For you. That's got to be a weight off your mind."

"It really is."

Uncertain what else to say, she fiddled with her necklace, fingering the cross and savoring her deepening renewal of her faith. But as she swung the cross pendant along the chain, an easy silence warmed between them, encouraging her to say the words she'd pushed away for so many years.

A loud thump and guffaw tugged her gaze to the bullpen and the activity around her. Now wasn't the time or place for full disclosure. But maybe they could meet later? Would Dax be open to that after she'd pushed him away in Gulf Shores? "So there's another reason for my call. I've been thinking about what you said the other day."

"And?" Hope wafted through the air as his breath caught on the word.

Could she really do this? Caitlin closed her eyes, sending a silent prayer toward heaven for strength. "Dax, like I said, I've been thinking. Well, more soul searching. And I want to talk with you … about … everything." She took in a halting breath and launched her heart into the deep end. "Can we meet sometime soon?"

Dax's deep, stunned chuckle sent shivers across her skin. "That'd be amazing … Caitie."

Caitlin closed her eyes again, relishing the sound of her nickname as it whispered between them.

"Is today an option?"

Her heart melted at his question. She glanced at her overloaded desk. Background checks waited for processing, a meeting reminder blinked on her desktop, and Bill McWorter looked to be headed right for her with yet another stack of case files. She frowned. She'd prioritized work over the rest of her life for so many years, needing the anchor for emotional survival. But now she had God. Maybe she could prioritize him and even Dax over the next case? Something felt right about the choice, and she smiled. "Yes, today can be an option. What time?"

"I'm still in Gulf Shores with Mom, but I can leave in thirty minutes and be in Montgomery by six tonight. Where do you want to meet?"

"What about our spot in Montgomery River Park? I'll bring dinner, and we can watch the sunset."

"I'm on my way."

Caitlin ended the call, hugging her phone to her chest, her heart filling with hope.

Bill pushed through her door. His eyes gleamed and a teasing smile crawled up his lips. "I'm guessing that smile isn't for me."

Her grin widened. "Nope. And I'm going to need the rest of the afternoon off because of it."

Montgomery's Riverfront Park spread out around Caitlin from the grassy tiered risers. Sunset wouldn't happen for another hour, but visitors already dotted the lawn and wandered along the river, taking in what promised to be a beautiful evening.

"Hey, you."

Caitlin's breath caught at the simple greeting. She lifted uncertain eyes at Dax as he towered over her on the grassy expanse along the river park. Panic quickened her pulse as old fears crowded her. *God, are we really doing this?*

Dax stared at her, his eyes soft and full of love, easing her knee-jerk terror to a skittering fear.

Willing her erratic pulse to calm, she smiled. "Hi, there."

Dax lowered himself to the grass nearby. She pulled a water bottle from her picnic basket and passed it over to him. He took a sip and let it dangle from his hand for a moment. He tossed a quick, mischievous look to her, then reached around her back and pulled her into his side. "That's better."

She flinched and eased back, hating the flicker of hurt in his eyes. "Dax, I ... I'm sorry. I'm still getting used to this. To the reality of us."

Understanding replaced his wounded gaze. "I guess I should have expected that." He fell silent.

Caitlin stared out at the river, grateful for the space and time. She'd thought of little else while she'd grocery shopped and driven to the park and hoped to have some sort of explanation by the time he arrived. Would raw honesty scare him off or help him see how hard she fought? Straightening her shoulders, she opted to trust the depth of his love. "I don't want to keep putting my life on hold, but I'm terrified. When Missy disappeared, I lost a big part of myself, my soul."

She sent a tentative look his way. Would he understand her battle? Appreciate how hard she fought not only for herself, but also for them?

Dax set the water bottle on the blanket and wove their free hands together, giving hers a light squeeze. The sun tinged the sky with a dusty pink, catching his hazel eyes and brightening them to gold. Compassion and love gleamed from their depths, but he remained silent.

"Mom said I needed to grieve losing her so I could move forward and have a life … a life with you. As much as Missy was a part of me, that was the past. I understand that now, and I let her go. I'm sure I'll still miss her, but the deep ache I carried around is gone."

Her eyes dropped to their joined hands as she continued. "You're right. There are no guarantees. I know what we have is worth facing this terror. But it's going to take time. Do we have … time?"

Caitlin's pulse raced in her ears. What if he said no? What if he said he couldn't wait? Could she—

Dax raised their hands to his lips, brushing the lightest kiss against her knuckles. "I'll wait forever, if necessary. You're worth it."

Tears of relief blurred her eyes, and she buried her face in his shoulder. His arms wrapped around her, holding her in a gentle hug. Caitlin soaked up the warmth of his solid support. They sat in the silence of long-time couples, Dax's fingers dancing along her shoulder and her forehead tucked in the crook of his neck. Her gaze drifted along the river as she treasured the simple joy of being with the man she loved.

Yes. I want a lifetime of this.

The Harriot II riverboat sat moored a little way down, bobbing in the river. She'd yet to take a dinner cruise on it despite living in the Montgomery area her whole life. Maybe she and Dax could go one night? She closed her eyes, allowing the possibilities and options to open up before her.

"Is it too soon to say I've missed us?" Dax's question rumbled in her ear, bringing a contented smile to her lips.

She brushed a quick kiss to his jaw, then laid her cheek back against his shoulder. "Not at all."

Dax pulled her into a long hug, pressing a soft kiss to her temple. "So what now?"

Caitlin nodded against his shoulder. "Guess that really depends on you. Well, your career anyway. What are you thinking?"

"Last I spoke with Gene—my producer—my options were narrowing. And since I didn't do as he said and hire a PR person to spin Pop's arrest, I'm guessing they've probably shrunk even further. I need to sit down with the Network and talk it over."

"What do you want to do?" The question murmured between them.

Dax pressed another kiss against her hairline. "Be with you."

Caitlin chuckled. "I meant for work."

"Oh, work." Dax's wry laugh rumbled between them, jostling her head against his chest. He sobered a moment later. "I honestly don't know. Football has been my life, but I had my own talk with God. He helped me understand football isn't who I am. If it goes away, it goes away. And I'll be okay." He tucked his cheek against her forehead. "What about you? Still happy being a cop?"

Caitlin bit her lip. Was she? Now that she'd released Missy

and begun her grieving process, her main reason for going into law enforcement was done.

But she was really good at her job. And so many families needed peace. She reached for her pendant, but her fingers landed on the treble clef instead of the cross. An idea formed. "Yeah, I am happy with the job. But I think I want to get back into singing—in church, in the theater, somewhere. It's a part of me. And I've really missed it. I always loved singing with your mom when we'd go down to Elba."

"She loved it too."

"How is Susan?"

A long breath slipped between Dax's lips. "Hanging in there. She loves Pop. And she's standing by him. He'll be in the Gulf Shores jail until the plea and sentencing. I'm renting her a condo down there, so she can see him pretty often. Once he's sentenced, who knows where he'll be."

"There's a federal prison here in Montgomery. It's not out of the realm of possibility his lawyer could request a location closer to home."

Dax hmphed. "That's good to know."

"What about you? How close do you want to be?"

"To you?" He tightened his arm around her waist, lifting her over his leg and settling her in between his knees.

Caitlin chuckled. "This is perfect." She leaned back into his chest and watched the sun sink in the horizon. The dusty pink deepened into a bright mauve. "But what about the distance to your dad?"

Dax tensed. "Good question."

Caitlin ran her hand along his arm in a soothing stroke, but her voice turned teasing. "Well, I am a cop. That's pretty much a requirement."

Dax snickered, the tension easing as she'd hoped, and linked their hands together. "I'm not going to walk away from him, so I guess, yeah, I want to be close enough to visit fairly regularly."

Caitlin squeezed his hands in silent support, pleased that, despite the reality of Mark's crimes, another family wouldn't be destroyed. She shifted deeper into his embrace. "Did I ever tell you, Maddox Dean Carpenter, that I love you?"

Dax's chest hummed with a delighted sigh. "No, you never did. But I knew it all the same. Just like I think you knew I loved you."

"Loved?" A mock-arched tone laced her response. She turned in his arms and watched his cheeks wrinkle, his smile filling with promise.

"Then, now, and always."

As Dax lowered his lips to hers, Caitlin sank into the kiss, finally giving her heart free rein to dream of their future together.

Chapter Thirty-Four

Tuesday, September 25
Montgomery, Alabama

The next morning, Caitlin, Mom, Ethan, and Shannon followed Homewood Place Assisted Living Facility's caseworker into the dining room. Light streamed in from the series of windows lining the back wall, brightening the buttercream walls to almost white. In one corner, a group of ladies sewed quilt squares and discussed their grandchildren's antics. Pots and pans banged in the kitchen as the dietary department cleaned up from breakfast and prepped for lunch.

Caitlin surveyed it all with a pleased smile. The staff had been friendly and welcoming during the tour, and all of the residents appeared content and happy. Although the residents were predominantly women, the handful of men in their ranks would provide Daddy some male company. She'd even seen a sign boasting a facility-wide fantasy football league. While Daddy probably couldn't follow the particulars, he'd at least enjoy football-related conversations.

Homewood Place was the first of three facilities they had scheduled to tour that day. But in Caitlin's opinion neither of the others could top it in location or set up. Unlike what she'd seen on their websites, here, Daddy could have his own private apartment, decorated in any style that suited him. And the family would only be thirty minutes away, allowing them regular and drop-in visits.

The caseworker gestured for them to take one of the tables. She flashed a kind smile as she set a file folder of information in front of Mom. A beautiful drawing of the facility gleamed out from the slick white cover. "Everything you need is in here, but let me know if you have any questions. That apartment I showed you will open up by the first of next week. That resident is transitioning to another facility closer to her family. I need to know something soon to reserve it for Mr. Fitzhugh."

They settled around the table, Caitlin and Ethan bracketing Mom, Shannon right across from her. Mom flipped through the papers until she found the financial sheet. Her mouth dropped open, and she paled.

Caitlin looked to Ethan, who then met Shannon's gaze. Mental calculations and awareness of Daddy and Mom's needs filled the silent conversation.

Mom grimaced and set the papers aside. She surveyed the dining room, and her gaze landed on the happy group of ladies. "It's homey. And I think your daddy would be better off in his own private apartment than in a place where he'd have a roommate. His retirement benefits will cover some of the cost, but ..." Her eyes returned to the monthly financial estimates.

Ethan squeezed her shoulder. "Do not worry about this, Mom. Shannon and I already talked. We'll make up the difference. The contract I just closed is more than enough."

"And I'll pitch in too." Caitlin covered the price list with her hand. "Money is nothing compared to getting you and Daddy the help you need now."

Mom lifted misty eyes to Caitlin, then to Ethan and Shannon.

"I love you all, so much. I couldn't be more blessed or feel more loved."

Shannon grinned and leaned into Ethan's side. "Well, the feeling is mutual, Laurie, for all of us."

Mom closed the file folder with a decisive nod. "I guess we'll cancel the rest of the tours and sign your daddy up here, then?"

They all agreed, and Mom waved over a housekeeper, asking her to contact the case manager.

Movement caught Caitlin's gaze through the windows. A handful of residents meandered on the sidewalk into the back garden, followed by two staff members carrying boxes filled with what appeared to be art materials.

Caitlin patted Mom's shoulder as an idea occurred to her. "Since we have a week, maybe we can set up some times for Daddy to visit and get a bit familiar with the place before he moves in? It's going to be an adjustment, but maybe that way, it won't be such a shock?"

Mom's eyes brightened. "That's a great idea, Caitiebug. Thank you."

Ethan cleared his throat and glanced to Shannon, who gave him a quick nod. Caitlin's brows wrinkled. *Something's up.*

"Now that that's been settled, Shan and I have our own news." His flashed a quick smile and grabbed Shannon's hand. "Since we won't be able to have children naturally, we've decided to try other options." He paused, but excitement radiated from his dark eyes. "We're going to complete the paperwork to become foster parents and also to adopt."

Shannon eyes lit with joy as she watched Ethan. A moment later, she turned to Mom and Caitlin, peace loosening her shoulders and relaxing the worried lines that had creased her forehead ever since the testing had begun. "We're giving both ways to God and letting him decide which route he wants us to take. And we're even open to it being both, if that's what happens."

Mom took Shannon's hand. "That's perfect. When will you start the application process?"

Ethan grinned. "This week. We have a meeting scheduled with an adoption attorney on Thursday, and we filled out the online foster care application last night. It'll be a week before we hear anything from them. Then we'll have to take a training course and undergo a home inspection, and jump through a few other hoops."

Shannon nodded. "Adoption is a much longer process and could take years from what I understand. But there may be a possibility of adopting a foster child too."

Caitlin eased around the table to wrap Shannon in a long hug. "Y'all are going to be just the best parents—no matter how God chooses to make it happen."

Shannon pulled back and held Caitlin at arm's length, her gaze sharpening with a silent question. *How are you with God?*

Thrill skimmed Caitlin's heart. Her cheek curved in a sheepish, one-sided smile. "I'm good. We're good."

Shannon pulled Caitlin back into another long hug. "I'm so proud of you, SIL," she whispered.

Shannon settled back beside Ethan, snuggling into his side as his arm dropped around her shoulders. A mischievous glint lit her eyes. "And speaking of new relationships in our lives, any word from Dax now that the trial's over?"

Caitlin slipped her hands off the table.

Mom leaned toward her with a chiding grin. "Caitlin Jennifer Fitzhugh, you've been holding out on me." Her delighted exclamation ratcheted up the temperature flaming across Caitlin's cheeks.

Ethan's grin widened to a smirk. "Caitie and Dax sitting in a tree, K-I-S-S—"

Longing to punch him in the shoulder, Caitlin settled for rolling her eyes. "How old are you?"

Shannon chuckled and laced her fingers with Ethan's. "A child. I'm married to a child."

He pressed a quick kiss to her nose and gave her an impish grin. "At least I'll relate well to our future kids."

Shannon shook her head, but love and a deep adoration radiated from her gaze.

Caitlin tugged at her pendants. "But now that you mention it. Dax and I ... are ... back together."

A delighted cry fell from Mom's lips. "And?" Maternal curiosity slathered the simple question.

Caitlin couldn't hide her grin. "And, while we haven't talked specifically about the future, I'm feeling like it's a done-deal." Caitlin could see Mom flipping through her mental calendar. She lifted her hand, hoping to forestall Mom's dreams. "But don't book the church just yet, Mom. Dax still has to figure out his work situation, so he may be in Atlanta for a while."

As Mom, Shannon, and Ethan discussed potentials, Caitlin's gaze found the clock on the wall, focusing on Dax's more immediate future. Adding an hour for the time difference, she calculated his schedule. He'd texted her when he left Susan's house in Elba that morning. Given the distance, he would be hitting Atlanta's outskirts by now. Which meant his meeting with the Network higher-ups was still a couple of hours away.

God? Please be with him no matter what comes out of this conversation. Give him the right decision and peace when he makes it.

Caitlin pulled her eyes from the clock. "He's meeting with his bosses later today. Said he'd call as soon as he knew something."

Shannon gave her hand a supportive squeeze. "I'm sure God has the perfect plan already worked out for him. Who knows? Wedding bells may be ringing sooner than you realize."

Heat stole up Caitlin's neck. "We'll see. I'm pretty sure he's on board, but timing is everything—especially with so much still up in the air."

Mom cleared her throat, garnering everyone's attention. "No matter when and how everything comes together, I am very excited and overjoyed for you." She let her gaze drift around the table as her smile grew misty. "Actually, for all of you. God is so good."

Caitlin closed her eyes, savoring Mom's peace, Ethan and Shannon's news, and her future life with Dax. Yes, she finally could see God was good.

And even more so, he was good to them.

Chapter Thirty-Five

Tuesday, September 25
Atlanta, Georgia

Dax tapped on Gene's office door and glanced around the open work area behind him. As he'd made his way to the fourth floor, coworkers had displayed varying degrees of interest and support. Most had watched him, gauging his own level of anticipation or dread. But a couple of the nosier guys had tried to pump him for information. Their interest more salacious than sympathetic.

Dax shrugged off the sensation creeping along his shoulders. Gene had offered to sit in on his meeting with the human resources and Network directors. His support mattered more than anyone else's here.

Gene's gruff response finally mumbled through the door. "Come on in."

Dax twisted the knob and ducked inside Gene's office. Why a sports network hadn't designed its doors with former athletes in mind, he still had no idea. But it might be a moot point anyway. Gene lifted a friendly gaze and held up his hand as he finished a call on his earbuds.

Dax looked around the office while he waited. Signed photos of Gene with former players covered one wall, and floor-to-ceiling bookshelves the other. Blinds screened the stunning view of downtown Atlanta.

Dax had a smaller office without the view. His own gameday photos, his Titans retirement jersey, and even an article about the college national championship win decorated its walls. But despite his nameplate still being on the door, when he'd unlocked it that morning he'd felt an odd sense of disconnect. If today was his last day at the Network, would it be that big of a deal?

Gene ended his call and rose, extending his hand. "Good to see you, buddy. You ready for the meeting?"

Dax shook Gene's hand with a firm grip as peace filled him. Yes, he was. No matter the outcome.

They walked to a conference room down the hall. Through the windows, the two directors talked in a heated conversation. Before Gene tapped on the closed glass door, Dax placed a hand on his arm. Gene turned curious eyes toward him.

"I just wanted to officially say I'm sorry for leaving you out of the loop and putting you in such a difficult spot, Gene. You're a good friend and great producer. I should've done better by you."

Gene's brow flickered as he absorbed the apology. "Thanks. You're a good man, Dax." He glanced back to the door, then to Dax, who nodded.

Dax took in a quick breath, but the peace remained. *Whatever you have, God. I'm ready.*

Joe Patterson, the Network Director, gestured to two seats across from him and Ben Green, the HR Director. "Gentlemen, come in. Ben and I were just discussing options."

Ben scrolled through his iPad. Gene and Dax took their seats, then waited.

Joe clasped his hands in front of him. "Dax, first off, let me extend our sympathies to you about this stressful time you've experienced. It had to be a shock."

Dax nodded, but remained silent, waiting for the real meat of the meeting.

Ben finished scrolling and set the iPad aside, fixing Dax with a serious look. "I've reviewed your contract with the Network, and I'm sure you're aware of the morals clause that's in it."

Dax didn't remember the specifics but wasn't surprised that clause would be a main factor in whatever decision the Network made. Usually, morals clauses were limited to the person signing the contract, but Dax could see how the issue of his dad's arrest would make the Network squirm.

Ben tapped the iPad, and the screen lit up with a lock screen of the Network logo. "The clause specifically relates to your personal actions and behavior. There's nothing detailing acts done by family members. But I'm sure you can see the Network's position, what with all of the press this issue has received."

Joe glared at Ben. But when his eyes returned to Dax, they were filled with compassion. "Since you went viral, we can't have you as a face for the Network. It doesn't matter that your father did the crime, and not you. However, because of the circumstances, we've also got some wiggle room."

Ben crossed his arms. "Very little wiggle room."

Dax blinked at Ben's irritation. Apparently, whatever Ben had recommended had been overruled. Curious, Dax waited for Joe to continue.

"We can't have you on air as a face of the Network, but we don't want to lose your skill and talent. Therefore, management is creating a color commentator position for you." Joe's cheeks curved in boyish smile, as if pleased to be playing the role of hero.

Dax let the offer roam through him. He'd told Zeb he could be punted down to some sort of sideline reporting job. But a color commentator? That was better than he could have imagined. He would be offering his insights from a player's perspective while the analyst called the play-by-play. Even though it wasn't the player profiling he'd done for the last five years, it was still well within his wheelhouse and interest. Possibly even more so since he'd be back to enjoying the game as it happened.

Joe's voice gained urgency. "It'll mean travel every weekend for games during the season, but it keeps you on the roster. And once this all dies down, maybe after a few seasons, then we can look at bringing you back into the studio."

A slow smile crept up Dax's lips as an idea began to take shape. "I understand the travel requirements, but that also means I won't be bound to Atlanta, right?"

"Not to Atlanta, no," Gene said. "However, you would need to remain in the market area. You'll either fly or drive to each location. But you can pretty-well live wherever you want in the South."

Hope surged through him. *God, could this be an even better option than the ESPN job?* He had one other issue to clarify before he jumped on the offer.

"Would it be a problem if I brought someone with me to the games?"

Ben's eyes narrowed as he considered Dax's request. "Someone?"

Dax rubbed his hands on his legs. They hadn't discussed a formal relationship, but he was certainly all-in—and for the long haul. Based on their lengthy goodbye at the pier last night before he'd driven to Elba, he was ninety-nine percent sure Caitlin would agree. "My ... girlfriend?"

Gene's brows lifted with wary concern.

Heat flushed across Dax's neck as he realized how the word could be misinterpreted. "No, she is my girlfriend ... or she will be … we just haven't made it official. And one day soon, it'll be more permanent."

Joe glanced to Ben then Gene. Dax watched the concern over other sticky relational issues leech from Joe's gaze. "Oh. Ah, yes. That's perfectly fine, but obviously, we won't cover her expenses."

"Of course. And with her job and schedule, she won't be able to come every time. I just wanted to make sure it was okay when she did."

"Does this sound like it's a good deal?" Joe asked.

Dax reached to shake his hand. "It's better than you or I could ever think or imagine."

An hour later, contracts signed and filed, Dax settled into his office chair one final time and called Caitlin. He smiled as her new profile picture appeared on the screen. He'd snapped it just as the sun set the night before when she wasn't paying attention. The reds and pinks of the sunset perfectly highlighted her pale skin and set her auburn hair on fire. In a word, she was stunning. And she was his. "Hey, babe. It's done."

Caitie's voice warmed with love, even as concern tinged her words. "How'd it go?"

Dax ran a hand over the back of his neck as the reality washed over him. "Better than I could have hoped." He gave her a brief run-down of the meeting and the job offer. "I'll start as soon as the next game and can move to Montgomery any time I want."

Caitie's gasp ricocheted between them. "That's incredible. I'm so happy for you."

"For us, Caitie. For us." The line went quiet as he absorbed the truth of his words.

Finally, she cleared her throat. "Last time you lived here, you rented a friend of a friend's house. Can you do that again, or … do you want me to start apartment hunting for you?"

Curiosity and eagerness flowed around her words, as she seemed to test the waters between them.

Dax held his breath, then took the plunge. "I think I'd rather have my own place. What do you think about actual house hunting?" The implication of their future as man and wife hung silent, but very much spoken. Was it too soon? Like he'd told Gene and the others, he and Caitie hadn't discussed how they pictured their future. But he wanted a life together. Did she?

"Um … yeah. I like that idea."

Dax's tense shoulders eased. "Great. I can put my stuff in storage and stay with Mom until we find something. It's not as close to you as I'd like, but it at least knocks an hour off the time."

"That's definitely better." A smile wrapped around her words, and Dax wished she was right in front of him.

Soon, buddy. Soon.

He ended the call with an "I love you" and a promise to talk more that night once they were each home. He ran his finger along her picture on the phone's screen, then clicked it off. He rose and took a long assessing look at his office. Packing wouldn't be too much of a chore. Network binders lined his bookshelves, and the usual office stuff cluttered his file drawers. It would take less than five minutes to remove his memorabilia from the walls and shelves. He could be out of there in under a day.

The condo would be another matter. But nothing compared to what waited for him on the other side of packing. He had a future. With Caitlin. With football.

And God had orchestrated them both.

He shook his head, marveling at how much his life had changed in a few weeks. How it would transform even more in the coming ones. His gaze landed on his left hand. Yes. He was ready. And he was pretty sure she was too.

Dax grabbed his phone and tapped Preacher's number. After updating Zeb on the meeting and the future move, Dax reached the real reason for the call. "Hey, by the way, I'm going to need to borrow Gina for a few hours sometime soon."

"Gina? Well, yeah, I'm sure she won't mind, but what's up?"

Dax's heart swelled, savoring how right the conversation felt. "I, uh, need a woman's perspective on something."

Confusion laced Zeb's tone. "Something?"

Dax shook his head. He would have to be more specific. "Okay. Okay. On jewelry."

And for the first time in all the years Dax had known him, Zebedee Reeves was speechless.

Chapter Thirty-Six

Monday, October 8
Atlanta, Georgia

Three weeks later, movers shut the van door in front of Dax's condo building and climbed into the truck cab. Dax patted the driver's door. "I'll meet you at the house."

The driver turned over the engine, then steered the rig out of the parking lot. Zeb and Gina waited with huge grins on their faces. "Can you believe this is really happening?" Zeb asked. He tugged Dax into a hug and clapped him hard on the shoulders.

Dax shook his head. "Believe me, I'm still pinching myself every so often."

Caitie had started house hunting almost as soon as they'd gotten off the phone the day he'd met with the Network director. Two days later, she'd sent him a link to a secluded house in Pike Road, Alabama situated on a few acres with a pool and a recently renovated, modern-styled interior. After hearing her delight as she described it, Dax couldn't have cared less about a walk-through or even seeing pictures. It was already perfect.

He'd put in a full-price cash offer and the contingency that closing could be done in under thirty days. The owners had readily accepted, and Dax began the process of packing in between traveling to games. All seasoned professionals, his new commentary team came together with an easy camaraderie that quickly made them SEC fan favorites. Between the team and the extra time with Caitlin, Dax now couldn't imagine ever returning to studio work.

"So life in the ATL is done." Sadness threaded between Zeb's words, tainting the joy on his face.

"Don't listen to him, Dax." Gina wrapped Dax in a long side hug, her baby bump now too prominent for a full one. "You're going to have a great life. And we both are ecstatic for you."

Dax pulled Zeb into his other side and squeezed his shoulder. "I wouldn't have gotten through the last two months without y'all. You are just as much family to me as my parents."

"We're always only a phone call away. And be sure to let us know how the sentencing goes."

He, Caitie, and Mom would go back to Gulf Shores next week. Both attorneys and Pop had agreed to the ten-year plea sentence, but where he would serve the time remained unresolved. As was the possibility of other robbery charges.

Dax had asked Peter about Caitie's suggestion of the federal prison in Montgomery, and Peter seemed confident it could be arranged, but they wouldn't know until the formal sentencing. He also hoped the charges for the robberies in Florida could either be pleaded out or served concurrently, but those sentences would come later.

Dax's lips lifted. "You're my first call."

Zeb helped Gina into their Mercedes G Wagon and shut the door. Gina shot a pointed look to Dax. "You got everything?"

Dax ran a hand over the pocket of his jeans and, feeling the bumpy outline, grinned. "Yes."

Gina wagged her finger at him. "I want pictures, you hear."

Dax squeezed her hand. "You'll get them when the time comes."

Zeb leaned across Gina to fist-bump Dax. "All right, then. Be safe, my man."

Dax waved them on, then gave his home for the last five years a final look. Without a second thought, he climbed into his truck, ready to start his new life.

Caitlin waved as Dax pulled into the long driveway of his new home in Pike Road. She, Mom, Susan, Ethan, and Shannon clustered on the front porch, watching him come down the long blacktop drive. She looked around, trying to see the place through his eyes.

Mature water oaks edged the property line. A small pond, complete with a family of ducks, sat off to one side of a red barn that probably housed a horse or two at one point. Now, it would serve as a general storage building or maybe a future weight room.

She chuckled as the truck rolled closer and Dax's reaction became clearer. Jaw dropped and eyes wide, he didn't seem to know where to look first. Delight and satisfaction stole through her. *Pictures couldn't do it justice.* She still couldn't believe he'd bought the place based on her recommendation alone.

Dax honked the truck's horn twice in a quick greeting before he pulled to a stop behind the other cars. Up at the road, the moving van cut hard, barely making the sharp turn into the drive, but soon rumbled up the blacktop. It jerked to a stop. The air brake split the quiet, sending the ducks squawking.

Tucking her hands in her jeans pockets, Caitlin ambled to Dax's truck and pulled open his door. She flashed a teasing grin, then turned to give the place her own once-over. "What do you think of your new home?"

Dax waved to the rest of the family. "It's incredible. The

realtor's photographer did a good job with the pictures, but it's even better in person."

"If you're impressed now, wait 'til you see inside."

He tipped his head to peer through the open front door, likely catching at least a glimpse of Caitlin's preferred white walls and dark slate floors.

"It's amazing, and so are you." He placed a long, sweet kiss against her lips.

Ethan's teasing hoots echoed from the wide porch, heating Caitlin's cheeks. But she wrapped her arms around Dax's shoulders, sinking into his embrace as if she had been born to be there.

And maybe I was. Thank you, God.

She gave him a long squeeze and stepped back. Grabbing his hand, she led him to the porch. "Come on. I'll give you the nickel tour."

Moments later, more hugs in engulfed Dax, soaring Caitlin's heart even higher. But she broke up the festivities. "Plenty of time for that later. He needs to figure out where everything goes so the movers can get started."

She walked him through the house, savoring the gleam in his eyes, ecstatic he loved the house as much as she did. They finished the tour with the master bedroom. When Caitlin pushed open the door, Dax gasped. A full-length wall of marble, the gray veining delicate meanderings in the stone, anchored the white paint and dark slate floors. "A big change from the French Country of your last place, huh?"

"It's perfect." Dax wrapped her in a hug from behind, tucking his head on her shoulder. "Let's get moved in."

Caitlin's breath caught at the words. If their relationship continued to progress, yes, she would someday move in with him. But until then, was this the right house for Dax?

In her imaginings of their future, had she pushed this particular house too hard? He hadn't looked at others before he put the offer in. Were the walls too white? The slate too dark? She loved the combination, but did he? Really? She stepped out of his arms, now uncertain of her choice.

Dax brushed his knuckles against her cheek. "I mean it. You picked a beautiful home for me."

Relief whispered across her heart. "Okay, then. Where do you want everything?"

With so many hands and so few items from his condo, unpacking took only a day. Dax savored the quiet moments when he caught Caitie pondering one room or another and silently encouraged her mental planning. He'd told her he could wait forever for her, and he would. But that wouldn't keep him from hoping their life as husband and wife could start sooner.

At nine o'clock that night, Ethan dragged a still-excited Shannon to their car while Laurie and Mom headed to theirs. Mom would stay with Laurie, Caitie and Ethan's mom, for the weekend, and there was no arguing Mom out of it. Despite Dax's invitation to stay with him, she had put her foot down, saying there would be plenty of time for visits later, but Dax needed to settle in on his own.

Now alone with Caitie, he stuffed the last pizza box from dinner in the trash while she gave the kitchen counter a good wipe-down. "I don't think I've ever had more fun unpacking."

She grinned, shaking out the rag over the sink. "Ethan and Shannon are a riot together. And of course, being able to tease me unmercifully is always a plus for Ethan." She paused. "Maybe Luke can come home for Thanksgiving or Christmas this year."

Dax grabbed her hand. "I'd love to get to know him in person rather than just over Skype."

"I'm sure he'd like that." She fell silent, her eyes scanning the open kitchen and living area.

Dax followed her gaze. Despite the couch, TV, a leather armchair, and some football memorabilia, the rooms looked sparse. Her art collection would do wonders for the blank walls. He glanced at her. "Penny for your thoughts?"

Caitie blinked, then blushed an adorable shade of pink. She had been thinking much the same thing. *Caught you.*

He wrapped her in his arms and placed quick kiss on her forehead. "I love you."

Caitie snuggled into his embrace. "Back at you, Carpenter."

A long time later, Caitlin shifted in Dax's arms. "It's getting late. I should head out. Mom wants us to go to church with her tomorrow."

Dax peered into her eyes. "You okay with that?"

"It'll be good to be back."

"And if that's not the right church, I'm happy to try out others with you until we find where we fit."

Caitlin's heart melted. *Thank you, God, for this incredible man.* She placed a soft kiss against Dax's lips. When she pulled back, he tightened his arms around her. She lifted a curious look toward him.

"Before you go, I need to ask you something." Dax slid his fingers into his pocket, yanking something free, then holding it up in front of her. It glinted, the overhead lights catching the gold band and clear stone that sat snugly between his thumb and index finger.

Her mouth dropped open. Her eyes flicked from his fingers to his face. *That isn't what I think it is ...*

But then he said two words.

"Marry me?"

Tears blurred her vision.

Dax's chuff blew against her cheek, uncertainty filling his voice. "I know I said I would wait forever. And I will. There's no rush to set a date, or do anything else. But I want you to know for sure. I'm in this. I want you in my life. And if nothing else, the ring can be my promise of that. But—"

Caitlin covered his lips with her fingers, silencing the heartfelt words, and gave him the only answer she could. "Yes, Dax, I would love to marry you."

His eyes gleamed as she curved her hand around his cheek. "Really?"

She nodded. "And one thing I've learned today. I don't want to wait forever. I'm done with putting my life on hold. I want to be your wife, and, in the future, the mother of your children. And I'm ready to fully trust God with you and them."

Dax swung her up into his arms and twirled her around. Delighted laughter pealed against the bare walls around them. As he slid the ring onto her finger, the last of her fears melted away, leaving only hope, joy, and a deep, abiding trust in God's plan not only for her life, but also for their future.

Thank you for reading When Secrets Come Calling. I hope you enjoyed it. Your feedback and connection really matter.

If you would be so kind, please leave an honest review of the book on Amazon and/or Goodreads. Reviews are like coffee and chocolate to a writer and are the best way to say thank you for an entertaining escape.

If you would like a free story, access to book club materials, or to simply check Felicia out, click this link or use the QR code below.

Acknowledgments

This book was a thrill to write. The cold case investigation was totally out of my women's fiction wheelhouse, but I fell in love with the characters as they took shape in my mind. I'm so grateful they chose me to tell their story. Playing in the romantic suspense sandbox is quite fun.

I owe Ms. Martha Williamson unending thanks for creating the television show Signed, Sealed, Delivered. The DLO team and the supporting characters have inspired so many viewers with their flawed but healing journeys over the course of the show's canon. As a writer, I would not be who I am today without SSD. But as a person, I would not have some incredible women I now count as friends, and even sisters, in my life. To the POstables!

Ginormous thanks and much love to those soul sisters, Christine Labozan, Jan Miller, and Tammy Steintl. I can't imagine my life without you in it now. Not only have you been virtually beside my every keystroke with this book, your love and friendship are priceless. Group hug!

To Sylvia Cave, thank you for your wisdom, insight, and experience in the psychological realms. Caitlin and Dax's struggles are richer because of your input.

Deep appreciation also goes to Bert Moore, criminal attorney, and Kaye Towner, former county deputy sheriff, for their expertise in the legal field and law enforcement. I also drew heavily on J. Warner Wallace's Cold Case Christianity. Any mistakes in the book are mine, and should not reflect on their wisdom and experience.

Thanks to sports writer and author Del Duduit for his insights and direction for Dax's career as an SEC commentator.

Much thanks and appreciation to Bryan Canter for his layout and formatting, to DiAnn Mills and Hope Bolinger for their stellar editing work and to Hannah Linder for the stunning cover. This book definitely wouldn't be what it is without you.

And lastly, to Carol Ogle McCracken, Alice Hale Murray, Mike Logan, and Ginny Cruz, y'all are just the best friends a girl could have. From Bible studies to road trips to laughing until we cried and crying until we laughed, I treasure every moment we've spent together. Love y'all bunches!

About the Author

Felicia achieved master's degrees in Healthcare Administration and Speech-Language Pathology, but has written since childhood and dreamed of authoring books that teach and inspire others. An award-winning fiction and non-fiction freelance writer, she has published several devotions and sweet romance short stories.

Her passion, however, is writing women's fiction and romantic suspense with strong female characters who work through their traumas and tragedies using biblical principles and counseling techniques. Her radio devotional, Build Faith for the Journey, airs Saturdays on Christian Mix 106.

As a child, Felicia lived in Kansas, Texas, and Louisiana before her family settled on a horse and cattle farm in Kentucky. As an adult, she lived in Tennessee for two years and later spent ten years in the Florida panhandle soaking up the sand and sun. But then God moved her once again. This time out of the South and into the mountains of Colorado. When she's not glued to her laptop, Felicia enjoys hiking, meandering with her thirteen-year-old Frenchie, and looking forward to the next story.

Made in United States
Troutdale, OR
08/04/2024